One Thousand and One Arabian Nights

OXFORD STORY COLLECTIONS

Fairy Tales from England
Fairy Tales from Grimm
Fairy Tales from Andersen

Tales from Africa
Tales from China
Tales of Gods and Men
Tales from India
Tales from Japan
Tales of the Norse Gods
The Odyssey
Tales from West Africa
Tales from the West Indies

Moby Dick
Irish Myths and Legends

One Thousand and One
Arabian Nights

Geraldine McCaughrean

Illustrated by Rosamund Fowler

OXFORD
UNIVERSITY PRESS

To Ethel and Leslie

OXFORD
UNIVERSITY PRESS

Great Clarendon Street, Oxford OX2 6DP

Oxford University Press is a department of the University of Oxford.
It furthers the University's objective of excellence in research, scholarship,
and education by publishing worldwide in

Oxford New York

Auckland Cape Town Dar es Salaam Hong Kong Karachi
Kuala Lumpur Madrid Melbourne Mexico City Nairobi
New Delhi Shanghai Taipei Toronto

With offices in

Argentina Austria Brazil Chile Czech Republic France Greece
Guatemala Hungary Italy Japan South Korea Poland Portugal
Singapore Switzerland Thailand Turkey Ukraine Vietnam

Oxford is a registered trade mark of Oxford University Press

British Library Cataloguing in Publication Data
Data available

Cover illustration by Paul Hunt

ISBN 978-0-19-275013-6

11

Typeset by AFS Image Setters Ltd, Glasgow

Printed in Great Britain by
Cox & Wyman Ltd, Reading, Berkshire

Contents

CHAPTER ONE

The Marriage of Shahrazad

Stories are carried from the desert kingdoms of India and Persia and Arabia—but who can tell if they are true?—of the twin kingdoms of Sasan and Samarkand al-Ajam. Their rulers were brothers: the tall and glorious King Shahryar and his smaller brother King Shahzaman. The foundations of their cities and palaces were not moved by the shifting ocean of Arabian sand. Their domes and minarets on a horizon were as beautiful in the eyes of desert travellers as foaming water or banked rain clouds.

Just as his cities were wonderful to the eyes, so the young Shahryar was wonderful in the eyes of his people, for he ruled wisely and generously. The heart of Shahryar was lovely, for he took pleasure in the life that Allah gave him. Above all, Shahryar took pleasure in his wife—a lady as lovely as the moon reflected in lily pools. Only the queen of King Shahzaman, his brother, equalled her in beauty.

One morning King Shahryar took it into his heart to visit his brother in the kingdom of Samarkand al-Ajam and called for camels to be mustered and loaded with presents. Bales of damask cloth, flasks of attar of roses, and panniers filled with oriental spices were heaped across the camels until their legs bent like an archer's bow. In the inner chamber of his palace, King Shahryar kissed his lovely wife goodbye and, of course, veiled her face so that no other man but the King should accidentally glimpse her beauty.

The streets of the royal city of Sasan were filled with fragrance as the caravan wound its way from the palace to the eastern gates. Just as they were leaving the city, King Shahryar remembered the small personal gift of red sulphur he had laid ready in his bedroom, intending to carry it to King Shahzaman. He hurried back to his palace alone and climbed the stairs, his calf-skin shoes making no sound on the stone staircase. As he opened the bedroom door, his heart jumped inside him like a startled hare. In one moment it leapt with delight at the sight of his wife's face, and in the next it leapt with anger that her veil was gone. A servant from the palace stables was sitting beside the queen. In one hand he held the crumpled veil and in the other he held the queen's hand.

When King Shahryar rejoined his caravan of camels, he wore his unhappiness like a black woollen cloak: he stooped under its weight. No word passed his lips until he reached the royal city of Samarkand al-Ajam, the home of King Shahzaman, his brother. The distant city walls trembled like a mirage, for his eyes were still full of tears.

An old man, richly dressed, came out of the gates towards them, making small and weary gestures of welcome—as though his strength was not equal to his message. But as they drew closer to one another, King Shahryar recognized his own young brother, wearing his grief like old age. His body was like a tent smothered by a sandstorm as it bowed under the weight of his unhappiness.

'Put faith in no one but Allah,' said Shahzaman, pressing his forehead against his brother's shoulder. 'There is such wickedness in the world.'

They walked away from the whispering of camel drivers and grunting of the camels to share their secret in the shadow of the city wall.

'Who can I tell but you, brother?' whispered Shahzaman, looking around him for fear of being overheard. 'My wife has taken my love and emptied it into a pool of mud. She has uncovered her face in front of the palace cook and shined on him with her eyes and waited on him with her hands. Oh, Shahryar, you cannot know what good fortune you have in your lovely, loving wife.'

At the sound of his brother's words, King Shahryar, King of all Sasan (let it not be spoken twice) wept salt tears. 'Oh, Shahzaman! I wish I had married a camel on my wedding day! My wife has uncovered her face in front of a stable-boy and shined on him with her eyes and waited on him with her hands—and I killed them both this morning with my own sword.'

Shahzaman held his head and cried aloud. 'My wife and the palace cook were put to death this morning. What shall we do, brother? It is true what the poet says:

> *Women are worthless,*
> *Women are liars:*
> *They seem to be roses,*
> *But grow into briars.*

All women are fickle!'

3

So night fell in the hearts of King Shahzaman of Samarkand al-Ajam and King Shahryar of Sasan. When Shahryar returned to his city, a pall of sadness settled over all the people of Sasan for three long years.

Sadness crept like a spy into the rib-cage of young King Shahryar. It snuffed out all his candles of joy and left his heart to blunder about in utter darkness. Unhappiness crept to the back-door of his heart and unlocked it, letting in the enemies of Allah: doubt and harshness and . . . fear. Yes, let it not be spoken twice—the tall, valiant, and courteous King of all Sasan was afraid. At night, when his courtiers were in bed and his maidservants were sleeping, the candles in his chamber trembled with loneliness, and the black tent of night flapped around his heart. The creases of the empty pillow beside his head made faces at him, and the faces reminded him of his wife. Then, hitting the pillow with his fist, he vowed to hide the pillow's creases under a new head.

'Wazir!' he shouted. 'Fetch my Wazir!'

The King's Wazir, his sole adviser, ran to King Shahryar's chamber bleary with sleep, and kissed the hem of the bedspread.

'I will not spend another night alone in this bed,' shouted the King.

The Wazir clapped his hands with joy. 'Oh, you wish to marry again, most courteous and mighty king! All Sasan will delight in the news.'

'How can I marry again,' Shahryar stormed, 'when all women are faithless, and none of them will love a man for more than a day?'

'No one could love the magnificence of your lordship for less than a thousand years,' said the Wazir, shaking with fright.

'I *know* that women are fickle. If anyone dares to dispute it, I'll have him fed to the palace dogs in pieces for a week—and then put him to death myself!'

'All women are fickle,' said the Wazir, who had a certain store of wisdom.

'It is perfectly obvious what I must do,' said King Shahryar, recovering his just and even temper, renowned throughout Sasan. 'Fetch me a pretty, talented girl at once and I will marry her this morning.'

'I will, sir, with all my heart, sir . . .' said the Wazir, anxious only to be gone. But with one word the glorious young King stopped his Wazir at the door.

'Worthy old man,' he said. 'Invite the executioner to the wedding and furnish a room for him inside the palace. I shall behead my new bride tomorrow morning before she can stop loving me. Fetch another young woman to me after the execution, and I shall marry again. While the executioner's sword is sharp, I need never be alone at night. Have I not more wisdom than my own Wazir in solving this problem?'

'With such wisdom what need have you of me, your miserable Wazir?' agreed the Wazir, and he crept backwards out of the King's presence. In the corridor outside he was obliged to stop and lean his head against the wall: his heart had turned into a lead anchor which stopped all movement but for the seasick rocking of his soul.

And so for three years, the golden ruler of all Sasan married every day: a thousand brides, a thousand executions, a thousand spaces in the crowded streets of the bazaar, two thousand empty sandals, a hundred thousand pricks of conscience in the heart of the King's Wazir.

So the stories say—but who can tell if they are true?

The stories also say that the Wazir had two daughters,

Dunyazad and Shahrazad, and that during those three dark years in the history of Sasan, Shahrazad, daughter of the King's Wazir, crossed the river that separates childhood from womanhood.

One morning at breakfast, the King's Wazir took his beard in both hands and wept salt tears into his pewter dishes.

'Dearest father, why are you crying?' his daughters asked. The Wazir looked at Dunyazad and her elder sister, Shahrazad—and he covered his face with his hands.

'Tell us, father,' said Shahrazad. 'Is the dear King ill? Nothing else could make you so unhappy.'

He shook his head. 'I cannot truthfully say that the dear King is ill . . . O sweet Shahrazad, you know that there is no king more glorious in all the realms of India and Persia and Arabia than King Shahryar. And there is no man more fortunate than I am to be his Wazir and to advise him. But there is a matter about which he will not take my advice. My words fall like blown sand on a sleeping traveller: he rises the next morning and brushes my advice away with a wave of his hand.'

And the Wazir recounted the sorrows of the last three years. 'The dear King has taken the notion into his heart that no woman can be trusted. A woman, he says, will love a man one day and hate him the next. She will marry a man one day and fall in love with his servant the next morning. I cannot convince him that there were many good women among his brides.'

'Many? Brides? Has the King married many times?'

'He marries every day, Shahrazad. His bride keeps him company during the hours of darkness . . . (Let it not be spoken twice, but the valiant King is a little afraid of being alone at night.) But the morning after his wedding, the dear, good King has his new wife's head cut off so that she cannot fall in love with anyone else. And it is my task to find him another bride . . . and another . . . and another . . .'

'Poor father,' said Shahrazad. 'Now I understand why the halls and corridors of the palace are so empty. I understand why I see no noblewomen in the market place and so few silken sandals outside the marble mosques. Now I understand why you are weeping.'

'The city is as empty of young women as the sea is empty of drinking water,' said the Wazir. 'The dear King has cut off all their heads. But that is not why I was weeping. I must send both of you away today—at once. If the dear King should find out that I have a beautiful daughter of marriageable age, you would have to become his latest wife. And he would not leave you your life the morning after the wedding.'

Dunyazad began to cry. But Shahrazad covered her face with her veil so that her expression could not be seen.

'But that is not why I was weeping, either, my beloved daughters. There are no more noblewomen in the city, and I will not empty the kingdom of Sasan of all its young women. When I cannot or will not carry out the orders of the dear King, he will certainly, in his graciousness and wisdom, see fit to put me to death.'

Dunyazad cried all the more, but Shahrazad's face was hidden by her veil and she was silent. Finally she said: 'Dearest father. If you believe that we shall never meet again after today, you cannot refuse me one favour.'

'I would not refuse you a favour even if you were not going away,' said the Wazir. 'You have never asked me for anything. What would I refuse you?'

'Then marry me to the dear King Shahryar. In this way I will die as a queen, and one less daughter of Sasan will die because of me.'

'O Shahrazad. You are the oasis in the desert of my dry old soul. Do not empty yourself into the King's hands. He will only spill you.'

'Father! Do not let your sorrow make you speak without respect for our glorious King. Mention to him that you have a daughter. Please, I beg you. If Allah wills it, our dear King will marry me.'

King Shahryar, ruler of all Sasan, was delighted with Shahrazad.

'Her face behind her veil is like the moon behind a cloud,' he said to the Wazir. 'Why did you not bring me this one before?'

'She is my daughter, noble king, my beloved daughter . . .' And seeing that the King's heart was already set on a marriage, the Wazir covered his face with his arm and left the royal chamber, not staying for the wedding feast which began in the self-same hour.

During the festivities, Shahrazad took her little sister to one side and whispered to her:

'You know that the dear King, in his graciousness and wisdom, will not cut off my head until the morning. I would like to see a friendly face when I wake. Come to my royal husband's bedroom in the morning.'

'I will come,' said Dunyazad.

'And if you come, perhaps Allah will put it into your heart to say this . . .' and she lifted her sister's dark hair and spoke a few words into her ear.

The sound of the King's Headsman sharpening his sword

in the courtyard woke Shahrazad where she lay in the royal bed. King Shahryar was already awake.

'Are you ready, wife?'

'If it is time, my gracious husband. My little sister Dunyazad is knocking on the door. Let me say goodbye to her, and then you may take what joy you can from cutting off my little head.'

Dunyazad stood on the threshold, her face uncovered, and King Shahryar captured her face in the cage of his memory, thinking to marry her, too, when she came of age.

'If you have come to ask for your sister's life to be spared,' said the King, 'I must tell you that it is impossible. A woman's love is as long as the stroke of a pen that has seen no ink. Do not waste your tears.'

'Gracious King,' said Dunyazad, bowing to the ground. 'In your graciousness and wisdom, you know what is for the best. But let me say goodbye to my sister, for the swordsman is waiting in the courtyard and I shall never see her again.' The King stood aside: Dunyazad and Shahrazad kissed one another.

'Dearest sister,' said Dunyazad. 'How we shall miss you, father and I. How we shall miss your voice singing in the garden, your flute playing on the terraces, and the aroma of your cooking. But I know when we shall miss you most of all. The nights will be so long without your wonderful stories. No one in all Arabia can tell stories as you do. The nights will be as empty as the sea is empty of birds. Do you remember how father laughed when you told the story of the Everlasting Slippers? Do you remember how we all cried when you told the story of the Keys of Destiny—and how the maidservant almost choked on her dinner when you amazed us with the secret language of the animals? I would give up my place among the ladies of this palace just to hear one more story. Won't you tell me one last story, Shahrazad?'

'No, little sister. It is time now. My dear husband the King has many things to do today; I must not keep him waiting. It is a pity, for tonight I would have told you the story of . . . No matter.'

King Shahryar overheard their words. He remembered in his heart how the black tent of night flapped around him when he was alone in the dark.

But he said: 'You have some of the wisdom of your father, Shahrazad. My days are busy. My courtiers are waiting. No worthless wife must delay court business, and surely every second that passes makes it likely that your life will outlast your love for me. Woman's love is as long as the hairs on a chicken's egg. You can do only one more thing to please me: give up your head. I can see the swordsman from this window. Hurry down to him, and I will watch from here.'

In the courtyard, the stones underfoot were already hot. Shahrazad bowed to the ground before the King's window and then she coiled up her hair and bowed low before the King's swordsman.

CHAPTER TWO

The Voyage of
Sinbad the Sailor

IN his heart, King Shahryar pictured the nights of his childhood when his mother told him tales from beyond the furthermost borders of Araby.

'One word, Shahrazad,' he called from his window. 'What story were you going to tell to Dunyazad tonight?'

'The story of Sinbad the Sailor, dear husband,' said Shahrazad as the swordsman placed his foot on her back. 'An adventure drawn up from the liquid mountains of the sea where there are as many wonderful beasts and fabulous islands as there are trees in a forest.'

'Shahrazad, I have it in my heart to hear the story. But I have affairs of state to attend to. You will tell it to me tonight. Swordsman, come back tomorrow at the very same time.'

Just as the tent of night began to flap around King Shahryar's heart and set the candles in his eyes trembling

11

with fear, Shahrazad came to his bed and lay down beside him. Leaning on one elbow, she began:

A story is carried from Baghdad—though who can tell if it is true?—of a young man called Sinbad the Porter. Sinbad was known at all the local inns for his beautiful singing voice, and he would often sing in return for a coin or a bite to eat. He was summoned one day to a great house built of white and wine-coloured marble on the skirts of the city. An old man was sitting on the vine-covered terrace, and asked him to sing—which he willingly did:

> *Oh I have carried golden treasure*
> *Half across Arabia's sands,*
> *And I have seen the cost of pleasure*
> *Pouring out of rich men's hands.*
> *But do not think of me as rich, sir,*
> *Because I carry treasure chests,*
> *For I count myself much richer*
> *When I lay them down and rest.*
> *I am just a poor young porter—*
> *All my meat is caught from rivers,*
> *All the wines I drink are water—*
> *All I carry, I deliver.*

The song pleased the old man, and he took a great liking to the porter.

'The pleasure a good song gives can't be paid for with money alone,' said the old man. 'Let me give you something of mine. I shall give you the story of my life, which is moderately interesting. My name is Sinbad too. But I am Sinbad the Sailor.'

I was born the son of a rich father who died and left me a lot of money. Being a particularly clever boy, I made the sensible decision to invest the money. I invested it in drink and expensive food and stylish clothes and in buying myself a lot of friends at the local inn. Before long I found that my investment had left me with hardly a penny. To tell you the truth, I did not want to be poor in my old age.

So I sold everything I owned and bought instead a silk-sailed ship and cargo. I employed a captain, and we set sail for the rest of the world, turning a furrow through the sea as straight and certain as an arrow through a blue sky. I was confident of making my fortune as a merchant.

One day a solitary island came into view from the mast top—two or three trees and a smooth, grey beach the colour of the atolls in the great Western Ocean.

Some of the sailors were tired of the blood swilling in their veins with the motion of the ship, and we took it into our heads to draw alongside the island and walk about on dry land. The captain was sleeping below decks. We did not trouble to wake him: a friendly fire, a baked fish, a short walk, and we would be ready to set off again. Two of the men even brought a laundry barrel from the ship to do their washing in.

Ali lit a fire, and I made a tour of the island, but there was not a lot to recommend it. We were just deciding that no one could live there, without fresh water, when suddenly Abdul caught sight of a fountain—a geyser, rather—at a great distance from us. Its water gushed higher and higher, seemingly to the height of a castle tower, then dropped out of sight.

'I have been aboard ship for too long—the ground still seems to be moving,' I said, embarrassed by losing my balance and falling over. Then the captain's voice drifted to us on the wind.

'Aboard! Aboard! Or you are all dead men!'

'The island is sinking!' someone cried.

'The island is moving!' shouted another.

A deep roaring beneath us was followed by a second eruption of water from the geyser. It spouted so high that the spray reached us on the wind and soaked us to the skin in a second.

Amidst the spray, I could just see the captain giving orders for the ship to pull away. The space of water opened between our landing-party and the vessel. Some men ran to the water and leapt in. Others shouted at the captain, calling him names or begging him to pull ashore again. Only one or two of his words reached us across the opening gap.

'Whale! . . . Fire has woken the whale . . .'

Well may you hold your head in wonder, friend. We had indeed moored alongside a giant whale, and the fire we had lit on its back had disturbed it out of a sleep centuries long. The sandy silt of the ocean had washed over the whale, and the winds had brought seeds and spores and planted its sparse vegetation. But as it rolled in pain, our fire beginning to burn through its hide (and making an awful stench), the shallow-rooted trees were washed away like toothpicks, and the sand swirled round our knees as we stumbled to and fro. The whale dived.

One sailor was thrown high out of the water by the massive tail—believe me, friend, those tail-flukes were larger than galleon sails—and the tail fell on us like the greatest tree in all the gum forests of Arabia.

To the end of my days I shall weary Allah with my thanks. The barrel full of my fellow sailors' washing rolled towards me across the water. I pulled myself across it and floated away, while my sailor friends swam down with the whale to the kingdom where only the fish can breathe. Friend, friend, it makes me sweat salt-water only to think about it.

The ship had long since gone. I was alone on the ocean with the smell of scorched whale in my nostrils. I began to paddle with my feet, and my lonely voyage, as you can imagine, was so long and tiring that I do not remember reaching land.

I woke up beside my barrel on a white beach to find, to my great surprise, that I was alive. I also found that the fish had eaten many holes in my feet, and only with pain and difficulty did I climb the beach and explore.

I saw no one, friend, and nothing. Under the trees the undergrowth was thick—a perfect home for wild animals. Why else did I climb that tree? But from the topmost branches I could see a long, long way.

I saw no one, friend, and nothing. In another direction, however, I glimpsed a shining white dome. Surely it was a fine mosque at the heart of a splendid city. Its white curve seemed so massive that I was almost afraid to approach.

When I finally reached it, I walked around it five times before I gave up hope of finding a door. Its whiteness was dazzling in the sun. I tried to climb up it, but the white surface was so polished and smooth that I slithered down to the ground again every time. I exhausted myself in the mid-day heat, and that is why I was sitting on the ground in the shade of the white dome when the sun went dark.

I have seen tropical suns set like a single clap of hands. I have seen the moon forget its rightful place and push in front of the sun. But this was no eclipse or sunset.

Looking up, I saw that the sun had been blotted out by the shape of a gigantic bird. Its claws were as large as the tusks of elephants, one toe the thickness of a tree-trunk. Its wings were as huge as my terror, and its feathers as black as my miserable fate. For now I realized that the white dome I was sitting under was nothing other than the bird's unhatched egg. And as slowly and certainly as a ship on a whirlpool is sucked circling down, the huge bird was wheeling down towards me.

'Why have you stopped?' said King Shahryar.

'Oh, my dear husband,' Shahrazad replied, 'I am surely the most worthless of wives, for I have wearied you all night with my story-telling, and already it is dawn. Your swordsman is waiting for me in the courtyard. I can hear him sharpening his sword.'

'But what became of Sinbad the Sailor?' Shahryar demanded. 'How did he escape being eaten by the bird?'

'Ah, dear husband, the things that happened to Sinbad are so strange and so many that I could spend another night in telling you his story . . .'

So King Shahryar rose and went to the window and leaned out.

'Come back tomorrow, swordsman, at the very same time. And you, Shahrazad,' he said, turning to his wife, 'you must return this evening to finish the story.'

'To hear you is to obey,' Shahrazad replied.

CHAPTER THREE

Sinbad the Sailor:
The Valley of Diamonds

On the next night Shahrazad reclined on one elbow, rested her head in her hand and continued the story of Sinbad the Sailor.

From the well of my memory I drew up the strange and wonderful tales I had heard at Baghdad harbour. I recalled travellers' descriptions of the Giant Rukh—a bird whose wing-span half covered the sky. Undoubtedly, I was squatting in the shadow of just such a bird, and my only hope of life lay in staying hidden under the egg.

A vast, stinking warmth enveloped me as the rukh settled over her egg, and I found myself somewhere between the clawed feet, a pouch of bird-down pressing on my head with all the weight of a feather bed. It pushed off my turban which unwound at my feet. That was when I formed my plan of escape. Lying down alongside one horny talon—as thick and rough as a log—I tied myself securely to the rukh's claw, using the cloth of my turban. Then I went to sleep to escape the pains of fear in my heart and the pains of hunger in my stomach.

I woke up in time only to wish that I had stayed asleep. The rukh had risen off its egg and was climbing a furlong with every beat of its wings. The egg below soon looked no bigger than a white bean; the whole island soon looked no bigger than a pea.

I wished to commend my life's good deeds to Allah so that He might be merciful to me, but I could remember lamentably few. So I vowed to behave much better if Allah, in His mercy, would grant me the opportunity. Still the bird soared higher until I thought it must roost among the beams of the sun. The air was so thin that my lungs shrivelled to the size of walnuts and the blood abandoned my head. I regained consciousness just as the rukh swooped down below the rim of a black canyon and glided down into a valley.

'Oh, Allah is truly merciful!' I cried. 'He saved me from the gulf of the ocean and from the vault of the sky and has set my feet on solid ground again.' Fumbling at the knots of cloth, I rolled away from under the rukh and bundled together my turban.

'Oh, Allah is full of subtlety,' I shrieked. 'Was a drowning too good for Sinbad or starvation too merciful? Was it not bad enough to be eaten by the rukh? Was Fate preserving me for this miserable pit?'

For everywhere I looked were bare black rocks, and the sides of the canyon were sheer. Between every rock and strangling every boulder, huge black serpents coiled and writhed about. The rukh which had brought me to this pit of despair stretched out its grotesque head and snatched up a serpent as though it were a wriggling worm. Then with a scrabbling of gravel it ran forwards and took off, spiralling up to the narrow blue slit of sky a mile above me. It scarcely interested me, but indeed it was not gravel which the rukh scuffed up. Everywhere, but everywhere, the ground was sprinkled with precious stones—diamonds, emeralds, sapphires, and rubies— more treasure than even the greed of a young Sinbad had ever imagined. And shall I tell you, friend, my only thoughts at seeing this undreamt-of wealth? I wept because the diamonds hurt my feet to tread on.

Those hideous land serpents rippled as hugely and shined as blackly and were as many as the swelling waves on a night sea. The roots of my soul shrivelled, and I fell on my face waiting to be swallowed, strangled, or poisoned by their licking fangs.

Just then—I tell no lies, but believe me if you can—a slab of raw meat fell on my head.

'A serpent is crawling over me,' I thought, praying for a quick death. But as the juices trickled through my hair I decided I was in fact wearing a side of mutton. Perhaps it was a hint from Allah that I should eat hearty before I was eaten, so I crawled out from under the meat only to be narrowly missed by another side of mutton, bouncing down the canyon wall.

Have you heard the rumour, friend, of a place called the Valley of Diamonds? Well, I can vouch that the place exists. There are indeed merchants who grow rich on the diamonds, but they do not—they dare not— climb down among the snakes. Instead, they pitch slabs of raw meat into the ravine. The diamonds and so forth became embedded in the meat, then the giant rukhs, hunting for food, fly down and carry the mutton out of the ravine. Let my story tell you what happens next.

When I realized what was happening, I gathered up as many jewels as my pocket would hold, crawled back under the slab of mutton and clung on to it as mortal man clings to life.

A rukh came hunting for food to feed its chick.

I and my meat were lifted off the ground in the grip of its giant claws, and soon the serpents in the valley looked no bigger than bloodworms in a barrel. The bird carried its food to a nest in the crook of a mountain ledge. It immediately began tearing at the meat with its gruesome beak and pushing pieces into the pink gullet of its chick—a creature as big as a cow.

One peck slashed open my chest, the next would certainly rip out my heart.

'Oh Allah!' I cried. 'Did my mother's care and my father's money make me fit for nothing but to be breakfast to a baby rukh?'

Just at that moment, an avalanche of rocks tumbled past the ledge, and a great din of shouts and hoots up above frightened the rukh off its nest. One solitary merchant lowered himself on a rope to the ledge and began prodding the meat.

'There are no jewels there, my good fellow,' I said.

At the sound of my voice, the merchant leapt backwards. At the sight of me crawling from under the meat, he fell on his knees and began praying. I suppose I was *not* as clean as on the day my mother bore me—caked in sea salt and bird-lime, and red from head to foot with meat juices and blood.

'Forgive me, friend,' I said, 'for I know that cleanliness is close to Allah's heart. But if you would be so good as to help me off this unpleasant ledge, I would willingly share with you the treasure whose weight so discourteously prevents me getting to my feet.' So saying, I fainted, quite overcome with hunger, weariness, and pain.

I received from the merchant the most precious of Allah's gifts—hospitality. He fed and cared for me, and only grudgingly accepted half my immense riches. He found me buyers for my diamonds, emeralds, sapphires, and rubies. And, when I was fully recovered, he directed me to a coastal harbour where my new-found wealth bought not just one ship but a whole fleet.

Unfortunately, not one captain among those who sailed in and out of the harbour had heard tell of Baghdad. Imagine it, friend! that some of the islands of the world have drifted on the winds and tides so far from the world's centre that the inhabitants have never heard of Baghdad!

I sent the fleet in all directions, one following the Dog Star, one the Pole Star, one the Pleiades, and one the Red Planet, with instructions to trade at every port until they found knowledge of Baghdad. I myself boarded the ship with the richest cargo, opened the sails fully, and ran before any and every wind. For who sends the wind but Allah?

'Who sends the wind but Allah?' I crowed, sighting an island one morning.

But the captain said, 'Some devil sent this one,' and he bent his head on to the wheel and wrung his hands. He ordered the sails to be reefed in, and the ship turned to put the island behind us, but no sooner had we turned than a pirate ship rushed down on us. We lay between the ship and shore with not an inch of sail blowing.

The captain recognized both the island and the approaching ship, and he cursed his fate for bringing him to those waters. I begged him to tell us why he was lying full length, beating the deck with his fists. I begged him to tell us what to expect. But he only moaned pitifully and said, 'Expect death, young man. Expect to die!'

'But what am I thinking of,' said Shahrazad, breaking off suddenly. 'I have told you the story of the First Voyage of Sinbad and now I presume on your patience to tell you the awful events of the Second Voyage.'

'Don't interrupt the story with your chattering,' said King Shahryar. 'Go on, go on.'

'But your courtiers are knocking on the door, my most eminent and conscientious lord, and I still owe you your rightful wedding present—my little head in a silver dish.'

'Worthless woman!' said Shahryar, stamping to the chamber door. Opening it he shouted at his startled Chancellor, 'Do you know the story of the Second Voyage of Sinbad the Sailor?'

The Chancellor fell on his face in the doorway and kissed the carpet between the King's bare feet. 'Forgive me, my most powerful and intellectual lord, but I cannot truthfully say that I do.'

'You see!' said King Shahryar, turning on his wife. 'Are you suggesting that I go without the Second Voyage of Sinbad rather than keep my own headsman waiting? I forbid you to leave this room until I have come back tonight and heard the story.'

'O patient and even-tempered husband,' said Shahrazad. 'Forgive my lack of judgement, for I am only young and foolish. To hear you is to obey.'

King Shahryar dusted his hands together with satisfaction and strode downstairs to his audience chamber while, outside in the courtyard, the old Wazir walked fretfully up and down and the Royal Swordsman sharpened his sword.

CHAPTER FOUR

Sinbad the Sailor's Second Voyage

'B e quick,' said King Shahryar the next night, throwing himself down on his bed alongside his wife. 'Sinbad's treasure ship is trapped between pirates and some dreadful island. Why was the captain so terrified?'

'Ah well,' said Shahrazad, 'he knew the stories about those waters. But I ask myself who had told him the stories, for no one had ever escaped alive from the Island of Cannibals.'

'The Island of Cannibals . . .' whispered the King, savouring the fear that slid down his throat like a raw mussel. 'Tell me, Shahrazad.'

'Not I, but Sinbad must tell *this* story,' said Shahrazad, 'for surely *I* can know nothing of such terrible things . . .'

The pirate ship was manned by a crew of dwarfs—

wizened, yellow, little men whose fathers were surely monkeys for they swarmed aboard like a pack of chattering apes. They stood no higher than a man's thigh, but they bit and scratched and leapt on us from the rigging where whole hoards of them swung about, shrieking and jabbering and baring their long yellow teeth.

Our clothes and skin in tatters, we huddled together at the stern powerless to fight these darting, treacherous ape-men with our slow fists and short, feeble cutlasses. They took control of the ship, let out all the sails, and steered us at full speed for the island—to give it its true name, the Isle of Zughb.

In the shallows, they carried us ashore, four or five ape-men supporting each sailor. Then, as the last of us was thrown down on the sand, they all leapt aboard our ship and drew away from shore.

'Allah be praised,' I said. 'They may have been the most ugly creatures living, but at least they did not kill us—they were obviously thieves of mercy.' O Sinbad, what kind of fool did your parents feed and educate? Did I sit on that beach and call those ape-men thieves of mercy? They were no more merciful than the housewife who puts cheese in the traps to feed poor hungry mice!

Behind the beach stood a towering fort surrounded by a high wall. Facing us was a gate worked all in ivory which stood half open, so we went inside and looked about.

We saw no one, friend, and nothing, but for a few cooking pots—as huge as horse troughs—some barbecue skewers longer than spears, and a few broken benches. Littering the deserted courtyard were several hundred white bones—put out for the owners' dogs, or so we assumed.

As no one answered our greetings we curled up in our cloaks and slept—and I believing that my greatest misfortune lay in losing my cargo and ship. Fool that I was, fool that I was.

At sunset we were woken by the earth shaking under us. The ivory gates swung fully open, and a grotesque giant shuffled in and bolted them behind him. His head could only have pleased his mother: his cheeks hung down to his chest like a camel's dewlaps; he was as bald and tusked as a walrus, and the folds of skin under his eyes would have made hammocks for sailors; his ears draped over his shoulders and he barked a great deal, dragging his knuckles along the ground so that his nails, like two farm harrows, ploughed up the soil.

The giant lit a fire, sat down beside it, and then looked us over thoughtfully. We were no surprise to him: the monkey-men had simply made their regular delivery. A barricade of fat fingers trapped me against a wall and rolled me into his fat palm as though I were a sweetmeat. The giant poked and prodded me, but as I was still thin from my earlier shipwreck I did not please him. Instead he picked up the fat ship's cook between finger and thumb and cooked him on a spit over the fire, crunching him up with obvious satisfaction and spitting out the larger bones.

Almost at once he fell asleep for the night, leaving us desperate with fear but unable to climb the high, smooth wall of the fort.

Every day was the same: the giant went out in the morning, bolted the gates, and came back in the evening with a ravenous appetite. He would choose the fattest sailor from the crew and roast and eat him barbecued for supper.

'O Allah, decider of all fates,' we cried out, legless with terror, 'could you not have let the ship founder or be swallowed by a whale? This is no way for a Believer or native of Baghdad to meet his end. We should have thrown ourselves into the sea when we first saw the pirate apes.' In short it seemed time to act.

There were only a handful of us skinny sailors left. I suggested that the giant would soon start eating us two at a time. 'In order to defend ourselves we must attack,' I said. 'But first we must know our escape route. Let's tie these benches together into a ladder and be ready to climb the wall tonight . . .'

That evening, after the ship's second lieutenant had satisfied the giant's hunger, we watched the ugly brute settle down to sleep and then we crept to the fireside. Hauling two of the skewers across the coals, we heated their points white-hot and, carrying them as undertakers carry coffins, we ran at the head of the sleeping cannibal. His snores blew our turbans off, but on we charged and plunged the white-hot spits into his red-rimmed, blue-lidded eyes.

The bo'sun fell into the giant's cavernous mouth, as the cannibal let out a yell like doomsday. We were thrown in all directions as the grotesque beast staggered to his knees and slapped the ground trying to squash us like flies. Because he could not see us, we were able to lean our makeshift ladder against the wall and climb out, pulling the benches over behind us—for they were to serve as our raft.

But we had no sooner pushed off from the shore, paddling with our hands, than a female giant with the same dewlap cheeks, ears flapping as she ran, appeared on the beach leading the blinded cannibal by the hand.

Truly the sight of them was so repulsive that the shallow shoreline waves wrinkled up their noses.

The giants stood howling at us from the beach, baring their fangs and barking as great black conger eels bark on the hook. Then they picked up boulders and threw them at the raft, swamping it with pitching waves and smashing some of the boards. Only three of us were left clinging to the raft when it drifted beyond range of the falling rocks, and limped out on to the open ocean.

For a day and a night we watched for land until our eyes were as dry as pebbles. And then we slept.

'Wake up, wake up!' I cried shortly before dawn. 'The sea's as still as the milk in a cat's saucer. We must have entered a lagoon.' Lying on our raft, we waited for the sun to tell us what kind of land the sea had brought us to. Little by little it lit a circle of scaly coral which totally enclosed the raft so that I could not tell how we had sailed inside. I was remarking on the multicoloured scales of the reef, when the sea-monster whose coils had surrounded us, lifted its multicoloured head and sipped a sailor off the raft.

Round and round its coils writhed, spinning the raft in a whirlpool of snake. At night it was hidden by darkness. But its loud hissing made us long to hear waves breaking on Arabian beaches before we met our end. In the morning I was all alone—the sea-serpent had licked my last companion off the deck and left me one more day in which to praise Allah.

It seemed time to act. I tore up the benches from the edge of the raft and raised wooden walls and a roof, so that I was floating in a lidded wooden box.

'At least if I am to die,' said I, 'Sinbad will have a respectable coffin as befits a Believer.'

Round and round the sea-snake wheeled, spinning the crate in a whirlpool of serpent. Then in the night it nosed me up and down, hissing like a punctured elephant, but truly it found Sinbad and his coffin an indigestible meal and swam off by first light to wreck the ships of Believers and Unbelievers alike. May Allah grant it a short life.

My flimsy box was sighted by a merchant ship. The sailors mistook it for a crate washed overboard from a cargo ship and were greatly amazed to prise open the lid and find a creature of my kind inside.

The sailors did not press me for my story, and I rested below decks for several days, interested only in eating and sleeping, though they told me that I cried out in my sleep: 'O Allah maroon me on the Island of Zughb, if I ever see Baghdad again and do not stay at home to grow old!'

'The captain is from Baghdad,' said the second mate. 'But we won't be docking there again. He will have to sell the ship at the next port we come to. Times are bad in shipping and he is nearly ruined.' The sailor shook his head disappointedly. 'And they say the captain has a rich cargo waiting in a Baghdad warehouse, but he won't sell it in case the owner comes back to claim it. Come back from the dead after seven years! Sinbad won't come back. He went down with a whale to the kingdom where only the fish can breathe.'

I dropped from my hammock and begged them to take me to the captain. The old man did not recognize me at once, but I remembered his face so well as the ship pulled away from the whale-island, and his voice shouting 'Aboard! Aboard! Or you are all dead men!'

I was so grateful to the good captain for keeping my cargo, that I gave him half its value and one of the ships that had found its way back from the far distant Diamond Valley. For I am almost embarrassed to tell you what wealth awaited me at home. My friends, the trade-winds, had shepherded my scattered fleet to Basra harbour, and there the cargoes had been sold for more dinars than can be counted on an abacus.

The captain came to visit me here when he was in port, bringing stories from the liquid mountains of the sea where there are as many wonderful beasts and fabulous islands as there are trees in a forest. I was tempted, Allah forgive me, to set sail again on other voyages and I met with other adventures.

'But I have stolen too many moments from the span of your life,' said Sinbad the Sailor to Sinbad the Porter. 'May Allah reward you and all those who have an attentive ear and can listen with their hearts to an old man's stories.'

'Sinbad sailed on five more voyages, my attentive and unsleeping lord.' Shahrazad slipped from bed and began to dress, for bright morning stood in the window and the Royal Swordsman stood in the courtyard below. 'I wonder how many ears have heard him describe the fight between the great rhinoceros and the elephant . . .'

'Shahrazad, aren't you afraid of the Swordsman?' her husband interrupted her.

'No, my lord,' she answered with honesty (for in her heart of hearts she had no fear of the Swordsman—only of his sword). She continued to dress quickly and cheerfully.

'Shahrazad, aren't you even afraid of Death?'

She looked at him with her head on one side. 'O fearless, long-lived King,' she said, 'I know that Death is huge and ugly and threatening, but so was the jinni in the Tale of The Fisherman and the Bottle, and you know how *that* story ended.'

Shahryar searched the library of his memory for the Tale of The Fisherman and the Bottle. For who but Shahrazad could know that the story was as new as tomorrow, a half-hatched story with scarcely a word to fly on.

'No, Shahrazad, I have questioned my heart and it claims not to know The Tale of The Fisherman and the Bottle.'

'Oh, dear,' said Shahrazad, opening the door on to the staircase. 'Poor heart.'

'. . . Wife!' said Shahryar, his temper flaring up. 'I do not like there to be stories *lying around* in this kingdom without me knowing of them. Come back tonight and tell me The Tale of the Fisherman and the Bottle. The Swordsman can wait another day. I command you.'

'To hear you is to obey,' said Shahrazad, and turned another way along the corridor.

CHAPTER FIVE

The Fisherman and the Bottle

The fisherman was well known hereabouts (said Shahrazad) though I forget his exact name. He used to be a familiar sight on the beach, throwing his net into the surf to catch bass and mullet. He was almost as old as he was poor, but his faith and trust in Allah comforted him.

Arriving at the sea shore and starting to work, he looked at the sky and said:

'O Allah who sends some days red with mullet and others silver with bass and still more black with mud, is it to be a day of the third kind? My net is caught on the bottom, Allah.'

When he finally dragged the net ashore, he found nothing in it but a dead donkey. Moving along the beach, he cast again, and again his net caught on the sea-bed. Looking at the sky he said:

'O Allah who makes fish, donkey, and fisherman, do

32

not grant me the blessing of a second donkey.' He undressed, dived in, and freed the net. This time he pulled in a small mountain of broken clay pots full of black mud.

'O Allah who makes and breaks every man's life, I thank you for this generous gift of broken pottery and mud, but consider how much greater my thanks would be were you to fill my nets with *fish*.'

He cast again, and yet again the net snagged against the rocks.

'O Allah, did my father or mother offend you before I was born, or is this simply Allah's idea of a joke?' said the fisherman, looking at the sky.

But when he hauled the net ashore, this time it contained a rather fine copper bottle. It was green with age, but once emptied and cleaned it would sell for a few dinars in the bazaar. The lead stopper was still in place, and the mouth of the bottle was sealed securely with an elaborate wax seal.

Now the fisherman's education was small and his ignorance was large. He did not recognize the Royal Seal of Suleiman, first and greatest of all Believers and King throughout the empires of Arabia, who lived two thousand years ago. So the fisherman broke the seal with his knife and prised out the lead stopper.

'What nodding-headed man sealed up an empty bottle,' he muttered, 'and threw a thing of value into the sea?'

He shook it vigorously upside down, but only a dust as fine as smoke trickled out: a dust so fine that its weight was less than air. It wreathed upwards from the bottle's neck, changing colour in the light. As dawn expands into daylight and shadow grows into night, so the dust expanded into a vapour. Just as a seed grows into a tree and a second grows into a year, so the vapour grew into a tower of weaving colours as tall as the sky. Then, just as a distant caravan in the heat-haze of a desert becomes little by little distinct, so the floating colours hardened into the leg, the arm, the hand, the head—the body of an immense jinni. The arch of his foot overshadowed the fisherman, and the lowness of the sky forced the creature to bend his head and neck.

A flat, square head overgrown on all sides with reddish stubble; his nose hung like a jug in the centre of a white face pitted and blotched with red. His mouth was as deep as the mines of Africa; the eyes were as yellow as sulphur beds and the purple veins beside them bubbled horribly.

For a moment the fisherman forgot his prayers, his name, and all the powers of speech. Amazement stupefied him. Then the sky's beams shook at the sound of the jinni's voice.

'O great Suleiman, defender of Allah, the one true god, I beg forgiveness and will never again—but you are not Suleiman, O smallest worm.'

The fisherman shook his head (as best he was able while leaning over backwards to gape up at the jinni). 'Who let me out of the bottle?'

'I did, sir. Me.'

'In that case, weasel, I have brought you interesting news,' said the jinni, picking a small cloud out of his beard and blowing it away like a dandelion head. 'It should interest you. It touches you closely.'

'News?' squeaked the fisherman. 'Me?'

'News of your death, O smallest and foulest one. Today. Now.'

The fisherman let out a piercing shriek. 'But what have I done?'

34

'Choose the way I should kill you,' said the jinni without pity, 'but make it horrible or I will think of a more dreadful way.'

The fisherman could only repeat: 'What have I done? What have I done? Pardon me, Allah. Pardon me, O vastest one, but what have I done?'

'Listen, child of a sickly frog,' said the jinni, swatting a flock of birds as they flew past his shoulder. 'I'll tell you my story, but prepare to die when I have told it. I am Sakhr al-Jinni, the ifrit, who rebelled against Suleiman, son of Daud. My army was defeated and my life fell under the foot of King Suleiman. How I crept and wept and flattered, until the King, thinking I was sorry, said: "Calm yourself, Sakhr al-Jinni. Promise to obey me and to obey Allah, and I shall forgive you." Forgive? *Me*? Sakhr al-Jinni, Terror of the Lower Hemisphere? I told him: "You will wait a lifetime for my obedience and Allah will wait an eternity before I become a Believer!"

And so Suleiman stuffed me into this bottle and sealed it with his seal and hurled me into the deep ocean, where I washed and swashed about like a lake squeezed into a cup or a whale squeezed into an egg.'

'But Lord Suleiman died two thousand years ago!' exclaimed the fisherman, and the jinni let out a terrible groan as he remembered his imprisonment.

'For the first hundred years I swore that if anyone freed me from that copper bottle I would grant him three wishes—however greedy.

'But nobody came.

'For the next two hundred years I swore that if anyone freed me from that copper bottle I would give him and all his tribe everlasting riches.

'But nobody came.

'For the next five hundred years I swore that if anyone freed me from that copper bottle I would make him ruler and owner of all the people of earth!

'But nobody came.

'For the next thousand years I swore . . . and I swore, but now my oaths were terrible. My patience was gone, my fury was bigger than the ocean I was floating in. I swore that if anyone freed me from that copper bottle (*unless, of course, it was the all-powerful Lord Suleiman*) I would make him the first to feel the scourge of my revenge! My old enemies are long since dead. You will have the honour of standing in their place while I cut you to atoms! I have sworn it.'

With that the jinni drew a cutlass brighter than sheet lightning, and began warming its edge in the sun's furnace. He had been looking forward so eagerly for two thousand years to boiling his victim in terror before mincing him, that he looked down once more to enjoy the fisherman's despairing face.

The fisherman, however, was looking up at him with one finger against his nose and one eye winking.

'Tsk, tsk,' said the fisherman. 'Come now, you don't really expect me to believe that, do you?'

The jinni's anger shook the ocean and caused a tidal wave in furthest China. 'The curses of ten thousand dogs on you and all your tribe,' he bellowed. But the fisherman only shook his head and smiled knowingly.

'No, be honest now, where did you come from just now? I know I was shaking out this old bottle when you—when you loomed up, so to speak. But ignorant as I am, I know what can be done and what cannot, and I also know when someone is enjoying a joke at my expense. I couldn't fit one leg into that bottle.' And the fisherman demonstrated, trying unsuccessfully to squeeze one foot through the narrow bottleneck. 'A sheep cut into small pieces would barely fit inside.'

'But I am a *jinni* . . .' said the ifrit, pouting slightly.

'Well *I've* certainly never met a jinni of half your size' (said the fisherman with perfect honesty), 'who could do such a thing. Take that cutlass for instance—two thousand years in the sea and no rust to show for it? A jinni who wore that sword and climbed inside such a small bottle would surely ruin himself. No, no. It's no good trying to fool me. You may be clever, sir, but it would take true genius to fit a jinni of your magnitude and magnificence into a bottle like this. Speak truly, where did you come from and what put it into your heart to make fun of a poor old fisherman on such a lovely day?'

It seemed that the jinni would burst with frustration. 'Ignorant little worm,' he shouted, shaking his fists and tearing holes in the sky with them. 'Can you not be made to understand the power of Sakhr al-Jinni, Bringer of Death to a thousand such fishermen as you? Watch me! And shake in your rope-soled sandals, for this is the least of my powers and I am more skilled still in killing stupid, ignorant, witless old fishermen!'

Then, just as an old man's sight grows blurred, the body of the jinni broke up into a tower of weaving colours. And just as a rushing river shrinks to a trickle in summer, so the column shrank to a modest fountain of colour. And just as rocks crumble into sand, so the smoke left only a light soot—a fine dust—that trickled back into the bottle.

Snatching up the lead stopper, the fisherman pushed it in on top of the jinni and pressed home the two-thousand-year-old Royal Seal of Lord Suleiman.

'So, Bringer of Death to a thousand fishermen, Terror of the Southern Hemisphere, lie there for another two thousand years. I shall tell my fellow fishermen that this beach is haunted by a hideous ifrit so that they never have my bad luck in drawing up such a monstrous fish. And may Allah send me the quickness of wits, even in the slowness of old age, to put any such jinni as you in its right and proper place!'

So saying, he hurled the bottle as far out to sea as his old arms would let him. And so it was that one humble Believer escaped a cruel and terrible death.

And so it was that Shahrazad, thousand and first wife of Shahryar, ruler of all Sasan, escaped her own death, delighting the King with stories night after night. Each morning the Wazir, her father, would wait in the courtyard a short way from the Royal Headsman, holding the silver dish on which he must one day present the head of Shahrazad to her jealous, bitter husband. And each day he carried the dish away empty, though he felt a little older each time he climbed the stairs to his rooms to tell the news to little Dunyazad.

On the morning of the fifteenth day, Shahrazad promised to tell the Tale of Pearl-harvest that self-same night, and King Shahryar found that the poet was wise who wrote:

> *Day seems short*
> *When night's a foul and sleepless waste;*
> *Day seems long*
> *When night's a warm and friendly place.*

CHAPTER SIX

The Tale of Pearl-harvest

Can a river forget its source, a sunbeam forget the sun? Can the anchor on the sea-bed forget the ship, or the tail of a snake forget the head that went before it? Can today forget yesterday? Can a man forget his father and grandfather? The Kalifah al-Mutasid Billah, although he was a mighty Commander of the Faithful and sixth Kalifah in the line of Abbas, took pride most of all in being the grandson of al-Mutawakkil, the grandson of Harun al-Rashid.

The young al-Mutasid Billah travelled his kingdom widely, to see for himself the lives of his people and hear the small voices of the weak, which are never heard in palaces. The story runs—though who can tell if it is true?—that one such journey took him through a pleasant orange grove in a quiet country place.

It was the hottest part of the day (when travellers do well to draw aside respectfully and let the sun pass by) and al-Mutasid Billah sent messengers to the owner of the grove, asking for the shelter of his roof. He did not, however, mention his name. The owner sent word that he wished himself more worthy of the honour but would welcome any traveller with every hospitality his poor home could afford.

The house was plain to look at, but the hospitality of the humble orange-grower surpassed anything offered to al-Mutasid on all his journeys among the common people. The ruler, his wazir, his companions and servants were given drinks of sherbet water-ices, pomegranates, melons, and sweet confections, all served in a room as beautiful as any at the Royal Palace. They lay on silk cushions fringed with gold, among Persian carpets and low cherrywood tables covered with finest Egyptian linen. Shantung silk hung at the windows, and perfumed candles burned inside lamp-holders of chased Indian silver. A fretwork silver screen separated the room from the stone-paved kitchens and drab exterior rooms, and behind it someone was playing exquisite music on a lute. The rich and gorgeous furnishings were showing many signs of wear, but the music drifting through from the outer room transformed both room and food into a small paradise, all the more alluring to al-Mutasid because it was so unexpected in this out-of-the-way orange grove.

Just then the elderly owner came in and bowed low before al-Mutasid Billah and asked if his poor hospitality had left them discontent in any way.

'We lack only your company and your name. Come and sit with us and tell us about your life and how you came by the finest lute-player in the kingdom!'

'O gentle and generous guest, I am usually called Abu al-Hasan Ali ibn Ahmad of Khurasan. The hand you have heard playing the lute is that of my beloved wife, Pearl-harvest. Her hands are older now, but they still play a pleasant tune.' The lute-playing had stopped meantime, and their host left to speak to his wife when the party asked to hear more music.

When Abu al-Hasan returned, al-Mutasid was standing up, his servants and courtiers were halfway to their feet. His look was that of the cobra on a rat.

'Speak before blinking an eye,' he stormed. 'Who are you and have you anything to say that will stop me cutting off both your hands?'

Abu al-Hasan fell on his face in front of his guest, gibbering with fear. 'I am usually called Abu al-Hasan Ali ibn Ahmad of Khurasan,' he said distractedly, 'and I need my hands to tend the oranges!'

'Your excuse is disallowed. Do you know who I am?'

'I have not yet enjoyed the honour of knowing your name, noble sir, but if my hospitality has offended you in any way . . .'

'I am Kalifah al-Mutasid Billah, Commander of the Faithful and grandson of the all-esteemed al-Mutawakkil.'

Abu al-Hasan crawled forward and kissed the ground between the feet of the Kalifah.

'Speak before the sunlight touches the ground: why is this room furnished entirely with things stolen from my grandfather's palace? See here, his heraldry is woven into every cushion, every curtain; it is in the carpet's weave and engraved on the silverware. Thief! Villain! What wickedness did you commit to lay your hands on these things?'

Abu al-Hasan breathed deeply and raised his head. He smiled as the mouse smiles who hears that a cat has died.

'Be seated in comfort, lord of all living lords, and I will tell you the wonderful story connected with these

41

furnishings. Allah give me quickness of tongue to put your heart at ease before the food of my table has settled itself in your stomach.'

Still with the look of an angry scorpion, Kalifah al-Mutasid sat down, fixing the old man with unforgiving eyes. And Abu al-Hasan began his story:

While I was still young, I inherited from my father the most successful and thriving jewellery shop in Baghdad—where al-Mutawakkil had his palace. That most honourable of grandfathers was at that time a tree in the flourishing summer of his life, and his wealth was beyond calculation by mere accountants. He had a fine harem of wives and a retinue of the most beautiful slaves—male and female—that money could buy in the market.

One morning I was sitting in the shop when a young woman, totally veiled, came in. I went to serve her and showed her some pieces of jewellery without really paying her much attention. But when she asked the price of one particular bracelet, her voice was as sweet as a babbling spring and I looked up without a thought—and instantly drowned in the standing water of her eyes. My poor soul clung to the long curling black rushes that fringed each pool, but could not swim against the current of love, and it drew me down into the black vortex at the centre of her brown eyes. She did not lower her eyes from mine until I thought I would collapse, surfeited with their light like a man faint from sunstroke. Through the muslin veil I could see that her mouth was like a small red flower filled with white hail.

'Give me this bracelet,' she said, without breaking the spell.

'Take it,' I murmured, 'as a gift from one who has earned his living from beautiful jewels but never seen beauty before today.'

She was gone, like a fly taking flight, and I wondered whether I had dreamt her. But the shop itself seemed to be holding its breath and indeed the bracelet had gone, unpaid for.

The same thing happened the next day, although the rim of her yashmak seemed a little lower and a hairline of bird-black hair framed those miraculous Babylonian eyes. Believe me, I cast my heart on to the waters of those eyes, and there it floated and there it sank. When she left the shop my heart went with her: I had also given her outright every ruby and emerald in my shop. 'Take them,' I had said, 'from one who has lived too long if tomorrow holds no sight of you.'

The very same thing happened the next day and, when she came in, my shop seemed two windows lighter and my own face called to me from the reflecting pools of her eyes.

'Take these as a gift from one who will die of thirst if he does not drink again at the watering place of your eyes,' I said, pressing on her all the diamonds and pearls in my shop. As she leaned forward to take them, the veil fell away from her face altogether, and I cried out as the sharpness of her beauty ran me through.

I was lost under folds of love as a man is lost under the folds of a fallen tent. I locked up my shop and followed the lady—all the way to the gates of the great palace. Fear should have barred my way, but without thinking of the consequences I found a small window in the palace wall and climbed in through it, feet first.

Feeling about with one foot for a ledge or chair, I felt

a small pair of hands take my foot and place it on a wooden stool, and as I climbed down, an angelic little page-boy took my hand to steady me. Looking me up and down, he said:

'You must be Abu al-Hasan Ali ibn Ahmad of Khurasan. Couldn't you have come any sooner?'

'What do you mean, pretty child? I don't even know why I came or what I intend to do. I followed a lady here: she dragged my heart behind her as a ship drags its anchor in a storm. But how shall I find her among all the harem and slaves of Kalifah al-Mutawakkil? And what shall I do if I find her?'

'Please, please,' the small boy interrupted me. 'Do stop your quacking. The lady in question is Pearl-harvest, the Kalifah's lute-player. Her room is on the third level of the eastern wing at the end of the fourth corridor. What you do when you find her is entirely your own concern. But she has been wearing our ears thin with descriptions of your face, your hair, your arms, your eyes, and so on and so on. In short, sir, abandon hope: she has made up her mind to have you.'

'Abandon hope? If I cannot marry Pearl-harvest of the Babylonian eyes, I shall throw myself off the highest tower of the palace and never be thought of again . . .'

'Quack, quack. There you go again. If you only wish to die for love, it is easy in the palace of al-Mutawakkil where every door is guarded by Ethiopian wrestlers. But if you wish to live long enough to see Pearl-harvest again you will need to undertake certain risks. You will, of course, be killed instantly if the Kalifah al-Mutawakkil finds you in the women's quarters of his palace.'

On the instructions of my beloved Pearl-harvest, the boy had laid everything ready. He brought me one of the

Kalifah's own robes—a hooded kaftan—in which I disguised myself.

'Every evening,' the boy said, 'the Kalifah tours the women's quarters and enjoys the sight of their faces, for he only of all men has the right to see them unveiled: they are his property.'

'And is he not mad for love of Pearl-harvest when he sees her face daily?' I asked, sick with jealousy.

'Allah enlighten you, sir! Among the women of the palace Pearl-harvest is a buffalo among horses. She is not even one of the wives in his harem. She is just the lute-player. The Kalifah is nose-deep in love with his new wife, the lady Sweet-Friend of Kurdistan. If he found you with Pearl-harvest, sir, al-Mutawakkil would kill you more for stealing her music than her beauty. But hurry now. You must begin your tour of the women's quarters before the Kalifah begins his. And we, the friends of Pearl-harvest, cannot spend another day listening to her glowing descriptions of your *eyebrow*, sir. Go to her now, and live or die as Allah wills it.'

In the gorgeous palace of al-Mutawakkil there were many hundreds of doors. The page-boy explained that as the Kalifah passed each door at night, he would place a grain of musk in a saucer by the door. He gave me a bag of musk seeds and told me to do the self-same thing, patrolling the corridors at a slow and stately pace and remembering to place a grain of musk in every saucer—so that the guards would not suspect that I was an imposter.

Every corridor seemed as long as the road from Ain Sefra to Niemey and every staircase as long as the Nile. As I passed each door, I opened it and, shutting my eyes, put my head inside. A woman's voice would say: 'Allah

45

send you sweet dreams, master, and many sons,' and I would shut the door again and place a grain of musk in the saucer by the doorpost.

'The Kalifah is early tonight,' I heard one guard say to another as I passed.

Allah forgive me, I opened the very occasional eyelid and saw such beauty as flowered on the walls of the hanging gardens of Babylon. But I had no heart to lose to the beautiful harem of al-Mutawakkil, for mine was already given.

Up above me, in marble corridors, panelled with cedar and hung with silver lamps, I heard the hem of a robe swish against the golden fringing of a carpet and knew that the Kalifah al-Mutawakkil had begun his evening round. He was descending the building as I worked my way up it. I heard doors open and shut and the distant murmur of goodnights. Not knowing which way to turn, I looked back along the corridor at the row of saucers, each containing a musk seed. As soon as the Kalifah came to a saucer already filled, or passed a guard who had already seen him, I was certain my secret would be discovered.

To the amazement of the huge Ethiopian guards, I set off to run, thinking not to escape downstairs but simply to see my beloved Pearl-harvest once more before I met with my death. Up the staircase to the third level of the eastern wing and along the fourth corridor—halfway along it I heard the Kalifah coming in the opposite direction. At any second he would turn the corner and see me.

'Son of sunshine, O joy of Sasan,' a voice called through the bedroom doors, 'King Shahryar, son of Shahbillah, are you awake yet? The sun's face has slipped from behind the veil of the horizon, and the mullah is calling all Believers to prayer.'

King Shahryar grabbed up a cloak and left the room, calling for water to wash himself before morning prayers and leaving Shahrazad with a mouth full of words but no ear to receive them.

A moment later, the Chancellor came into the Royal bedroom backwards (for fear of seeing the face of the King's wife) and said: 'Our glorious King sends word that the Tale of Pearl-harvest must be continued tonight. Is that understood?'

'To hear his words or the words of his messengers is to obey,' said Shahrazad, smiling as the Chancellor tripped over a rug.

CHAPTER SEVEN

The Tale of
Pearl-harvest continues

'At any second the Kalifah al-Mutawakkil would turn the corner and see me,' said Abu al-Hasan, continuing his story to the Kalifah's grandson.

I put my hand to a door handle and slipped inside, throwing back my hood to wipe the sweat from my face. A young woman sat in the middle of the floor, as pretty as a single jasmine blossom. She at once saw that I was not the Kalifah and lifted the hem of her muslin gown across her face. I waited for her to scream, my fingers in my ears, my terror pouring through my skin.

But she did not scream at all; she only said:

'You must be Abu al-Hasan Ali ibn Ahmad of Khurasan. Couldn't you have come any sooner?' Seeing that I was still too afraid to utter a word, she went on: 'I am Sweet-Almond, the sister of Pearl-harvest. She has stretched my ears to the size of a rabbit's with her words of love. But she did speak truly when she said that your face is as lovely as the hyacinth and clematis. And you have passed all her tests of love to come this far and risk your life so perilously. I will take you to her without delay.'

She veiled herself, and led me to a communicating door to the next bedroom. There I found Pearl-harvest as a man lost in the desert finds a cool stream. She was sitting in the middle of the floor wearing no veil and singing to herself. When she saw me, she jumped up and put her arms round my neck. 'Couldn't you have come any sooner?' she said.

Pearl-harvest explained that I was in no danger at all: 'The Kalifah places the grains of musk in the saucers because, with so many doors, he easily forgets which ladies he has visited and which he has not. When he finds the grains that you have left, he will think he has been there earlier in the evening.'

'But when the guards see two Kalifahs in one night . . .' I said. But she told me that the Ethiopian guards were not allowed, on pain of death, to speak words to the Kalifah and so could say nothing.

'We can escape, then and be married,' I exclaimed, holding her in my arms like a bouquet of flowers. 'Kiss me and sing me a love song, then bring your most valuable belongings and come with me. We will leave Baghdad and find a new land beyond a new sea where you will be no one's slave but your husband's.'

Pearl-harvest silenced me: 'You are my heart's blood,' she said, 'but the arms of the great al-Mutawakkil are long, and I am his property. Let us live or die as Allah wills it, but I have only this to say on the matter: I shall hold you, as the sea holds the land, until we are separated.'

As we spoke there was a rattle at the door, which made Pearl-harvest tremble like a deer. The Kalifah had come. She threw a large cushion behind the door to block it while she looked around in panic for somewhere to hide me.

Now, until that moment of immediate danger, I had seen only the beauty of Pearl-harvest, but now I looked at every detail of her room. It was furnished with the most exquisite taste and splendour, as was the whole Palace. The floor was covered in Persian carpets and scattered with silk cushions fringed with gold. Low cherrywood tables under Egyptian linen were piled with fruit bowls and jugs of wine. Shantung silk hung at the windows, and scented candles burned in lamp-holders of chased Indian silver. A chest, upholstered in velvet so as to make a fine wide seat, stood in the alcove of a fretted silver screen. Lifting up the padded lid, Pearl-harvest signalled for me to climb inside.

'Forgive my careless and slovenly ways, my sweet lord,' I heard Pearl-harvest say as she cleared the doorway and allowed the Kalifah to enter. 'Allah send you sweet dreams, O master, and many sons.'

But al-Mutawakkil did not simply close the door and pass on to the next bedroom. He came inside, told her to veil herself, and brought his wazir into the room as well. Feet shuffled, robes rustled, the smell of musk crept in through the seams of the chest, and then the wood surrounding me groaned under the weight of a heavy man. The Kalifah al-Mutawakkil, Commander of the Faithful—imagine the honour—had sat down on my hiding place.

'Pearl-harvest, you know that the walls of this palace keep secrets badly,' said the voice above me. (What was this? Were our secrets found out and our lives lost?) 'You probably know already that I am about to be married again

50

to the most lovely wife in all Araby—Sweet-Friend of Kurdistan. My love for her is so new, so strong, so happy, so . . . Well, Pearl-harvest, a girl of your years will not understand me, for you have never suffered the sickness of love. But I tell you, this love sits on my chest so heavily that I can barely breathe, and my happiness is so great that I fear it will choke me or swell me up like a bullfrog. For truly, to fit so much love into so small a man is like the old story of the jinni held prisoner in a small bottle. My wazir advises me that there is no remedy for this happy pain except to hear a love-song. Is it possible, despite your inexperience in affairs of love, that you know a love-song to soothe me?'

Now Pearl-harvest was as filled with love for the humble Abu al-Hasan as the Kalifah was for his new wife. She was filled with love as a ship's sail is filled with wind. So when she took her lute on to her lap and opened her mouth to sing an old song, new words and music poured from her soul: a music that might have been blown from the flower trumpet of an arum lily.

Her song began:

> *O sister, can you guess*
> *How deep in love I am?*
> *Or why Allah should bless*
> *A woman with a man?*
> *And such a man as he!*
> *Who thunders like a weir*
> *In the river of my blood*
> *And drowns my every fear*
> *In his white, courageous flood!*

and her song ended:

51

What love could equal mine,
The happiest of happy brides?
Not ninety-nine times nine
Who loved until the sea's last tide.

When Pearl-harvest finished singing, tears were glistening in the beard of al-Mutawakkil. He wrung his hands with wonder, and rocked to and fro on the bench.

'O Pearl-harvest, ask anything of me in return for such a song. What could you ask that I would not give you?'

Obediently, Pearl-harvest said: 'I desire nothing but to sing for you from time to time and delight your heart when I am able.'

But the Kalifah insisted that she should name some valuable reward—the contents of a gold mine or a cargo ship to carry her name along all the trading routes of the Seven Seas.

'If I must fix a reward,' she said finally, 'let it be my freedom and the furnishings of this one room. Forgive me, master, if I ask too much.'

'A woman without greed is as rare as a sea without water. Take your freedom as of this moment and accept my blessing, and look for the blessing of Allah who loves plain women better than beautiful ones.'

Plain women, indeed! I almost called out from the chest that only a blind man in the dark could call my Pearl-harvest a plain woman! But I held my tongue and, within the hour, felt two of those huge Ethiopian guards lift the chest in which I lay hidden and carry it downstairs. Behind and ahead, more slaves carried alabaster fountains, lamp-holders and carpets, curtains, cushions, and porcelain finger-bowls. This strange procession of sleepy porters moved the entire contents of Pearl-harvest's room down to the wagon yard beyond the palace wall.

I climbed out of my hiding-place and walked home through a night giddy with moon and star.

And, by first light, Pearl-harvest came to the shop, followed by six cart-loads of furniture. The silver screen you see behind you occupied one whole wagon.

We sold all the jewels—hers and mine—and moved away from Baghdad to live a peaceful life here in these orange groves. We are neither rich nor poor, but the shop in that crowded arcade in the casbah was too small for our love, which daily grew and grew—rather like the jinni in the old story when he escaped from his small bottle.

Now, sir, the joys of my life have been crowned by a visit from the Kalifah al-Mutasid, sixth Kalifah in the line of Abbas. My regrets will be few if your worship can take pleasure in cutting off my hands.

When Abu al-Hasan finished his story, the young Kalifah al-Mutasid clapped his hands together and roared with delight. He wrapped Abu al-Hasan in his arms and congratulated him on his wife and on his quickness of tongue.

'Sweet-Friend of Kurdistan was my favourite grandmother!' he exclaimed. 'Not only will I spare you your hands, Abu al-Hasan Ali ibn Ahmad of Khurasan, but I will spare you any taxes from now until the time of your death. Live in peace and prosperity or as Allah wills, and tell your wife, if you will, that my eyes are round with wonder at the thought of her beauty.'

The sun in its midday fierceness had long since passed. The Kalifah and his court mounted their horses again and left the orange grove for other parts of the kingdom. Watching them leave, from a small balcony, was the slight figure of an old lady. The heavy black cotton of her headscarf hid her white hair and her skin like yellow hammered vellum, but it revealed a rather splendid pair of elderly brown eyes. Pearl-harvest offered thanks to Allah, and then her husband joined her on the balcony and they stood holding hands as the oranges in the groves sank into darkness like a thousand and one orange suns.

As Shahrazad finished the Tale of Pearl-harvest, her own heart had sat listening like a quiet guest at the story-telling. Now it fell flat with fear as Shahryar turned on his wife with speechless rage. It seemed as though he would lift her from the bed and fling her on to the kindling fire in the centre of the bedchamber.

'The Kalifah al-Mutasid had less sense than a camel's tail, and Abu al-Hasan less hope than a man chest-deep in quicksand. Didn't he keep the furniture and sell the woman at the very next cattle market?'

'Oh, no, my perceptive and gentle husband, for she loved him as dearly as he loved her,' said Shahrazad aghast.

'Execrable and foul-mouthed woman. Your stories are full of lies and deception. Did Pearl-harvest not belong to the Kalifah when she let Abu al-Hasan see her face and shined on him with her eyes and waited on him with her hands? She had no right to do so. She was made of oil and water as all women are, and even if her husband locked her in the innermost room of his house and bricked up the windows and nailed shut the door, she would pour herself through the keyhole into the mouth of another man before long.'

Then suddenly the angry thunderclouds in the King's black eyes all shed their rain and he hid his face from Shahrazad and wept. 'The people in your stories are not liars,' he said. 'They are nothing but lies that you drop from your mouth to deceive me. They do not exist. The world of men is not as you paint it. People are worthless and their mouths are as full of lies as the rukh's egg is full of rukh.'

Closing her eyes, Shahrazad urged her heart to rescue her.

'O just and injured husband, that is very true. The animals everywhere testify to the truth of what you say. Their stories are full of the crooked cunning of Man, and they warn their children nightly to beware of Man's tricky and deceitful ways.'

There was a silence. King Shahryar turned over and looked at her in amazement.

'Do you understand the language of animals, Shahrazad? Your father did not tell me.'

'I understand enough to have heard some of their stories and memorize them. But were you to have me tell them I would, for your delight and ease, speak them in Arabic.'

'Do the animals truly know the cunning heart of Man?' asked Shahryar, wide-eyed with fascination.

'Not as you do, O Prince of Learning, but they have learned a little about it from The Tale of the Lion's Revenge on Man-kin. Judge for yourself.'

CHAPTER EIGHT

The Lion's Revenge on Man-kin

All this happened early in the morning of Time before the golden trees that covered the Sahara had crumbled into the yellow dust called sand, and when Animals and Man spoke one language. A goose woke up from a nightmare screaming, and ran about, head stretched out and wings beating with fear until she collapsed on a flat rock with fright and exhaustion. When a lion strolled out from a nearby cave and sauntered up to her, she was too overcome to move.

'Gentle creature,' he said (for he was a cultured and finely bred young lion who had led a sheltered childhood). 'What is your name?'

'My name is Goose and I am of the Tribe of Bird,' she said, curtsying respectfully.

'I see you have been frightened. If it is not too painful to recount, please do tell me how.'

The Goose recounted her dream—a blind nightmare

without pictures in which a voice whispered:

> *Goose, poor goose, beware, beware*
> *And warn the chicken and the hare;*
> *Warn the fish and warn your wife*
> *Man-kin comes to take their life.*
> *Warn the deer and warn the cow*
> *Man-kin's coming even now.*
> *Never trust and never thank him*
> *For no foe is worse than Man-kin.*

The Lion scratched thoughtfully.

'I had just such a dream once, and when I told my father his fur turned quite a pale yellow and he told me never to live in the same province as Man-kin. Personally, I've never seen the beast.'

The Goose was still white with fright—even to the tip of her beak—and seeing that the young Lion had an exceptionally lean and muscular flank, fine strong paws and claws as sharp as cuttle-shell, she said:

'It is clear to me what must be done. This Enemy of Animals must be destroyed. We must find a champion who will defend us against this cruel and merciless beast. And now I look at you, who better than the Prince of Beasts and the finest lion among the whole Tribe of Cat? Your fame will sound through sky, earth, and water when you have killed Man-kin.'

The Goose went on flattering the Lion until he agreed to hunt down and exterminate the Enemy of All Animals. He strode off, cracking his tail like a whip, and the Goose paddled along behind him, trying to keep up.

They went on until the Lion's nose was offended by a cloud of dust scuffed up in their path. In the middle of it was a donkey, rolling on its back, then jumping about kicking its feet in the air. The Lion, who had led a sheltered childhood, wrinkled up his nose.

'Come here, animal,' he said, 'and tell me, if you have a brain in your head, who you are and why you are behaving in this way.'

'O golden-furred master, I am Donkey of the Tribe of Ass and I have escaped, if only for a day, from the awful Man-kin.'

The Lion laughed: 'Whatever size is this beast Man-kin that an animal as large and as hard-hoofed as you is frightened of him?'

'Ah, I see that you do not know this terrible creature, Golden One. Coward that I am, I would not be afraid of Man-kin if he only wanted to kill me. He does worse than that. He puts something leather on my back and ties it so tightly under my stomach that I can barely breathe. He puts a metal bone between my teeth and sits on my back, pulling on the metal bone with strips of leather to turn me this way and that. Then he pokes me in the neck with a sharp stick until I run faster than my mother or father intended me to run, and when I cannot run any more he screams such words in my ears that my brains curdle like sour milk. When I'm old he will use me as a pack animal, and I will carry big water jars that bang together and squash my heart flat inside me . . .'

'Take me to this contemptible beast, O Donkey, and you will have helped in the Revenge of All Animals on Man-kin,' roared the Lion.

'Who me?' answered the Donkey. 'Forgive me, O Lion. I am undoubtedly your miserable slave, but I only ran away yesterday and although I'm sure Man-kin will catch me again, I intend to enjoy this one short day of freedom.'

So the Lion went on ahead of the Goose until he met a deer whose leaps were as long and elegant as the sun's daily leap from eastern to western horizon.

'O elegant creature of the twig-like legs,' said the Lion (who had led a very sheltered childhood). 'Who are you?'

'I am Gazelle of the Tribe of Deer,' said the Deer, trembling as four reeds tremble under the weight of a dragonfly. 'Be merciful, O beast of the sunshine fur, and don't delay me in my flight from Man-kin.'

The Lion laughed with disbelief: 'How long are the legs of Man-kin that he can chase a creature as fast-footed as you?'

'Ah, I see you don't know this terrible creature, O silk-haired Prince,' replied the Deer sadly. 'Sometimes Man-kin carries spines on his back which he plucks out and fits to a smooth branch and sends flying like hornets straight into the heart of Deer-kin. To give him speed of movement, he has also enslaved Horse of the Tribe of Horse. He forces her to carry a piece of leather on her back and a metal bone between her teeth. He nails shoes to her feet and keeps her captive at night by tying her feet together with hairy hemp rope. I pity the poor Horse, for Man-kin only wants to kill me with his "arrows". He works the Horse to death, harnessing her to a watermill in her old age to turn the wheel from morning to night. O Lion, let me go, for pity's sake. I hear the metal pounding of Horse's hooves coming closer and closer.'

No sooner had the Deer leapt out of eyesight than a fine black horse galloped into view rolling its glorious eyes and foaming at the mouth. But there was no Man-kin on her back, only a strange leather seat.

'Oh, do not delay me, gentle animals. I am running away from Man-kin and I know he is close behind me!'

'Wait, O Horse of the Tribe of Horse. I am Lion Prince of Beasts and I have sworn to make the Revenge of All Animals on Man-kin. Stay and see me hold him between my paws while I eat him from head to foot.'

But Horse had already gone, and all that stood on the path ahead was a huge and shaggy animal as ugly as an ifrit.

Growling the growl of a falling tree, the Lion leapt at the creature's throat crying, 'You must be Man-kin, big and horrible as you are to look at, and I have brought the Revenge of All Animals in my teeth and claws!'

'O excellent but sheltered Lion,' quacked the Goose, arriving in the nick of time. 'This cannot be Man-kin unless he is in all respects like a Camel, gentlest of all creatures.'

'Aioee!' wailed the shaggy animal as the Lion sprang on her. 'I am indeed Bactrian of the Tribe of Camel. Doesn't Man-kin make me suffer enough without you tearing out my throat?'

The Lion was filled with apologies to the lowest rib of his chest, but the Camel could not be consoled, and lay down on her side sobbing pitifully.

'It was hopeless anyway,' she said, 'to think that I could ever escape from Man-kin. He can be no more than a mile behind me, and I was too tired before I even began running. Man-kin loads me down with Things and Objects and Goods and Merchandise. I was once like my cousin Dromedary, but look at the groove Man-kin has worn in my hump with his Things and Objects and Goods and Merchandise.'

The Lion and the Goose examined Bactrian's back and, indeed, his hump was so worn in the middle that it looked altogether like *two* humps.

'Take heart, good Bactrian,' said the Lion. 'I have taken upon me the Revenge of All Animals on Man-kin, and your unhappiness has made me all the more determined to tear him and shred him and eat every morsel of him.'

'Lose heart, O well-intentioned but sheltered Lion, for Man-kin has broken my heart and will certainly break yours.'

But the Lion had gone. He ran ahead so hot-headedly that Goose could not keep up, and so Lion was alone when he met with the next beast.

It was a poor, slow-moving creature standing up on two legs like a chicken, but bent under a weight of wooden planks and metal nails. Its fur was all worn out but for a patch on top of its head and its skin was wrinkled. At the sight of the Lion it fell on its face and crawled towards him weeping as though its heart would break.

'O glorious king, O Allah increase the strength of your paw and paint your name in letters of gold on the blue vellum of the sky's frame. Surely your power is large enough for me to creep under your protection and be safe. I have suffered so much at the hands of my enemy, Man-kin.'

'Poor beast,' said the Lion, quite moved to tears. 'What kind of beast are you that Allah has put you inside such a weak and ugly body but given you the knowledge of flowing and delectable words?'

'May Allah preserve your Lordship. I am Carpenter. Man-kin made me work from morning till night for no money or food. I have run away from the city where he lives, but he is coming after me. He has no one to build his homes for him any more. All is not lost, however, if only I can find your father's cousin, Leopard of the Tribe

61

of Cat. He at least must be made safe even if I die serving him.'

Now the Lion, who was in a highly excitable mood, leapt about on his paws feeling hotly offended.

'Why the Leopard? Why must he be made safe? eh? eh?' and he pushed the Carpenter in the chest so that he fell over on top of his tools.

'Glorious but sheltered Prince of Beasts, he sent for me to build him a stockade—a strong cabin that would keep him safe from even the attacks of Man-kin. He intends to wait until Man-kin has exhausted himself beating on the cabin and then leap out of the cabin and make the Revenge of All Animals on his enemy.'

'Oh!' roared the Lion. '*I* have taken upon me the Revenge of All Animals. The Leopard stepped out of his rightful place in the Order of Living Things when he sent those orders. You will build *me* the cabin instead.'

The Carpenter wrung his hands apologetically and simpered at the Lion: 'What would become of your honourable servant, Carpenter, if I offended the Leopard? Let me go and make him his cabin and then I will return and build you a palace, a veritable palace.'

The Lion lifted the Carpenter between both paws as though he would bite off his head. 'Build a cabin for me *first*, or I shall bite you to death here and now. Leopard can wait.'

Carpenter took out a rule, measured the Lion, who stood head erect and chest thrown out grandly. In a few moments a solid box was built with a sliding door at one end.

'It seems very narrow . . .' said the Lion, eyeing the door.

'Plenty of room inside, O most courageous, intrepid and fearless of all beasts.'

So the Lion squeezed in leaving only his tail outside. With a flick of the wrist the Carpenter twisted the tail, packed it in with the rest of the Lion, and nailed up the cage door. The Lion, stuck round with splinters and the points of nails, roared with pain and shame. But Carpenter of the Tribe of Man-kin only danced a jig round the cage before stacking twigs round it and setting it alight from end to end, shouting, 'Yellow dog of the desert! Man-kin may be ugly and weak but he has enough lies and cunning in his heart to drown all courage and strength and beauty—and to burn all Cats!'

'Oh, no! No! No, sweet Shahrazad!' said King Shahryar, unable to remain silent for another word's length. 'Men may be treacherous, but I know no one in the kingdoms of Sasan and Samarkand al-Ajam put together who is quite so cruel and heartless as the Man-kin in your story. Burn the most glorious of beasts? What are you thinking of, Shahrazad?'

'Ah, did I not say that the world was only young when it happened? Perhaps it had learned less kindness, my kind and compassionate lord, than this kingdom has learned under your gentle rule.'

Shahryar looked sharply at Shahrazad his wife, and went to sleep without saying another word.

CHAPTER NINE

The Everlasting Shoes

One night, Shahrazad arrived in the King's bedchamber only to find him already asleep. Thinking she had come late and missed her opportunity to tell a story, she crept under the covers and lay in the hollow of the King's arm, searching the beehive cells of her heart for honey words to sweeten his temper in the morning.

Knowing that her art lay more in story-telling than in pleading or flattery, she opened her lips and whispered: 'Merciful Allah sees and knows me, small as I am. Perhaps Allah who writes the story of every man's life from its first letter to its last full stop, will grant me opportunity to tell Shahryar one more story and delight his heart with one more tale.' So saying, she closed her eyes and slept, as beautiful as a frost-covered reed floating on a river.

The next morning, King Shahryar, floating in the slack water between the ebb-tide of sleep and the flow-tide of waking, grumbled.

'Another day of listening to greedy merchants slandering each other. They expect me to make judgements on who owns a camel and who overcharged for a cow. The world is as full of greed, Shahrazad, as a duck egg is full of duck. I go to the audience chamber each day and my heart drops lower and lower like a bucket in a well—down, down, down—greed, greed, greed.'

'Would it raise your heart a little then, my melancholy and overburdened lord, to hear a story of a dreadful old miser who lived in Cairo once and suffered fittingly for his meanness?'

The King was instantly awake. 'But it's morning! I missed my story!' he said in astonishment. 'I lay down yesterday evening because my head ached, and I slept right through your story!'

'Ah well . . . Shall I tell it to you tonight, O bright and inexhaustible King?' said Shahrazad.

'Oh, first I shall hear the story of the miser. Tell the other tomorrow.'

So giving thanks to Allah, Shahrazad helped the King to dress and brushed his hair which, in her eyes, seemed as dark and soft as the black swan's winter down on the palace lake.

There was once a chemist in Cairo (said Shahrazad that night) who was almost as famous for his wealth as he was for his *meanness*. They said of Abu Kassim that he was born with arms too short—they never did reach his pockets. What is money for but for spending and giving to those who have none? But Abu Kassim buried his money as though it would grow, and hid it in drawers as though it would perfume his clothes.

But thanks to his miserliness, his clothes were not perfumed at all. Far from it! He patched the same trousers and bathed in his shirt rather than send it to the laundry. And his shoes were quite the surest sign of penny-pinching. For twenty years he wore the same shoes. Holes in them were patched so often and so cheaply with strips of leather tacked on with round-headed nails that his feet looked like two armadillos. The soles were as thick as the skull of a rhinoceros, and Abu Kassim's shoes became a byword in the houses and halls of Cairo.

People would say, 'This soup is as thick as Abu Kassim's left shoe', and 'My mother-in-law's cakes are as heavy as Abu Kassim's clogs', or 'This egg smells as bad as Abu Kassim's right boot', or 'That joke is as old as Abu Kassim's slippers'. In short, all Cairo was well acquainted with Abu Kassim's shoes and the reason for their extraordinary size and weight.

On one particularly lovely day, when the sun reminded Kassim of a big golden coin and every jingling camels' harness put him in mind of moneybags, he decided to take his yearly Turkish bath.

Leaving his shoes on the step and his robe with the cashier, he allowed the hammam masseurs to sweat him and scrape him and soak him and wash him and dry him and perfume him. Lesser men would have shrunk from the task, but the masseurs at the Turkish bath prided themselves on achieving the impossible: Abu Kassim came up almost spotless.

In the meantime, a wealthy merchant, before even his caravan was unloaded, refreshed himself after a long and weary journey with a visit to the Turkish baths. He left his slippers on the step and said to the cashier at the door:

'You will frighten your customers away if you leave

those horrible slippers of Abu Kassim's on the porch. I shan't share a bath with that man: put me in another.'

The hammam attendant agreed, ran outside and, picking up Kassim's stinking shoes with a long pole, deposited them out of sight in a corner of the porch.

Consequently, Abu Kassim, on finishing his Turkish bath, came outside to find no shoes on the step except the merchant's handsome silk slippers, soled with calf skin.

'A miracle!' he exclaimed. 'Allah knew that I have always intended to buy shoes like these when I could afford it, and He has worked a transformation. What a saving of money!'

They fitted exactly, and he pattered off home and surprised his cook who could usually hear him clattering all the way up the street.

When the merchant could not find his own slippers, his nose told him that Abu Kassim's shoes were still in the porch, and he rooted them out.

'Now I know how that rascal Kassim made his fortune,' he shouted. 'Stealing other people's property!' — and he called all his camel drivers and servants from his caravan, and they marched off in a band to Abu Kassim's chemist's shop.

There they broke down the door, seized the dumbfounded miser by the scruff of his scruffy neck, and beat him to the floor. The police were called, and Abu Kassim had to pay a large bribe to keep the matter out of the courts.

'And you can have back your detestable shoes,' said the merchant in parting, and threw them at Abu Kassim's head.

'This is entirely your doing,' Kassim whimpered accusingly at the fuming old shoes. The shoes did not defend themselves. So he picked them up and threw them—one, two—with all his strength over the garden wall.

They hit an old lady who was passing, and crushed her like a biscuit. Her relatives wailed and ranted and called out, 'Murder! Murder!' until the police arrived. Examining the scene of the crime, they found Abu Kassim's famous footwear and, when Kassim went to his window to discover the reason for the commotion outside, he was hauled over the sill and dragged off to prison in chains.

The relatives of the old lady demanded the death of Kassim. But a law (peculiar to Cairo) fixed the value of a life at twenty thousand dinars, and Abu Kassim was able to escape hanging by paying this to the relatives.

Parting with twenty thousand dinars was as painful to Abu Kassim as twenty thousand wasp stings. He howled with misery and kicked his ancient slippers round the house until his feet bled. Then he took them to the Nile and dropped them in, hoping never to lay eyes on them again.

They floated down the river, reeking and fuming, and the fish rolled over and died. Finally, the shoes caught in the nets of a fisherman—an ox of a man who, single-handed, could haul in a net full of tuna-fish. The nails in Abu Kassim's shoes snagged and tore the twine, and the weight of them stretched the mesh out of all shape, so that the net was entirely ruined by the time the fisherman dragged the slippers ashore.

'Ten thousand curses on that miserable dog, Abu Kassim. I would know these legendary monstrosities anywhere.'

When the fisherman squeezed his huge body through

the door of the chemist's shop, Abu Kassim recognized his shoes dripping in the great paw-like hands. There is no escaping the fate Allah sends. The fisherman tenderized Kassim as he tenderized squid and octopus on the rocks beside the Nile.

As a parting gesture, he threw the awful footwear against the rows of shelves, smashing all the chemist's stocks of precious minerals and herbs.

'O Allah take vengeance on you, contemptible objects,' Kassim sobbed, crawling out into his garden with the shoes and a trowel. Although it was late evening and already dark, he dug a large hole and buried the disreputable shoes out of all harm's way.

But his neighbours, watching from the bedroom window, saw Abu Kassim digging in his garden in the dark and, knowing his reputation as a miser, thought he must be burying treasure.

'That old miser, Abu Kassim, has run out of floor-boards to hide his money under. He digs holes in the garden now and buries it there.'

Abu Kassim woke to find all manner of people digging furiously in his garden, flinging his herb garden in spadefuls over the wall. Small boys were shaking earth through metal sieves, and metal diviners with bent twigs in their hands were walking up and down his melon beds. No one believed him when he shouted from the window that he had only been burying his shoes, and he had to dig them up again to prove his story, and then pay everyone in the garden—some one hundred and fifty-four spade-owners—a piece of gold to go away.

'I have to be rid of these appalling objects which are a blight on my happiness and a danger to my life,' he grizzled. And he walked many miles into the countryside before finding a canal and throwing the shoes into a weir-pool.

Unfortunately, on the other side of the sluices was a mill whose wheel was driven by the weir. The antique shoes which, as it has been told you, had soles mended to the thickness of a rhinoceros's skull, caught in the mill-wheel paddles and, shearing all the gears, brought the mill to a violent halt. Investigating, the miller instantly recognized the infamous slippers of Abu Kassim.

You have seen the size of a miller's shoulders, have you not? His strength comes from lifting sacks of wheat grain all day long. When the miller found Abu Kassim he picked him up like a sack of grain and flung him into the mill pond. Abu stayed there until the police arrived.

Even after paying for the damage to the mill, Abu Kassim was obliged to pay out the last of his money as a bribe to the police before he was set free. His shoes were, of course, returned to him at the prison gate.

'Ill-omened, everlasting slippers, cause of all my misfortunes, will you kick me all the way to my grave?'

Blubbering and babbling, he ran all the way to the High Court, and presented himself at the Kadi's bench waving the shoes above his head in a state of hysteria.

'In front of witnesses,' Abu Kassim cried, 'let it be known in all the regions of the Nile, I accuse my boots of malice and conspiracy. I hereby disown them. From this day forwards I will have nothing to do with shoes—of any kind whatsoever. Abu Kassim no longer owns any slippers. Abu Kassim no longer owns any money, but what of that? I beg your worships not to hold Abu Kassim responsible for anything *shoes* may do in the future!'

And he dropped the shoes in the middle of the court and ran out in his bare feet, cursing the whole tribe and family of Shoes, while behind him in the courtroom the Kadi laughed so much that he fell off his judgment bench.

While Shahrazad was telling the tale of the Everlasting Shoes, her husband King Shahryar turned his back on her. His face was buried in a pillow and his shoulders jerked up and down. Anyone who had not lived in the royal palace—as gloomy a place as the bottom of a poisoned well—anyone who had not lived in Sasan's royal city for those three sad years—might have thought that the King was . . . laughing.

But Shahrazad wisely said: 'I am presumptuous, my stern and sober husband, to weave stories out of such light and worthless stuff. Let me redeem a little honour in your beloved eyes and tell you a story that is full of heroism, wisdom, and merit. It is the story of The Keys of Destiny . . .'

'Tomorrow, Shahrazad, tomorrow,' said the King, emerging from his pillow. 'I'm quite tired out with laughing . . . with listening, I mean. I think I shall sleep now.' And just as a tropical sun sets in the blink of an eye, so King Shahryar, the sunshine of all Sasan, fell asleep during the speaking of his own full stop.

71

CHAPTER TEN

The Keys of Destiny

Without doubt you will have heard (said Shahrazad the next night) of the Sultan Muhammad ibn Thailun, who is remembered for the outstanding mercy and the justice of his rule over Egypt. When he came to the throne he said:

'Open the doors of the servants' quarters: if I find that anyone there is working wearily for a small wage I will lessen his work and increase his wages. Open the exchequer door: if I find that any tax collector has been taking more than the poor people can afford, I will give back the money and beat the tax collector. Open all the stable doors: if I find that animals are spending their old age doing heavy work, I will turn them out to grass and beat the owners. Lastly, open all the prison doors: if I find that my father imprisoned anyone unjustly, I will free him and make his life as pleasant as it has been miserable.'

Now the prisons were full of merchants who had been robbed of everything by Muhammad's father; they were full of poets whose verses had failed to please Muhammad's father; they were full of mothers who had refused to sell their daughters to Muhammad's father for his harem. And there was also one old man who had lain so long in the deepest cell that no guard at the prison could remember his crime. This old man was carried to the royal audience chamber and laid at the feet of Sultan Muhammad.

Now outwardly the young Sultan was very like his father, though their inner hearts were as different as the butterfly is different from its caterpillar or chrysalis. The old man looked up at Muhammad through drooping eyelids and said:

'The answer is still no, O Sultan Thailun. Let my Magic Book lie in your treasure chest until the moths eat every page. I will not translate it.'

The young Sultan called for a feather bed to be brought to the audience chamber and for a shawl of white lambs' wool to wrap around the old man's shoulders. While this was done, Muhammad went to his father's treasure chest and searched until he found a chest wrought in solid gold which held a little red earth and a strange, wonderful book written in gilt letters on the purple-stained skin of a gazelle. But though Muhammad knew many languages and his wazir more, the book's language was beyond their understanding.

He took the book back to the audience chamber and placed it in the old man's hands.

'I am my father's son, but I weep for the thing he has done to you. I do not wish to keep anything that rightly belongs to another man. If this book were the key to all the treasures of the earth I would give it back to you, its rightful owner. But if you tell me no other secret, old man, tell me your name and the circumstances of your sad life.'

The old man wept openly and turned the palms of his hands towards heaven. 'O Allah, who can both make a man and break him like a twig, I have lain in prison for forty years but you have released me to die in the sunlight.' Then he turned to the Sultan. 'Dear master, I will tell to a good man what I would not tell to a cruel one. I am Hasan Abdallah, son of al-Ashar. From this day forward I want you to have the manuscript: it is the only thing I have left of my journey to Iram, the mysterious City of Many Columns.'

My father was rich, and sent me to the most expensive schools so that I was able to marry well. But soon after my wedding, my father and his whole fleet of merchant-ships were swallowed to the very stomach of the sea. The family was ruined: my wife and I and my little children lived on the edge of starvation.

One day I went out to sell my wife's last beautiful dress to buy bread for the children, when a rich sheikh on a red camel jumped down in front of me.

'Hasan Abdallah, son of al-Ashar, I have come to Cairo looking for you!'

I thought of the food we ought to offer any guest to our house and thought for a moment of pretending not to be Hasan Abdallah. 'Clearly, sir, you have not heard of the changes to our circumstances. The house of Abdallah holds only one starving man and his starving wife and children.'

But he insisted on coming to the house, and I had to pretend that he was welcome.

My wife said: 'A stranger is the guest of Allah; he must be fed, even if we have to give him our children's food.'

The sheikh overheard her, however, and took out ten gold coins: 'Take this, Hasan Abdallah, and buy everything you need for a good family meal. Here, I kiss you as a brother so that you cannot refuse my gift.'

The mysterious sheikh, who never explained how he knew of my family, stayed on in our little home for two weeks. Every day he gave us ten gold coins so that slowly health and happiness returned to the household. My children were well fed and we thanked Allah for the sending of such a generous guest.

But after sixteen days, the sheikh leaned towards me during dinner and said laughingly, 'Are you willing to sell yourself to me, Hasan Abdallah?'

'I and everyone in my house belongs to you,' I said. 'So it must be between host and guest.'

'Oh, yes,' said the sheikh, 'but would you sell me your life for 1,500 dinars to provide a secure future for your wife and children?' He was serious: my wife knew it and began to cry.

'No! We shall sell the house and repay the money you have given us, but don't talk of taking my husband's life!' she begged.

The sheikh tried to calm her: 'I simply need a companion, my dear lady, for a rather long journey I am planning. I heard tell of the qualities of Hasan Abdallah and his recent hardships, and I am here to solve both our problems!'

My heart was silent inside me and would not tell me the right path to take. So I accepted the money and immediately became the property of the mysterious sheikh. The next day we went to the camel market and equipped ourselves for a desert journey.

The rising and falling waves of desert sand-dunes washed away ten scorching days. The white hammer of the sun beat on my head until time itself was beaten out of shape. On the eleventh morning we reached the edge of a plain of white sand—white like a plate of salt into which Allah himself might dip his bread.

In the middle of the plain stood a pillar of granite, taller than any column supporting the great palace of al-Mutawakkil in Baghdad; taller than any living tree. On top of it stood a copper statue of a boy with one hand stretched out, and on each of his five fingers hung a heavy key. The first was of gold, the second silver, the third copper, the fourth iron, the fifth lead.

The sheikh dismounted and unpacked a bow and a quiver of copper arrows. 'You're a fine archer, Hasan Abdallah. Shoot down those keys for me, will you?'

To tell the truth I was pleased to show my skill with a bow. With four shots I tumbled four of the keys from the five fingers of the statue. The keys seemed to fall slowly— as coins fall through water—and hit the ground without noise.

The sheikh, however, had laid himself down and was eating an orange, showing no great interest in the keys. 'Run and fetch them for me will you, young Hasan?' he said.

I gathered up the keys from around the base of the pillar like a playful dog fetching back a stick for my master. Oh, my bitter soul! Why was I not warned? Why was I such an eager puppet on the hand of that mysterious sheikh?

'You have pleased me a great deal,' the sheikh said, as I

hurried back like a gaoler rattling the keys. 'You have bought back your freedom by this fine display of archery, and as a token of my thanks for your pleasant company I would like you to keep the gold and silver keys for yourself.'

I was overcome. I held out the iron and lead keys (it seemed to me that he snatched them with great eagerness) and I hurried to fit another arrow to the bow to shoot down the fifth, copper key.

'What are you doing, donkey, son of a fool? Leave the copper one.' He knocked the arrow from the bow, and it stuck in my foot, making a deep, painful wound.

Remembering all his kindness to me and to my family, I stuck my two keys through my belt (as he did with his) and we remounted.

Allah sends good days and bad days: I thought that the days which followed were the result of a little bad luck. Any wound can become infected—any foot can pain its owner. Judge me! Would I not have jumped from the highest cliff into the deepest river had I known what lay ahead?

As the pain in my foot got worse I began to be feverish and developed a great thirst. So when we came to a grassy place spread with fruit-bearing trees, I climbed down painfully from my camel and limped across to sink my teeth in the peach-coloured, plush-skinned fruit.

With my jaws at full stretch and my tongue pressed against the skin, my teeth fastened in the fruit and would not cut through it—nor could they be drawn out. I could barely breathe, for the fruit fitted my mouth as an egg fits an egg-cup; and I could not swallow for my tongue was out of use. By wild arm-waving I tried to tell the sheikh that I was drowning, and he finally came walking across at a slow pace.

'You've got that stuck in there, brother,' he said from the seat of his great wisdom. And although he wrestled with my head under his arm, the fruit would not come out. He assured me that there was nothing to worry about and broke a twig off the overhanging tree.

It was crawling with ants.

As I fell back, exhausted with my efforts to breathe, chew, or swallow, he shook several of these ants on to the fruit.

'There,' said my companion, 'did I not tell you there was no need to roll your eyes and thrash about so excessively. The ants will soon eat the fruit away.'

'U aaa?' I said.

'How soon? Oh, no more than three days, I should say.'

That is why, good master, the story of my miserable life includes three pages in which I lay on my back in a field, aching with hunger and thirst with my mouth full of fruit and ants. My companion sat alongside me, giving a commentary on the progress of the ants.

When, after three days, the fruit-core broke between my teeth, my first words were, 'Water for the love of Allah!'

But in the course of waiting, my companion had drunk both the water in his goat-skin and in mine. 'Here I am delaying my journey for three days to take care of you: you surely didn't expect me to go thirsty while I sat?' he said reproachfully.

Remembering his kindness to my family, I saw that he was in the right. When we passed a stream that afternoon, you can imagine how my heart flew to the cool, sweet water, though my wounded foot carried me there slowly. I gulped it deeply down, but my friend felt no need to refresh himself.

Consequently, he was not alarmed for his health when, a little farther up the stream, we found a dead sheep lying in the water. I soon felt the effects of drinking at the polluted stream, as violent pains tore at my insides. The river water might have been acid, for it burned away inside me until the bumping of the camel was almost too much to bear.

'Your groaning is quite irritating, my friend,' said the sheikh. 'You should try to keep more fit, then you would not be so prone to these little ailments.'

Leaning on one stirrup only because of my swollen foot, my jaws still aching, I bumped along in agony behind my friend and, remembering his kindness to me and my family, tried not to groan too often.

The day cooled like an old fever, and I thanked Allah for sending the night so that I could sleep.

'Before you sleep, O Hasan Abdallah,' said my friend, just as I slid my poor body into the soothing water of sleep, 'climb that hill over there and say evening prayers for us both.'

'O considerate sheikh, I don't think I am able to do your bidding—what with the pain in my stomach and my bad foot . . .' But he reminded me of the kindness he had done me and my family, and I was ashamed. As I hopped towards the steep hillside covered with thorn-bushes, he called after me: 'Do not be tempted to sleep while you are on the hill. The night mists that settle over it tend to damage a man's health.'

I considered the state of my health often on that evening climb, clutching my stomach as I limped from sharp rock to thorn-bush, from squeezing foothold to trailing cactus. A wind as sharp as a Berber's sword sliced over the hill-top as I stood and said my prayers. A full moon was shining directly in my face, and when I looked back to our encampment my friend was tracing the long, long shadow that the moon cast behind me into the valley.

Turning out of the wind, I felt the full weight of my weariness, as the swimmer climbing ashore feels the full weight of his body. I stretched out on a flat rock, thinking to rest myself before climbing down. But sleep crept in at my ears and coiled itself around my brain; it took away my pain and wiped from my memory the sheikh's warning: *Do not be tempted to sleep while you are on the hill.*

'Shahrazad,' said King Shahryar, holding up one hand, 'the weariness of Hasan Abdallah has crept into my ears along with the words of your story. I must sleep an hour or two before morning. You may return to your own room or sleep here, as you wish.'

'And tomorrow, if you will permit it, my bright-eyed lord,' said Shahrazad, 'I shall reveal the secret properties of those five keys in the white desert.'

The King patted her hand in agreement.

Shahrazad did not return to her room. She curled up in the angle of the King's arm and watched sleep settle on him like dew on to a wide-petalled flower.

CHAPTER ELEVEN

The Keys of Destiny:
The City of Many Columns

The young and noble Sultan Muhammad was listening so closely to the old man's story that he almost forgot the beautiful book held between his hands—written in letters of gold on the purple-stained skin of a gazelle. Old Hasan Abdallah reached out and fingered the gilt-edged pages before returning to his story.

When I woke up—long before morning—the dank fog smothering the hill-top hid from me at first the full horror of what had happened. I only knew that my arms, legs, and head were heavy past lifting. When the chilly, rheumatic mist rolled back, the moon stood over me severely. And I saw that my body had swollen to twice its normal size. My arms were as thick as an elephant's legs; and my mountainous stomach cut me off from all sight of my feet, though I could feel that they had burst out of

81

their sandals. My head was bloated to the size of a wine-skin and, indeed, I slopped about as though I had been filled to bursting with gallons of liquid.

Unable to wave or attract my friend's attention, I came down the hillside in the only way I could—rolling my grotesque hippopotamus of a body over and over down the slope. Thorn-bushes punctured me, cactus plants clung to me, jutting rocks squelched me but, gathering speed and bouncing faster and faster down the hill, I slopped to a halt at my friend's feet. I secretly hoped I might be dead, but Allah disappointed me.

Some of the thorns had pricked holes large enough to let out a yellowish water, and my kind friend helped to deflate me by drawing his knife and plunging it into me in several places.

'I did warn you, friend,' he said. 'It seems to me that you are too lazy to take a friend's good advice.'

When my body had emptied itself, my skin flapped round my bones like clothes on a clothes-horse. But my friend hardly noticed my changed appearance, for he was busily lighting a fire inside a shape marked on the ground. It was the shape of my shadow, thrown by the moon when I was standing on the hill-top.

Beside the fire, the mysterious sheikh dug a neat, square hole—down and down until he uncovered the book you hold in your hands. Then in a little metal basin over the fire he heated a phial of phoenix blood and held the book inside the wreaths of pink smoke which filled the air.

'The lead key of Wisdom has taught me the way here, and the dangers of the journey,' said the sheikh. 'Now this Magic Book will show us the way to a place more wonderful than living man has ever visited—Iram, City of Many Columns.'

'Oh, forgive your worthless slave, I am filled with happiness to know that you will find so agreeable a place, but I have seen many cities and many columns and at this moment I wish only to see my wife and children again. Won't you go on alone?'

'Ungrateful child, born on a raining Wednesday, the City of Many Columns holds more wealth than the desert holds sand. Do me the service of shooting that small serpent behind you and bring me its heart without another word.' And he returned to reading the Magic Book by the light of the phoenix-blood smoke.

Having a great fear of snakes, I turned to snatch up the bow and arrow from our luggage. There, twisting like a whirlwind up into the sky, its fangs flickering like lightning far above me, a monster serpent drew itself up into the night sky. Its tail lashed forward and encircled me, leaving my hands time to fire only one arrow. The dying creature thrashed me against the ground as it writhed blackly along the earth. And now others appeared from every shadow and tree: the valley was infested with giant serpents.

Calling on Allah to save me, I cut out the serpent's heart and ran with it to the sheikh, who placed it in a new basin over the fire and boiled it down to a liquid.

'Has your heart changed in the matter of turning back?' he asked me.

'O sweetest friend, riches do not interest me. But save us from this terrible snake-pit, if you have any magic in you!' I begged.

He took off his robe and instructed me to rub the liquid into his shoulder blades. I rubbed until two swellings appeared. Then his skin opened and two wings sprang up, which grew and grew until they trailed on the ground.

As the serpents plaited themselves around our camp, my friend rose up into the air, beating his wings. Weak as I was, I clung to his legs, and so we flew out of the valley and on to a great plain.

Against the horizon stood Iram, City of Many Columns, behind a wall of blue crystal. The sand of the whole plain was powdered gold.

I have seen beauty in the ten scales of a flying fish's wing, but here beauty stretched from a liquid horizon of aquamarine to another of flexing copper, and made the diaphragm of the sky pant with ecstasy. The bricks of the city wall were alternate silver and gold, and in the wall were seven gates: one of ruby, one of emerald, one of agate, one of coral, one of jasper, one of silver, and one of gold. Landing in front of the golden gate, my friend couched his wings and we passed through into the city.

Every building was a palace whose walls were alabaster, whose fountains ran with milk, and whose window arches were inlaid with porphyry. But at the high heart of the city stood the greatest palace of all, whose terraces were supported by one thousand and one columns of red gold—terraces hung with enchanted flowers, whose perfume was never spent and which leached drops of amber that altered as they fell, into tear-shaped pearls. In the inner courtyard of the palace a magic garden planted in beds of musk was watered by three rivers: one of wine, one of honey, and one of rose-water. But at the high heart of the garden stood a pavilion carved from a single emerald, shading a throne of gold and ruby. And at the high heart of the throne stood a small golden chest filled with red powder to the brim.

The old man in the audience chamber of Sultan Muhammad fingered the golden chest from which the young Sultan had taken the Magic Book. The packet of red powder in it was the last of the red sulphur, treasure of Iram, City of Many Columns.

My friend, the mysterious sheikh, leapt and danced around the pavilion in a way hardly fitting for a Believer. He whirled me round (despite my reminding him of the pain in my foot, stomach, and various stab wounds) and asked if I was not the happiest man in Cairo.

'Oh, sir,' I said, scooping up handfuls of pearls and sapphires from the flower beds and winding them into the folds of my turban. 'The hour that returns me to Cairo will indeed make me happy, but I beg your leave to feel a little unwell at present owing to the sorry state of my poor body. But wait until my wife and children see these!'

He knocked the jewels out of my hands and emptied my turban. 'Son of a plank, did you steal your brains from a table? Do you not know that Death searches those who leave this city, and if She finds a single jewel—even so much as a flake of crystal—She will swallow us up? Leave it: it is trash. But we can take this, and one grain of red sulphur will transform any metal into gold. It will turn a stone into a diamond, a drop of blood into a ruby. Half of this is yours. With a palmful of this powder a man could buy Baghdad and the earth beneath it. With a pinch of this a man could buy the most beautiful wife in all the Believing World and keep her love for half a day. With a handful of this . . .'

'But shall I live to see you so rich, master? I would like nothing more but I begin to doubt it, since my life runs out through so many holes and I am almost too down-hearted to breathe.'

'Ungrateful son of a whimpering ferret. Did you shoot down the Copper Key of Death in the white desert? No! I promise you as a man of magic, Hasan Abdallah, you will live to a great age and be as rich as I am.'

Remembering his kindness to me and my family, I was ashamed of myself and begged to be allowed to cling to his feet when he flew out of Iram, City of Many Columns.

We flew over the great plain of powdered gold, over our camels in the valley of giant snakes, over the hill covered with thorn-bushes, over the polluted stream of cool water, over the orchard of jaw-breaking fruit, over the white desert where the Copper Key of Death still hung from the finger of the copper statue.

'Now that our journey is ending,' I said, 'will you not tell me the Fates attached to the other Keys? I know that Lead brought you wisdom, but what did the Iron Key bring you?'

'Wealth, of course!' he laughed. 'Wealth and happiness!'

'Then may I beg you to tell me what lovely fate you gave me when you so kindly let me keep the Gold and Silver Keys which I have hung round my neck?'

'Allah knows all!' he said as we arrived at the Gates of Cairo. 'Allah and the Magic Book and I alone know the secrets of the Keys of Destiny. When I die, Hasan Abdallah, I promise that you may have the Magic Book, and the phial of phoenix blood. In the meantime we shall live here in unimagined wealth. Now be content, as all Believers must be content.'

No man in Araby was more happy than my wise, successful friend: no man in Araby more miserable than I,

Hasan Abdallah. For let me tell you what misfortune awaited me in Cairo.

From the Gate I hired a litter to carry me home, thinking of the joy and commotion I would cause at my little house. But I found the door open to the cats and dogs of the street, and the roof open to the birds of the sky. My house was an empty ruin with less life inside it than a snail-shell that the thrushes have broken open. I suppose that Death came and filled my empty place at table after I had gone, and carried off my dearest people.

With the riches provided by the red sulphur, the sheikh and I built two palaces on the edge of Sultan Thailun's kingdom. The walls were of bone china and the roofs of transparent sky-blue sapphire—so there seemed to be no roof at all. The day pavilions in the perfumed gardens were tents of grey silk, shot with gold fibres and embroidered with texts of poetry. Deer browsed on lawns of camomile. Guests of every rank and nationality were invited to the sheikh's palace, given their hearts' desire, and could stay for as long as they wished. A party began on the day when his palace doors opened, and lasted for twelve years.

In all that time I neither took pleasure in a song nor smiled the smile of a happy man. I kept to the inner rooms of my empty palace and poisoned the scented air with sighs and groans. The pain of my wounds never left me and my heart seemed like the fruit of that evil orchard—eaten away little by little by the small ants of misery.

My friend criticized me for taking so little delight in the wealth he had brought me. But he was kind enough to send for medicines from China and the Islands of Knowledge beyond Mesopotamia, and he bought me beautiful slaves at every slave-market hoping to make me sick with love—the sickness which drives out all sicknesses. But although he was kind, I felt better when he was in his palace and I was in mine. For he could not help but laugh continually and slap my bony back, saying:

'Is life not the greatest of Allah's inventions! Is any man happier than I? Send him to me and I will buy his weight of happiness and put it in my cellars for the mice to eat. Hasan Abdallah, even the mice in my palace must be happy, for I have the Iron Key of Happiness and Wealth!'

I asked him if his grains of red sulphur could buy him one hour more of life, but he only laughed hugely and slapped my bony back again.

On one such cheerful visit he told me news which shook my hollow chest as the wind shakes a sail, but he laughed as he told me:

'That old rascal Sultan Thailun has fixed his greedy eye on our two palaces. He plans to attack and to take them for himself, for Cairo is a flea circus alongside the carnival I have begun here with my red sulphur! We shall send him back like a flea to his flea circus, shall we not, Hasan Abdallah?'

And he seemed so pleased with his joke that he laughed and laughed until he had to sit down; and still he laughed and laughed until he had to lie down; and still he laughed and laughed until he had to be buried because he was stone dead. Allah send me as happy a death— but, alas, I did not keep the Iron Key of Happiness and Wealth!

I arranged a funeral for my friend more splendid than any ever seen before or since. There are surely men in your kingdom now who remember the feasts and processions at the funeral of the Sheikh of Iram. And I buried with him the Keys he wore round his neck—the Iron and Lead Keys of Wisdom and Happiness.

As soon as the festivities ended I went to the sheikh's palace and sought out the Magic Book. The fire, the phoenix blood, the golden letters on purple-stained vellum, and the pink smoke—I remember them all when I found them on the onyx floor of the palace. They revealed to me the directions to the City of Iram, the secret of flight and wing-growth, the truth concerning the Keys of Destiny:

> *The Iron Key opens all doors to Happiness and Wealth,*
> *The Lead Key to all Wisdom and all Health;*
> *The Copper Key opens the doors of Death;*
> *The Silver Key brings Suffering and Pain*
> *And Gold unlocks all Misery and Shame.*

The sheikh, when he bought my life for 1,500 dinars was buying himself a slave to carry the Keys of Misery and Suffering, and I had worn their gold and silver round my neck for twelve long years! Oh how I clawed them from my neck. I put them together in the tin basin over the fire and watched the metal fusing together. Some of my pain left me at once.

But sometimes one minute decides the fate of a man. As the gold and silver melted and ran together, Sultan Thailun's soldiers stormed the palace. They took the gold leaf from the walls and the platinum nails from the floorboards and every valuable thing between. They scattered my magic fire and set alight the grey silk tents, shot with gold threads. Both palaces built from the riches of Iram were burnt to the ground, and Sultan Thailun captured both me and the Magic Book and the last of the red sulphur in its chest of wrought gold.

The old man held the precious box in his arms again after forty years and wept freely over it.

'My father could not understand the mystical writing in the Magic Book and commanded you to translate it. Am I right, Hasan Abdallah?' said the young Sultan.

'Forgive me if I was wrong, O son of your father, but with the wealth of the City of Iram the Sultan your father would have raised an army to crush all Arabia under his foot. Without Wisdom, he placed no value on the red sulphur, thinking it was a little dirty sand in the bottom of the chest, but he tortured me daily to find out the meaning of the Magic Book, then threw me into his deepest prison and, in time, forgot. But Allah does not forget.'

'No, indeed, old man,' said the Sultan. 'I shall use the last of the red sulphur to build you a country house and keep you in comfort. But all the red sulphur in Iram and elsewhere cannot replace your forty years, nor your wife and children . . .'

'On that subject I have something to say, if a worthless woman may speak in the presence of the great Sultan Muhammad.'

An old lady, dressed in prison clothes stepped forward from the crowd of prisoners Sultan Muhammad had released along with Hasan Abdallah. 'I am one of the many mothers whom Sultan Thailun imprisoned when we would not sell him our daughters to be wives in his harem. I sent my children out of the country—to Baghdad—and accepted my fate. My husband, you see, was away travelling when the Sultan came to me offering gold for my oldest girl-child. I thought until this day that my husband had died on his dangerous journeying, in the company of the mysterious sheikh who bought my beloved's life for 1,500 dinars. But today I see that I am not a widow and can tell you, Hasan Abdallah, that our children are safe in Baghdad, if Allah is just.'

So Hasan Abdallah and his wife were reunited. But such was the happiness of old Hasan that he let loose a flurry of tears and fell at the feet of the young Sultan. 'O master, when I tell you the last and terrible secret I kept from your father, you will undoubtedly throw us again into the deepest cell in your deepest prison. But let it be one cell this time so that my wife and I may be together until Death frees us from all imprisonment!'

'Never, Hasan Abdallah,' said the Sultan, amazed that Hasan could still think him so cruel. 'Truth is owed only to those whose hearts are strong enough to hold it.'

'The soldiers of Thailun your father, like dogs joyfully fetching back a stick, brought him the little tin basin containing the gold and silver keys. He asked me what they would open to him, but I refused to speak. In the hope of finding the treasure chest they fitted, your father kept the Keys of Misery and Suffering close by him—for all I know they were with him to the hour of his death! Can you forgive me for the years of suffering and unhappiness I caused your glorious father?'

The thoughts of the young Sultan did not show in his face, but he kept his promise to Hasan Abdallah and built him and his wife a fine house on the outskirts of Cairo. His children returned home with children of their own.

Can a river forget its source or a sunbeam forget the sun? Can the tail of the snake forget the head that went before it? Can a man forget his father? The young Sultan Muhammad did not forget Thailun his father, but the stuff of his memories—ah, that is a secret Allah and the Sultan alone knew!

CHAPTER TWELVE

The Land Abdallah and the Sea Abdallah

As Shahrazad finished the story of the Keys of Destiny, a silence fell between her and her husband and separated their two hearts. Through the windows of his eyes, Shahrazad saw King Shahryar's heart turn away and dress itself in the hard armour of hate, and she was afraid for her life.

'What a fine name the hero of that story had,' she said aloud. 'If I were a man I would wish my parents had called me that.'

'Muhammad? Certainly there is no better name than the name of Allah's Prophet.'

'Oh, you have again shown me my female foolishness,' she said, 'for I meant the name Abdallah, "servant of Allah".'

'Indeed, Shahrazad, it is a common enough name, and I wish that all the children who are named Abdallah by their parents grew up to be true "servants of Allah".'

'Ah, yes, my devout and prayerful husband. Then indeed there would be reason to rejoice if every man in Sasan were called Abdallah. Does it not put you in mind of the Land Abdallah and the Sea Abdallah in the story of that name?'

'Is the story written in the libraries of Sasan? I have never heard of it. Were the Land Abdallah and the Sea Abdallah true "servants of Allah" worthy of their names?'

'The King could judge for himself if he would spare his worthless wife's life for one more night and hear the story . . .'

So on the two-hundred-and-seventy-fourth night Shahrazad began:

The story is carried—but who can tell if it is true?—of a poor young fisherman called Abdallah who was a true Believer in Allah and His Prophet. He had heard it said that *Allah will provide for tomorrow*, so every day he spent all the money he earned. On a day when the fish were shoaling in the surf he earned many dinars, ate like a King, and saved nothing at all. On the days when fish were sleeping on the sea-bed, he caught little, earned next to nothing, and ate even less. Then his friend the baker would see Abdallah standing outside his shop trying to fill his stomach with the smell of fresh bread. And he would give him a bag of hot sesame buns, for his heart was as large and warm as a freshly baked loaf.

'You are Abdallah the fisherman and I am Abdallah the baker,' he would say. 'If one Abdallah cannot help another, he is no true servant of Allah and does not deserve his name.'

One day Abdallah the fisherman cast his net and needed all his strength to pull it in. Caught in the mesh, and emerging little by little from the water was a *man*— yes, surely a man, with a head, shoulders, arms, a chest, a waist—and a tail.

A tail? thought Abdallah. This is no man. This is a jinni like the one who was thrown into the sea inside a copper bottle. And he dropped his net, hitched up his robe and ran away.

'Wait, friend. Please help me get free of this net or I shall certainly drown in the sunshine,' called the fishman.

'You're a jinni and there is a proverb which says *Allah gives Man arms to fight with but legs to run away—and a man's legs are longer than his arms!*'

'So that's what those are,' the creature interrupted. 'Legs! I thought at first that you had split your tail in two. I promise you I am only a man and a true Believer in Allah, the one God.'

Abdallah's curiosity pulled him back like a fish on a line to gape open-mouthed at the merman.

The creature said: 'I am from the Kingdom Below-waves. We too have a proverb: *Allah gave Man arms to fight with but a tail to swim away—and a man's tail is longer than his arms!* My name is Abdallah.'

'Allah be blessed, so is mine! So I'm the Abdallah of the Land and you are the Abdallah of the Sea.' He helped the merman out of the net and sat down on the shore, while the Sea Abdallah lay in the shallows up to his neck, ducking his head from time to time to fill his lungs with refreshing sea water.

The merman described his Kingdom Below-waves and asked many questions about the Kingdom he called 'Middleworld' (because it stood below the sky and above the sea): 'Our legends have always spoken of a race of men who live on the mountain-tops above the water-line, and I have often begun climbing the sea's mountains, wondering if I could satisfy my curiosity. Your net fell on me today out of the dry air, and I found that the legends are indeed true.'

The Land Abdallah asked the Sea Abdallah what the legends of Middleworld said.

'They speak particularly of the food of Middleworld, for not only does Dry-man draw up fish from the sea, but he also eats the meat of strange, air-breathing beasts and picks delectable food from the branches of green coral and land-weed.'

Abdallah the fisherman immediately offered the merman a peach and an orange from his bag and promised to bring a basket of different fruits the following day if the Sea Abdallah would come again.

'I must give you something in return, brother Abdallah,' said the merman. 'What can I bring you? There is nothing under the waves that so delights the tongue as this, this . . .'

'. . . Peach,' said the fisherman.

'But there is much to delight the eye. I shall bring a basket of pretty sea fruits from the bed of the ocean to decorate your house—and we shall talk together again.'

When the Sea Abdallah had gone, the Land Abdallah threw down his net in disgust. 'What a fool I am. I could have sold this creature to a zoo for a fabulous sum, and now he has tricked me into letting him go. Besides, here am I with no catch at all today, so I have no money to buy fruit for the merman. He can bring pretty pebbles from the sea-bed, but I must pay good money at the market for food!'

He went to his friend the baker and told him the story. But Abdallah the baker said, 'There's no need to invent all this: one Abdallah owes it to another to see him through the bad times we all suffer.' And he gave the fisherman money from his till.

Abdallah the fisherman took nuts, pomegranates, dates, plums, and water melons to the beach in a basket. He felt foolish, standing in the surf in plain sight of Allah and saying, 'Abdallah? Where are you, Abdallah?'

The Sea Abdallah rose from the waves carrying on his head a basket of glorious jewels: emeralds, diamonds, seed-pearls balas, and opals.

'Allah, God of dry and wet!' exclaimed the fisherman, 'I shall be the richest man in the kingdom. Did your fellow men of Below-waves agree to you squandering such wealth on a poor citizen of Middleworld?'

'Allah bless us! These are the stones I cleaned from my flower beds this morning so that my wife could plant sargasso. There are many millions of these pebbles on the sea-bed, and they account for the great lightness and beauty of Below-waves, but they are an insulting gift to offer in return for such deliciousness.' And the merman smelled the fruit and splashed his tail with delight.

They agreed to exchange gifts every day: the fisherman bringing fruit of Middleworld in a basket, the merman fetching a tub of precious jewels from the sea-bed. And the Land Abdallah left the beach that day, as cheerful as the Sheikh in the old story who grasped the Key of Happiness and Wealth.

He went to his friend the baker and gave him half the jewels to repay his generosity and trust of the day before. Then he went to the jewel market and offered to sell the fruit of the sea.

'Arrest this man!' cried the jeweller. 'His clothes are as old as my grandfather and he smells of fish. How does a poor fisherman lay his hands on jewels like these without stealing them?'

Other tradesmen gathered round and kept tight hold of Abdallah: 'The Queen's jewelled collar was stolen yesterday,' said one. 'This is obviously the thief!'

So the police arrested Abdallah, beat him, and triumphantly dragged him bound and gagged to the Royal Palace. 'We have caught the thief who stole the Queen's collar,' they crowed to the King. 'This dirty ragged fisherman without one dinar to drop through the holes in his pockets was trying to sell these jewels in the market.'

The fruits of the sea were shown to the Queen, who held them up to the light in amazement. 'These are much finer than the jewels in my collar. Besides, I found the missing necklet in my treasure chest. Husband, won't you buy these perfect jewels from this poor, wronged man and have them made into a collar for our daughter the Princess?'

The King's anger shrivelled the police and the jewellers as the sun shrivels beetles on a hot rock. He released Abdallah and consoled him for his ill-treatment with wine and exotic confections, with syllabub and marshmallows. Then he asked to hear the fisherman's story.

'I received the jewels in return for a basket of fruit, from a courteous, honourable gentleman of the Kingdom Below-waves. I caught him by accident in my fishing net. We agreed to exchange gifts each day—jewels in return for fruit—for we feel almost like brothers, sharing the name of Abdallah as we do. I call him the Sea Abdallah and he calls me, his poor brother, the Land Abdallah.'

'Allah bless and keep you both—you have the same name as me, your King Abdallah!'

'We do have that honour, your Majesty.'

'But you are far from poor, citizen Abdallah. These jewels will make you as rich as your poverty has made you honest. My wife wants me to buy your jewels for our daughter.'

'Take them, sire, if Abdallah the fisherman is not too insignificant a person to offer gifts to a great king. If you will only supply me with a basket of fresh fruit, I can soon fetch more. Indeed these are only half the jewels I was given, for I gave half to my friend the baker who has fed me when I had not one dinar to drop through the holes in my pockets.'

The King let Abdallah go on his way, but his heart remarked to his brain that the fisherman was well named 'servant of Allah'. 'The poet says: *the poor remember their friends; but the rich forget them.* But the rich Abdallah did not forget his friend the baker. This is a good man,' said the King's heart to his brain.

Every day the Land Abdallah took to the beach a basket of land fruit—figs, melons, cucumbers, tomatoes, dates, berries, and apples. And every day the merman came with a tub of gleaming jewels—amethysts, beryl, turquoise, alexandrite, and heliotrope. The fisherman's wealth was soon larger than the King's, and he was a familiar visitor at the Palace.

Seeing that the Land Abdallah's heart was to be valued as greatly as his treasure, the King offered the young man his daughter for a wife.

The wedding was celebrated with a day of feasting on fish—squid, bream and flying fish; shrimp and lobster, sturgeon and crab. Then there was a day of feasting on meat—venison and beef, mutton and sweetbreads. The third day saw feasting on birds of the air—larks and swan, duck and oriole, geese, crane and pheasant. A fourth feast followed of fruits, and a fifth of delicate dishes—monkey, lizard, sesame pastes, turtle, cream cheeses, and honeycombs.

But the bridegroom left every feast during the morning music and carried a basket of fruit to the beach— nectarines, apricots, coconuts, paw-paw, squash, pears, grapes, and tangerines—and met his friend the Sea Abdallah beside the white mid-morning surf.

'Abdallah, my son-in-law,' said the King. 'It is not seemly for a Prince of the Kingdom to carry fruit baskets like a common porter. Will you leave your bride and guests when the dancing is just beginning?'

But the Land Abdallah kept his promise to meet the Sea Abdallah every day.

One morning the Sea Abdallah said: 'As the eye is more lovely than the mouth, so sight is more lovely than the word. Why do you not come down with me to the Kingdom Below-waves and see its strange and shining twilight?'

The Land Abdallah protested that he would drown in the Kingdom Below-waves, but the merman fetched a magic lotion with which he oiled the fisherman's body. Then he took him by the hand and led him into the surf.

At the Royal Palace the Princess waited, like a heron beside a stream, for the return of her husband.

CHAPTER THIRTEEN

The Land Abdallah in the Kingdom Below-waves

Below the sea the Land Abdallah saw canyons of pink coral and forests of branching octopus; he walked through the wrecks of galleons and orchards of waving sponges. Rainbows of angel-fish arched between the sea-bed and the dappled sky of waves; icebergs drifted above him like clouds. He saw the foundations of Africa set in the shifting silt, and the feet of towering cliffs, and plains where crops of sea-kelp wave while the tides are drawn up over beaches.

Sunlight trickled only feebly through the liquid air, but the valleys and cities of Below-waves were brightly lit by the phosphorescent glow of electric fish and the refracted light from a million million precious stones on the sea-bed. Moonstone, zircon, coral, jade, and rubies sprinkled the sand and decorated the reefs; and the fisherman wondered at the value he and his fellow Dry-men placed on such common pebbles.

A farm of open-mouthed oysters lolling pearls on their grey tongues marked the border of the Sea Abdallah's estate. He led his friend into a large cave, and introduced him to his wife and five daughters. The babies were munching on raw fish and dribbled bubbles from the corners of their mouths.

At the sight of the Land Abdallah they burst out laughing, the little children rolled on their backs, and the Sea Abdallah's wife leaned against the wall of the sea cave and laughed until air bubbles oozed from her eyes and rolled down her cheeks.

'What's this tail-less thing you've brought back with you, Abdallah?' she said. When her husband reproached her for her bad manners, she tried to control her laughing and said: 'Oh dear, husband, I am so sorry. Has your friend split his tail in an accident and bandaged it with that strange cloth?'

'She means your trousers, I think,' said his friend soberly. 'Perhaps you should remove them.'

'Take off my trousers in front of your wife?' said the Land Abdallah, appalled. But noticing that the mermen wore no clothes at all, he honoured the custom of the underwater world and took off his baggy Arabian trousers. The merman's wife stuffed her long hair into her mouth, but could not stifle her giggles even so, and swam out of the cave apologizing as she shook with uncontrollable laughter. The neighbours soon arrived, and a detachment of royal guards from the King of Below-waves. The King had heard about the Land Abdallah and wanted to see this tail-less proof that the legends concerning Middleworld were true.

The fisherman began to look at his legs with new eyes for they were so comic a sight at the Royal Court that the

King of Below-waves offered him a pension for life if he would stay as the Court jester.

Somewhat offended, the fisherman said, 'Indeed, sir, I have a court of my own in my breathing world, married as I am to a king's daughter.'

'Do you mean to make us believe that such a poor, split-tailed crayfish as you is given authority over the legendary men of Middleworld?' said the King, holding his sides and choking with laughter. 'What can you *do* with that forked prong on the end of your spine?'

'My legs? I can run and jump and ride horses—I could sit astride a porpoise and ride him through the waves roofing your world.'

The King seemed baffled: 'Why should you want to do such a thing when tailed Man can outswim a porpoise? Well, show us this running and jumping.'

So the Land Abdallah set off to run across a wide strip of fine sand. But the water dragged on his limbs and he floundered like a bear in mud. The gathered assembly laughed until they fell down like a row of dominoes.

'And it would seem that these "legs" wear out more quickly than fins,' said the King, hungry for understanding, 'for are they not frayed badly, young man?'

The Land Abdallah looked at his feet. 'They are my toes, your royal Highness, not frayed ends to my legs.' And he wondered why he had left his bride waiting (like a heron beside a stream) for his return.

The underwater army were mustered to review the dryman's legs, and his trousers were hung up in the Royal Museum as archaeological proof of Middleworld and its outrageous creatures. A feast was given in his honour, but since no fires would burn in the kitchens of the sea every dish was raw, and there was no meat other than fish.

Abdallah began to long for his native land of roast meat and dry trousers.

'Speak, son-in-law,' said King Abdallah, 'and tell us things of the wet world that we of the dry world have never heard! How were you received by the mermen and mermaids? Did they wish that Allah had made them land creatures with legs and lungs to climb up on to the dry land and enjoy the fruits of the sun?'

'Must I speak about it?' said the fisherman-Prince shuffling his feet.

The King leaned out of his throne and peered into his son-in-law's face. 'What's this? The tongue that fails to speak says more than a book. What monstrous beasts did you see?'

'Oh, I saw a whale who could swallow an elephant without chewing. I saw the dugongs who sing like women and lure sailors to their deaths. I saw where the flying fish build their nests, and the octopus which has eight . . .'

'Eight what, son-in-law? You have turned the key of your tongue in your mouth to keep some secret in.'

'Eight legs, my lord—a foolish and laughable creature,' but the Prince's thoughts were not of the octopus. And the King saw that his son-in-law had brought back from Below-waves a greater weight of sorrow than of jewels.

'Tell me, my son, if the salt-water sea has waterlogged your happiness and swamped all your cheerfulness.'

'Ah, my lord, forgive me my silence. In my heart are written the words of the poet:

> *The good Believer turns aside*
> *From all things bad, but chiefly Pride.*

My pride was hurt, father, in Below-waves—a small and unimportant matter for a Believer—but forgive me if I do not add to my shame by describing what happened.'

But the King had an even greater store of pride than the humble Abdallah, and pressed for the truth. He commanded his daughter to pester her husband day and night until she persuaded him to speak. She called on her father early the next morning.

'My dear husband has opened the doors of his silence and shown me his wounded pride. The mermen (let it not be told in public) laughed exceedingly at his legs and placed his trousers in the royal museum. Tail-less man was comical to them, and Abdallah was offered the post of King's jester.'

When King Abdallah heard this, his great anger swept down from the land to the sea—a dry, hot anger that drove the tides down the beaches and fried the fishes in the surf. He swore an oath which melted the icebergs, and muttered curses which popped the pods of seaweed as they echoed along the shores:

'By Allah who made fish and fowl and raised up fowl higher than fish, no merman will ever cross high-water mark or taste freshwater from the inland springs. No two-legged man will ever carry fruit beyond the wet-sand line nor marry a mermaid nor eat raw fish.'

As King Abdallah was swearing this oath, Abdallah the fisherman crossed the palace courtyard with a basket of fruit—mandarins, satsumas, cactus pears, cherries, strawberries, quinces, gooseberries, and passion fruits.

'Where are you going, son-in-law, carrying baskets of fruit like a miserable porter. Princes of the Blood Royal are not donkeys to grunt under heavy loads.'

'I made a promise to the Sea Abdallah that I would

meet him every day and exchange gifts on the sea's edge,' replied Abdallah. 'What Believer would break his word while he had strength enough to carry the gifts? My friend Abdallah did not laugh at me, and what good Believer would let pride come between him and his friend?'

'Remember the old rhyme,' said King Abdallah crossly:

> *A common man should draw the line*
> *At being virtuous all the time.*

'But father!' replied Abdallah. 'You married me to your daughter because I try to be a true servant of Allah in my dealings with my friends!'

It was useless to argue. The more wrong the King felt in his heart, the less pleasure he took in his honourable son.

'I have made a decree,' he said finally, 'by Allah who made fish and fowl and raised up fowl higher than fish. No merman will ever cross high-water mark and no two-legged man will ever carry fruit beyond the wet-sand line. If you meet the Sea Abdallah today, all your wealth will be confiscated and your marriage to my daughter will be undone—and you will be thrown into prison. Let it be known throughout the dry world that a state of war exists between us upright two-legged Believers and the fish-tailed scoundrels who dared to laugh at a royal pair of legs!'

And that, you see, is why no merman has ever been caught since in a fisherman's net: they keep away from the dry mountain-tops that rise out of their watery kingdom and hide themselves in their deep-sea caves, and keep their treasure to themselves.

106

'But did the Land Abdallah keep his promise to the Sea Abdallah and meet him on the beach?' asked King Shahryar.

'What do *you* think, my husband,' said Shahrazad, 'for you are a judge of people and a student of the teachings of Allah? Should he have obeyed his conscience or the decree of his father—a great king to whom he was tied by marriage and by affection?'

'A man should keep his promise to a friend before any other consideration,' said the King.

'Well then, the Land Abdallah would have pleased you greatly, my virtuous and loyal King, for he took his gift of fruit to the Sea Abdallah, who wept to have brought his friend to such a sorry situation.'

'Think nothing of it, dear friend,' said the Land Abdallah. 'Before I knew you, I had nothing, and today I have nothing—what have I lost? Before I knew you, I had no wife, and today I have no wife—what have I lost? Before I knew you, I had a fishing net and one good friend. Today I have a fishing net and two good friends, and though I shall not see Abdallah the baker again I shall meet the Sea Abdallah on different shores: I am sure that a friend in the kingdom of fishes will never let a poor fisherman starve.'

So the Land Abdallah flung his old net over his shoulder and left the kingdom of King Abdallah to fish foreign surf and meet his friend the Sea Abdallah on foreign beaches.

'That's a fine story, Shahrazad,' said the King, 'and it has a fine ending. A man could learn a lot from such a story. Did Allah reward His servant for his honesty?'

'That is not known to me, discerning husband. The fisherman carried his story out of the country and out of hearing of all ears. I know that Allah rewarded the four murderers for *their* honesty in the Tale of the Little Beggar.'

'Murderers rewarded?' Then King Shahryar thought in his heart, 'I will hear this story if it has anything to teach a listening heart. For the poet says:

> *A story teaches better than*
> *A mullah's sermon ever can!'*

CHAPTER FOURTEEN
The Tale of the Little Beggar

From the far side of the desert comes the story—though who can tell if it is true—of an unremarkable town full of unremarkable people. Among them lived a little beggar, remarkable only for his cheerful, friendly nature and his smallness of size. He was such pleasant company that townsfolk would often ask him home to dinner. (So Allah provides for his most humble servant.)

One night the beggar was a guest at the house of the tailor and his wife, who served him a fine meal of white fish. He was part-way through telling a long and hilarious story when a fishbone stuck in his throat. He made a face like a red guppy as he fought for breath, but the tailor and his wife, thinking he was clowning, only laughed and laughed until the beggar fell off his bench and collapsed in a heap on the floor.

'He's dead,' said the tailor, putting his ear to the

beggar's chest. 'Allah forgive us, we have choked our guest to death!'

'Allah forgive us,' his wife agreed. 'No one will eat my cooking again. We must keep this secret: the man may have relatives who will ask for the price of his life. He must be hidden.'

So they wrapped the little beggar in a blanket and the tailor's wife picked him up (for he was no bigger than a child). 'Oh woe, little child of mine. Don't fret,' she said, 'we'll soon make you well.' In this way they walked down the street, and whenever they saw a neighbour or passer-by, they called out: 'Are you a doctor, sir? Our child is ill with smallpox.'

The neighbours kept as distant as a ship keeps from a sandbank! A maidservant came towards them and they called out: 'Where can we find a doctor: our child has smallpox.' The maidservant backed away, but then she called out to them, 'My master is a doctor. Follow me and I'll lead you to his house.'

The tailor and his wife were obliged to follow, but when she went up the outside staircase to tell the doctor they were coming, they quickly carried the body to the top of the stairs and left it sitting on the second step. Then taking their blanket, they ran home and locked the doors of their house, thinking themselves safe.

The doctor, hearing that a patient was waiting in the street, hurried to attend to them. At the top of the stairs he tripped over the body of the little beggar, which unbalanced and toppled down the steps with much flying of arms and flailing of legs.

The doctor rushed to examine the body. 'Oh Allah forgive me, this poor little fellow was sheltering on my staircase and I've pushed him to his death.' The maidservant came out, hearing the noise, and she held her head in horror.

'Patients come to a doctor to be healed,' she said. 'This man came to your house well and leaves dead. What will become of your reputation as a doctor?'

'Perhaps this little beggar has relatives who will demand blood-money. We must hide this accident.'

The maidservant suggested that they throw the body over the balcony into the yard of the cook who lived next door. 'Rats come every night and steal the food he stores in the yard. If we drop the body into there, perhaps the rats will eat it and hide all trace of what you have done.'

So they dropped the little beggar over their balcony and into the food storage yard of the cook—who was at that very moment arriving home.

'Let me see if I can kill some of those thieving rats tonight. If I put out my candle perhaps I can creep into the yard and catch them in the act . . .' So picking up a huge club, he tiptoed into the yard.

By the light of a small and unremarkable moon he could just make out a small figure crouching against the wall.

'So it was not the rats, after all,' he shouted, 'there was a human thief to blame for all that stolen corn and sugar.' And he caught the little beggar a blow across the ear with his club. The body fell over and lay face down in an open sack of sugar.

'O Allah, forgive me! I don't know the strength of my own arm. I've killed this unfortunate little beggar for taking a handful of food I would willingly have given him. What if he has relatives and they demand blood-money—or the police think that I murdered him

111

deliberately? O miserable little beggar, why did you steal the food when you could simply have asked me for it?'

So he put the little beggar's body across his shoulders and crept out into the alleyways, intending to drop it in the canal.

Hearing someone coming, he stood the body down in a dark corner—since it was quite stiff and cold, it stood up splendidly on its two feet—and the cook ran home and locked his door and felt quite safe.

The person approaching was a slave who had spent all evening in an inn. Indeed, there was more wine in his veins than blood, and his eyes were floating in sloe gin. Glimpsing the rampant body of the little beggar standing in the shadows, he thought that he was about to be attacked and robbed. He seized the little beggar by his hair and banged his head against the wall several times screaming, 'Help me! I'm being murdered!'

The city police, by the light of their torches and the sound of flying punches, found a drunken slave beating a harmless little beggar as though he were an old carpet. The poor little man put up no defence, and did not land a single punch. When, on closer inspection, the beggar proved to be dead, the slave was dragged to the public court in the town square and tried for murder. The body of the little beggar was brought and laid on the judge's bench.

The judge—who was a good Believer and never touched alcoholic drink—quickly decided that the drunken slave was guilty. The slave swore an oath that he would never again touch drink since it had made him do such a dreadful thing.

'You might have saved yourself an oath, you pickled rascal,' said the judge, 'for you will not touch liquor again whether you swear it or not: I am going to hang you immediately.'

A scaffold was built in the town square, and the miserable slave was blindfolded, while the judge's clerk read out his crime:

'This drunken slave is to be hanged to pay for the life of a little beggar (of name unknown) whom he foully beat to death in the alleyway of the casbah last night while in a state of great drunkenness.'

The crowd said Hurrah and Boo, as is the way of crowds.

'Stop! Stop! This cannot be,' said a voice in the crowd. 'The ghost of this miserable slave would sour all my cooking and flatten all my cakes, and I should never sleep another peaceful night. I killed the little beggar when I found him stealing sugar from my yard,' said the cook, stepping forward. 'I killed him with this club.'

'So big a club for so little a crime?' said the judge. 'Will Allah be merciful to you when you show no mercy to a little beggar? Free the slave at once and hang this cook.'

So the cook mounted the scaffold and was blindfolded, while the judge's clerk proclaimed his crime:

'This cook is to be hanged to pay for the life of a little beggar (of name unknown) whom he killed for the small crime of stealing sugar—and for his efforts to hide his guilty secret.'

The crowd drew one breath, as is the way with crowds.

'Stop! Stop! This cannot be,' said a voice in the crowd. 'The ghost of this poor cook would make my hands tremble too much to practise my medicine, and I should never sleep another peaceful night. I killed the little beggar by kicking him down my outside staircase,' said the doctor, stepping forward. 'I dropped the body over my balcony into the cook's yard, hoping that the rats would eat it and no one know of my crime.'

'Is it the gracious act of a rich Believer to kick a poor Believer down his outside staircase?' said the judge. 'Since you earn your living by preserving life, you have earned your death by the death of this little beggar. Free the cook at once and hang this doctor.'

So the doctor mounted the scaffold and was blindfolded, while the judge's clerk proclaimed his crime:

'This doctor is to be hanged to pay for the life of a little beggar (of name unknown) whom he kicked down the outside staircase of his house for no very good reason—and for his efforts to hide his guilty secret.'

The crowd said 'Would you believe it?' to one another as is the way of crowds.

'Stop! Stop! This cannot be,' said a voice in the crowd. 'The ghost of this doctor would haunt my tailor's shop until I pricked myself with a thousand and one pins, and I should never sleep another peaceful night. Last night the beggar came to dinner and choked on a fishbone and died,' said the tailor stepping forward. 'I and my wife killed the little fellow though he was a guest in our house and though he was halfway through a long and hilarious story.'

'Strange hospitality to offer your guest,' said the judge. 'No laughter now for you who stopped the little beggar from finishing his joke. Free the doctor at once and hang the tailor. Allah, judge of judges, what a large number of killings to account for the death of one so small!'

So the tailor mounted the scaffold and was blindfolded, while the judge's clerk proclaimed his crime:

'This tailor is to be hanged to pay for the life of a little beggar (of name unknown) whom he choked to death with a fishbone—and for his efforts to hide his guilty secret.'

But the crowd had gone home, as is the way with crowds.

'Wait! Wait!' said the doctor, stepping forward.

'Oh, no!' said the judge. 'I forbid you to confess twice to the same murder. Hang the tailor before I decide to hang everyone connected with this death.'

'But there has not been a death,' said the doctor, who was standing beside the judge's bench. 'This body is still breathing.'

Truly, the sheet over the little beggar's face was rising and falling as gently as the surface of a puddle disturbed by one drop of water. The doctor opened his instrument bag and sprinkled a coloured pepper on to the beggar's face. The little corpse sneezed several times, sat up and spat out a large flat fishbone. So the doctor's reputation was saved.

'Allah bless and keep me,' said the corpse, 'I feel as though I had been thrown downstairs, hit over the head with a club, and beaten against a wall like a carpet.' Then, catching sight of the tailor and his wife among the witnesses in the court, he said, 'Ah, my hospitable host, now I remember. Allah bless you and your house for fetching so many people to help remove one small fishbone. I seem to have caused a great many people a remarkable inconvenience. Perhaps I can repay you all by finishing the story I began at the house of the tailor last night. If I could just remember which it was . . .'

'It was the story of the Ox, the Donkey, and the Farmer,' said the tailor, helping the little beggar down off the judge's bench, 'and we would be honoured to hear it from beginning to end.'

So the little beggar sat down in the middle of the courtroom floor and began the story of The Ox, the Donkey, and the Farmer.

CHAPTER FIFTEEN

The Ox, the Donkey, and the Farmer

A farmer kept two animals: an ox for ploughing his fields and a donkey for riding into town. But the farmer's legs grew to be long and the donkey's legs grew to be short, so that for his rare visits to town the farmer seldom bothered to saddle the donkey and walked there instead.

When the Ox came in from the fields at the end of the day, his knees buckling with weariness, he found the Donkey, all sleek and fat and smiling, on a clean bed of hay and with a full manger. Smiling was the Donkey's only exercise, and so he smiled a great deal to work up an appetite for the three big meals he ate each day.

'What a wonderful life you lead, brother Donkey,' said the Ox. 'My neck is sore from the yoke, my back aches from pulling, and my feet are full of mud. But you spend all day in the shade of the stable, and your only work is to think and smile!'

Now, the farmer outside the barn overheard the Ox and was sorry that his gentle animal was so downhearted. He stayed to listen to the Donkey's reply.

'Allah gave you a large head but a small brain, brother Ox,' replied the Donkey. 'Listen to me, if those small ears of yours are big enough to hear. Tomorrow, when you are pulling the plough, fall down and refuse to get up even if the farmer whips you . . .'

'But the farmer never uses a whip, brother . . .'

'All the better,' said the Donkey. 'Pant and wheeze and climb to your feet only to fall down again immediately.'

'Thank you, brother,' said the Ox. 'I do not understand what good this will do me, but you have told me many times that wisdom is measured by the size of an animal's ears and I will do as you say, wise brother Donkey.'

The next day during ploughing the Ox lay down and refused to get up. The farmer did not whip him but unhitched the plough, waited for him to stumble to his feet, and led the wheezing animal back to his stall, saying: 'The poor beast is sick. Unless he's better tomorrow I shall not be able to use him for the ploughing.'

'You see, brother,' said the Donkey, when the farmer had gone. 'If you take my advice you will eat no hay tonight.'

The next morning the farmer came to the stable and, seeing the Ox's manger of hay untouched, patted the beast's head. 'My ox is clearly ill and can't be put to work today.' (The Donkey winked at the Ox and smiled.) 'I shall have to use the Donkey instead.' And he hitched the Donkey to the plough and worked him all day until the animal's back ached and his weary feet were twice their thickness with mud.

'O brother Donkey, what wonderful advice you gave me,' said the Ox that night. 'Today I have done nothing but flick my tail to keep off the flies, and watch the sunlight trickle through the eaves.' The Donkey did not answer for he was already asleep—too tired to eat his hay. So the Ox ate from the Donkey's manger and left his own untouched.

The next day the farmer saw the Ox's hay untouched and again harnessed the Donkey to the plough. The miserable animal was obliged to pull all day until his neck was as bald as a vulture's head, and his muscles were knotted like rope.

'How right you were to tell me that wisdom is measured by the size of an animal's ears,' said the Ox that evening, 'for your advice was the best advice I have ever been given!'

But the Donkey was too tired to speak a word in reply.

The next day the Donkey worked at the plough until his ears were limp and the sweat ran down his tail. In the afternoon he lay down in the traces and refused to get up. But the Farmer fetched a whip and beat him soundly, saying, 'What a pity it would be if this weak and stupid animal fell sick like the Ox. With no animal to pull the plough I should grow no crops and make no money and have to sell this miserable Donkey for dog-meat.' The Donkey got quickly to his feet, though the Farmer kept his whip with him after that and used it freely.

'Allah gave you a large chest but small breath to speak the truth,' he said that evening to the Ox. 'You told me that the farmer never used a whip.'

'Believe me, brother, I never saw one in his hand. What suffering you have saved me from, brother, with your wonderful plan!'

But the Donkey only groaned and slept on his feet with his ears hanging down.

On the fourth day the Donkey thought of a plan to save himself more work at the plough.

'O my poor, dear friend,' he said, nuzzling up to the Ox. 'Imagine my sorrow when I heard the Farmer's terrible decision. I hold myself to blame for your awful fate.'

'What decision? What fate?' said the Ox, gulping his small supper of hay.

'I overheard him saying, "If that old ox is not any better tomorrow I shall have to sell him for dog-meat".'

The Ox rocked in his stall like the clapper in a bell and bellowed mournfully, 'What shall I do, brother Donkey? You always told me that wisdom is measured by the size of an animal's ears: *advise me!*'

'Well, brother Ox, eat up every scrap of hay and tomorrow morning greet our master like the young and healthy ox you are.'

The Ox took the Donkey's advice and, when the Farmer came next morning, frisked around his stall as only an ox can frisk. The Farmer patted his gentle ox on the head and opened the stable door to give both animals a sight of the farmyard.

'I want you both to see what I bought at the cattle market.'

The plough was lying along the ground, linked up to the usual shaft. But attached to the shaft was a brand new yoke with a harness at either side. He yoked the Donkey side by side with the Ox and led them into the field, saying (for any Donkey who might be listening), 'Who was it that first spoke that well-known saying:

> *Though Man may have the smallest ears*
> *They're large enough to overhear?'*

CHAPTER SIXTEEN

The Wonderful Tale of Ali Baba and the Forty Bandits

'Why is it,' said Shahrazad on the five hundred and twelfth night, 'that Allah sometimes deals such different fates to two brothers of the same parents?'

'My brother Shahzaman and I have experienced exactly the same fate at the hands of women!' her husband complained.

'Yes, my proud and haughty husband, the difference between you is only one of height. But just as you stand to the shoulder of a giraffe and your brother stands only to the shoulder of a horse, so it was with the fortunes of Ali Baba and his brother Kasim.'

Kasim became as rich as trees are rich in leaves, but Ali Baba could only scratch a living as a woodcutter. By great

122

hard work and by his wife's thriftiness, he came by two donkeys which he took into the forest daily to carry back the firewood.

While he was out with the donkeys one day in a rocky wooded valley, he saw a great cloud of dust ahead of him on the forest track. Because it was a wild, lonely and out-of-the-way place, Ali Baba hid himself, shooing the donkeys into the forest and climbing a leafy tree to hang like a squirrel in its branches.

It proved a wise precaution. The cloud of dust rose from the hooves of forty horses ridden by forty dervish bandits. Their hearts were as black as their beards, their clothes as black as their deeds, and their souls as black as their horses. Their leader was dressed in black astrakhan and rode a horse whose mane, like his, stood up in wild disarray. He halted his corps of bandits almost below Ali Baba's hiding place, beside the valley wall—a sheer cliff which rose, from ground to sky, all grey but for a few scrubby bushes.

'Open, Sesame!' he cried.

I tell no lies, but believe it if you can—in answer to his words, the cliff face opened its mouth—it yawned—it gaped. Where there had been solid rock there was suddenly a black cave, and the bandit chief walked boldly in, carrying his saddlebag across one arm. His forty men followed, each with bulging saddlebags, which were empty when the band reappeared.

They're hiding their plunder, thought Ali Baba, or I am no true Believer.

As his men remounted, the bandit chief faced the cave's entrance and pronounced the words, 'Close, Sesame!' No sooner had the final 'e' touched the air than the cliff wall had closed, like the sea closes over a rock-pool, leaving no sign that a cave had ever existed.

The sound of hooves and the flying dust settled to a stillness, and Ali Baba climbed down. He stood well back from the wall of rock, coughed nervously, and addressed it:

'Open, Sesame . . . please,' he said, and in less time than it takes a fly to blink, a cave appeared in the cliff wall.

'May Allah cross the threshold with me,' whispered Ali Baba and went inside, down a flight of stairs carved from solid rock, and into a sunless cavern. The door closed behind him.

The bandits had left a single torch to burn itself out in a bracket on the wall. By its light Ali Baba saw the spoils of a hundred years of thieving, the contents of a hundred thousand saddlebags, the booty of three generations of bandits. Sacks of gold had outgrown their clothes and burst through holes on to the floor. The lids of chests had been lifted off and turned upside down to hold more golden goblets, necklaces, bracelets and plates, after the chests had overflowed. Barrels of rubies were spilling their brilliant colour like wine across the floor. Gold coins were as plentiful as the drops in a waterfall.

Like a man who dreams quickly for fear of waking up, Ali Baba dragged two of the sacks of gold up the steps.

'If I am not too low in the esteem of Allah, may the magic words release me from this amazing place: Open, Sesame!'

Ali Baba found himself on the forest path and he was able to fetch treasure enough to load both donkeys until they were bow-legged with gold. Then he closed the cave behind him with the magic words. He let night go before him on the road, so that he could creep home in its shadow and deliver to his wife and son the wealth he had always dreamed of earning for them.

His wife turned the gold coins over like water in a bowl, cutting into them with her hands time and time again to let them trickle through her fingers. When she set about counting it, however, Ali Baba laughed and said:

'There is more gold there than can be counted on an abacus. What more do you want to know?'

'We must measure it in some way!' his wife insisted. 'We must know how much more than nothing we own!'

'It is enough to keep us in bread all our lives and to pay for a servant girl to help you in the house. Knowing that much, be content.'

They promised each other in the sight of Allah that they would tell no one about the gold or where it came from. For the bandits' eyes were undoubtedly sharper than their swords, and their ears sharper still: any revenge they took would be more terrible than fire's revenge on straw.

But Ali Baba's wife could not bear to be rich without knowing the extent of her wealth, and ran to her brother-in-law's house to borrow a measuring jug.

Kasim's wife had a great kitchen, and her winter store of grain was heaped like sand-dunes outside her larder. So of course she owned a large brass measuring jug. She had an even greater store of curiosity; seeing her sister-in-law's great excitement, and knowing that Ali Baba's earnings could buy woefully little grain, she ached to uncover the mystery.

Out of everyone's sight, she smeared a dab of butter in the base of the measuring jug and gave it to Ali Baba's wife, who ran home and measured the weight by which her happiness had increased since morning.

Kasim's wife, of course, called to collect the measuring jug and there in the base was a gold coin sticking to the butter. She showed it to her husband who was ferociously jealous—as only a brother can be when he has always thought himself the best and most successful in a family.

'What wealth have you come into, Baba?' Kasim said, laying a heavy hand on his brother's shoulder. 'Out with it now. Brothers should keep no secrets from one another. Allah tells us to share our good fortune liberally.'

There was nothing Ali Baba could do but tell his story to Kasim, who decided as his brother spoke the last full-stop to have every penny of the remaining treasure himself. He found his way to the cave, following Ali Baba when he went to fetch another sack of gold and silver coins. Waiting his chance, Kasim approached the valley wall, coughed respectfully, and said: 'Open, Sesame!'

In the time that it takes light to shine, the treasure of the dervish bandits was laid out in front of him.

He walked among the sacks and barrels and chests and bags, wondering which to take home first. Then dragging two sacks up the stone staircase he backed into the cave door. 'Open, Wheat!' he said irritably.

But nothing happened.

'Oh, sorry. Open, Barley!' he said, certain that he had chosen the correct cereal.

But nothing happened.

The commonest words are the most difficult to remember: he recited all the crops he could think of, but the magic words 'Open, Sesame' were as lost in his memory as a pin dropped into the sea.

Kasim was still stamping up and down the staircase when the bandit leader and his forty men came to the cave with more treasure.

'Open, Sesame!' said the robber chief, and in less time than it takes a bee's wings to beat, he stood face to face with Kasim.

Allah chooses the fate of all men, or Kasim would have chosen differently. The bandits cut him into slices on the spot—a thing that no Believer should do to another, for a man likes to be buried in one piece, does he not? Thinking that their secret was safe with Kasim (who could tell it to no one now) they left the cave and went about their murderous business.

Ali Baba went with his donkeys to fetch more gold, and brought back instead the parts and pieces of his brother.

As he had promised his wife, Ali Baba had hired a girl to help in the house. Allah guided his choice, for the girl, Marjanah, was an exceptionally bright, sensible and loyal servant. (Ali Baba's twenty-year-old son was quick to notice her pretty face and ready smile.)

'Marjanah,' said Ali Baba that night. 'I find I must ask your help in a rather unpleasant matter. I hope you won't regret starting work here under my roof when you hear what it is.'

'Master,' said Marjanah, 'I have neither mother nor father, and you have made a place for me under your roof and found me food when my stomach was empty. Ask anything.' So he took Marjanah out to where the donkeys were standing by the back door and, explaining the circumstances, showed her his brother's parts and pieces and asked if something could be done to give him a secret but honourable burial.

'Of course, sir,' she said and lifted the sacks down from the donkey. 'I shall carry your brother down to the cellar and find a tailor who can smarten him up for his funeral.'

'It must remain secret, Marjanah, or the robber chief will find out that I too know the secret of the Magic Cave.

Now I must tell his wife and have her come here to share the shelter of my humble roof and my family's food.'

Marjanah went to town, found a tailor (poor enough to sew iron to stone if he were asked) and led him, blindfolded, to Ali Baba's house where he sewed all night in the cellar. In the morning Kasim's body was a fine imitation of the living man; all his parts and pieces were joined up again, and he made a respectable corpse for his relatives to follow weeping to the grave.

No one would have known that Kasim was the man at the cave. Ali Baba decided that further trips there were out of the question. The strength of Kasim's greed and the weakness of his memory had separated Ali Baba from the dervishes' great fortune. But he was content with his small good fortune and would have continued praising Allah undisturbed if fate had not also favoured the robber chief.

Returning to the cave, the bandits instantly knew that their secret had not died with Kasim. Someone had collected up the parts and pieces of his body from inside the cave. Somebody else knew the secret words, 'Open, Sesame'. The bandit leader asked in town if anyone had been buried secretly or in several pieces: no one had.

If he had not torn his trousers in the late evening outside the tailor's shop, there would have been no more story to tell . . .

'Do you sew without use of your eyes that you can work so late at night by the light of a single candle?' said the robber chief as he waited for his trousers to be patched.

'Truly, sir, if Allah were to strike me blind,' replied the tailor, 'I could probably continue my profession. Didn't I sew together a man's body only last week, in a dark cellar, with no more candles than this?'

A painted signpost could not have directed the robber chief more surely towards the man he had sworn to kill. He paid the tailor two golden coins, blindfolded him, and had the old man feel his way along the route Marjanah had taken him. He led the dervish to the very door of Ali Baba's house, and the bandit—whose heart was as empty as the moon is empty of heat—drew a cross on the doorpost. The next day his men could burn the marked house to the ground and in it the mouths of any who knew the secret of the Magic Cave.

'Why have you stopped, Shahrazad?' said King Shahryar. 'I hope that is not the end of the story, for I hate stories that leave villains unpunished.'

'It is not the end, judge of all living judges,' his wife replied, 'but I have foolishly left too little time to finish the Wonderful Story of Ali Baba and the Forty Bandits before morning comes and occupies your ears with matters of state. I fear that my head will remember little of the story after it has left my shoulders, but I know better than to ask you to spare my miserable life another day.'

'You have some of the wisdom of your father, Shahrazad, for I would not grant you your life if you asked for it. However, your head cannot be spared until the Wonderful Story of Ali Baba is finished. See that you complete the story between the setting of today's sun and the rising of tomorrow's morning star.'

'To hear you is to obey,' said Shahrazad and, pressing her fingertips together, bowed low to the King as grass bows before the wind.

CHAPTER SEVENTEEN

Ali Baba:
The Robber Chief's Revenge

'Are you like those rascally old story-tellers who forget the beginning of their story before they have reached its end?' said Shahryar accusingly. 'Are you going to tell me that the robber chief had marked the wrong door with chalk or that the forty thieves all suddenly became good Believers and gave up their life of crime?'

'No indeed, my critical lord, for who am I to change the story from the way it is written? The chalk cross did mark out Ali Baba's house, and the forty thieves were quite intent on killing him and all his household by the first light of day.'

But Marjanah, the maidservant, who rose before the sun, saw the cross when she went to sweep the step. Thinking that some gypsies had marked the house in order to curse it or rob it, she took a piece of chalk herself and drew a cross on every other doorpost in the street.

When the dervish arrived with his forty armed men, they found a string of houses that looked as alike as the leaves of a single branch.

'It seems I must spend another two gold coins at the tailor's shop,' said the robber chief, chewing his beard in rage, 'before I can blunt my sword on that thief's neckbone.' And, of course, it did not take him long, with the help of the tailor, to single out Ali Baba's house once again.

This time he formed a plan that would make killing the whole family as easy as crushing strawberries with his tongue. He dressed himself as a merchant selling cooking-oil and bought twenty donkeys and forty large stone jars. Each bandit was commanded to bore a breathing hole in the lid of a jar, then climb inside with as many knives and daggers as could comfortably keep him company in that confined space.

'When the time is right,' said the chief dervish, 'I shall lift off the lids and you will leap out, killing everyone who has not been dead for at least a year! Is that clear?'

'To hear you is to obey,' said his men and climbed into thirty-nine of the jars. The fortieth was filled with olive oil.

'Brother woodcutter,' said the oil merchant to Ali Baba as their donkeys met in the street outside the little house, 'Allah is generous in offering me a starry night to cover my head tonight. But I fear my donkeys will be thirsty by tomorrow morning since I have neither food nor drink for myself or my animals. Won't you allow a humble oil merchant to buy water with this vat of purest olive oil?' And he showed the contents of the one oil-filled jar.

Without a suspicion in his simple head, therefore, Ali begged the merchant to keep his oil and spend the night under *his* roof, and enjoy what humble hospitality a woodcutter could afford.

'First Kasim's wife and now the oil merchant,' said Marjanah. 'Soon there will be as many people sitting round my master's table as sit round that dervish campfire shaming Allah with their unholy ways. Allah akbar! I've run out of oil!'

With forty tubs of cooking oil in the yard, Marjanah felt that their guest could spare them a measure of oil. So she went outside with a cup in her hand, and waited until her eyes became accustomed to the dark. Just as she went to unseal the lid of a jar, a voice inside it said, 'Is it time?'

Marjanah clapped her hand over her mouth and danced about on one foot until her heart slipped back down her throat and settled among her ribs. A silly, superstitious girl would have thought the jar contained an ifrit or a jinni, but Marjanah was an exceptionally bright and sensible servant. Her heart spoke with her brain and together they arrived at Understanding. Brushing against a dozen more jars, Marjanah heard men's voices say, 'Is it time?' and she whispered (in as deep a voice as possible), 'Not yet.'

Then she fetched a large cream cheese from the kitchen and stopped up the breathing holes in all the thirty-nine jars which spoke.

The meal ended, the family went to bed. The robber chief crept out to the yard and unsealed the jars whispering, 'It's time now.'

But no one answered.

What murderer can complain to his victim that his plans have all been spoiled? The next morning, to Ali Baba's amazement, his guest looked at him as though he would bite if he had teeth enough to do so. Then he led his donkeys away down the street without a word of thanks or farewell and went to the Magic Cave to mope about and plot revenge.

When Marjanah told Ali Baba what had happened, he praised Allah for guiding him to such a bright, sensible and loyal serving girl and said: 'After such a deed, the walls of my house are looking at you differently. In the house of a man with one son there is room for a daughter. From today you are my adopted daughter and not my serving girl.' (So Allah provides for his most humble servant.)

It is said that the snake with nothing to strangle will strangle itself. The robber chief had no need to murder Ali Baba, for now the woodcutter put all thought of the Magic Cave out of his mind and lived in comfortable poverty, eking out the gold from his three visits there. But the leader of the forty bandits—now the leader of none—lived for the day when he could shave Ali Baba's beard with a dagger and part his hair with an axe.

He disguised himself as a wealthy sheikh and returned to town a year later riding a camel. He encouraged the beast to fall down outside the front door of Ali Baba's modest house, spilling his rider and baggage into the road. The woodcutter was, of course, the first to help him up and offer him hospitality, according to the laws of Allah and His Prophet.

That evening Marjanah surpassed her usual skill and served a meal which delighted the tongue without weighing heavy on the stomach. When the bandit consulted his stomach he considered that to murder the cook might be wasteful. So he offered Ali Baba a fair price for his maidservant.

'I regret to say that Marjanah is no longer mine to sell as a maidservant,' said Ali with pride, 'for I adopted her as my own daughter.'

'Then perhaps I should ask for her as a wife!' said the sheikh.

Marjanah, who was serving coffee to the assembled company, looked quickly but closely at the sheikh in case she should indeed find herself given away to him before the day was finished. (For what gracious host can refuse the request of a guest under his roof—especially a wealthy sheikh.)

'I and my household are all your property, noble sheikh,' said Ali Baba, 'for so it must be between host and guest.'

'And would you like to be married to me, my pretty little gazelle?' said the bandit, catching hold of her hand.

Marjanah brushed herself against the sheikh and ran her fingers through his hair (shocking her father and outraging Ali Baba's son who until then had looked with pleasure at his new 'sister'). 'Shall I dance for you before you decide?' she asked the sheikh in a voice as thick and sweet as syrup.

She ran from the room and changed into dancing clothes—a white muslin veil and crimson robe—and she carried for her dance a pair of tiny cymbals on the finger and thumb of her left hand and a curved ivory dagger in her right hand.

Round and round she whirled, to the rhythm of her bare feet slapping on the floor and to the music of her cymbals and some music within her dark, foreign soul. Though she turned this way and that, and her plaited hair cracked like whipcord, her eyes never seemed to leave the wealthy sheikh who was spellbound by her weaving dance. Faster and faster she turned in the middle of the room until her plaits were flying out as level as a black horizon. Closer and closer to the floor she whirled, and the white ivory blade of the knife made a white whirling circle round her blurred crimson shape.

The sheikh rose to his knees and his eyes glittered with excitement, his right hand beating the floor in rhythm with her feet. He put his hand into his robe to pull out a purse of money as Marjanah added a chant to her dancing:

> 'And isn't that how,
> and isn't that how,
> and isn't that how
> the dervisha dances?'

she shrieked, and dropped on the sheikh, plunging the knife into his heart.

'What have you done, you wild, peculiar woman?' cried Ali Baba's wife, but Marjanah was too out of breath to speak.

'What have you done, daughter?' asked Ali Baba, heartbroken with shame.

'Knife . . . knife,' she panted, '. . . had a knife . . .'

'You foolish, wicked girl,' said her adoptive brother. 'He was reaching for a purse of money to give you.' He turned over the body of the sheikh to show her her mistake, and a purse of money dropped from his right hand and a long silver serrated dagger from his left.

'I saw it in the folds of his robe as I served him coffee,' said Marjanah, 'and recognized the face of your old enemy, the dervish robber chief.'

Then Marjanah removed the bandit's disguise, and

withdrew to her bedroom to change into the modest clothes of a modest Believer.

Ali Baba was so delighted with the bravery and resourcefulness of little Marjanah that he married her to his son to make her truly a part of his family. After a year or so, the woodcutter asked his courage if it was strong enough to make a fourth journey to the Magic Cave. He found the cliff face overgrown with weeds and mosses and the forest path empty of footprints. But a thousand years cannot dull the memory of Allah's Magic Places and when Ali Baba spoke the words 'Open, Sesame!'—in less time than it takes the heart to love—the cave entrance opened and the dervish treasure of three generations lay at his feet.

Ali Baba became the richest man in the whole province, and built a palace for himself and his wife on a hill in the town. He also bought a little farm for his son and Marjanah, and although the young man earned an income no larger or smaller than the average sheikh, he took it into his head—and said aloud on many occasions—that he was the richest man in the whole world.

CHAPTER EIGHTEEN

The Price of Cucumbers

One night Shahrazad was asleep in the King's arms when his tightening, frightening grip woke her.

'What's the matter, my lord?'

'What story were you going to tell me this morning,' he said, 'or promise to tell me tomorrow night?'

The dust of sleep was still thick on the lady's thoughts, and she could not immediately summon up a story.

'I have been watching you sleep,' he said, 'and thinking about the days and nights that have slipped by like earthworms through the earth since I married you. My brain instructed my heart, saying, "She has tricked you night after night. She has fooled you and you have enjoyed being fooled." Can you dispute, wife, that you have saved your life by trickery, telling me stories that tempt me to listen rather than to kill?'

Shahrazad did not answer.

'You know that a man's mind is a palace whose occupants are his separate thoughts. The mind of a king must be larger than most, for there are a thousand thoughts to be bedded down under the one roof. What room is there for *stories* in such a palace. The chambers of my head are crammed with your stories, Shahrazad. They run about during the day, interrupting and tripping up my sober thoughts of state. Should a King's thoughts be cluttered with such light, fanciful matters. No!'

But Shahrazad did not answer.

'I will not thank you for your stories, for they have been a deception—a device—a deceitful trick of yours to help you cling to your worthless and empty head. I must admire your cunning, Shahrazad, but such cunning is the very reason I must cut off your head.'

But Shahrazad did not answer. She only bowed to the King to show that she accepted his decision.

'Do you deny that you have been tricking me all these nights?'

'May Allah look away from me if I ever deny what my King and husband tells me is true.'

'Is that all you have to say!' exclaimed Shahryar.

'Ah, my husband, I fear that if I speak, the first word of another story will fall from my mouth, for the palace of my mind is overflowing with such meddlesome, troublesome stories. They teach me that trickery is rife in the world and that you are right, therefore, to beware of tricksters such as me. It is true that I enjoyed life, for every day was crowned with the sight of you, O Shahryar. But do not believe that I—a worthless and silly and slow-witted woman—thought I could cloud your eyes or deceive your heart. Allah forgive me: I only wished for the fate of the Arab who so foolishly tried to trick the Emir Muin ibn Zaid.'

'What fate was that?'

Shahrazad stamped her foot. 'Again I have spilt a drop of story at your feet, my lord, like a careless dairymaid spilling the milk. Surely you don't want me to tell you how the trickster was out-tricked?'

'Oh, yes, my trickster wife,' said Shahryar with a cold glitter in his eyes, 'for it may teach me how to trick you out of your life this coming morning.' Shahrazad wrapped the blanket of the bed around her head so that only her eyes were showing:

Riding out into the desert one day, the Emir Muin ibn Zaid was dressed like this against the flying prickle of a sandstorm. Out of the whirling sand came a poor Arab mounted on a donkey and, of course, they exchanged greetings.

'Where are you going, sir?' asked the Emir. Now most men who are rich as the Emir was rich are too mean to squander precious words on men below them in rank, but Muin was quite the most generous, hospitable and courteous Believer ever to have graced Allah's Sahara. (All this happened, of course, long before the reign of Shahryar of Sasan or Shahzaman of Samarkand.)

'Where are you going, sir?' was the Emir's question to the Arab.

'I am going to the court of the Emir Muin ibn Zaid with these,' and the Arab held up a small parcel.

'What is in there—something you wish to sell?' asked the Emir, intending to reveal himself immediately.

The Arab winked. 'A cunning man has no need to be so simple. You must know, sir—for everyone knows it— that the Emir Muin is quite the most generous, hospitable, and courteous Believer ever to have been entrusted with money. A cunning man could make good use of such a man.'

Muin decided not to uncover his face and again asked what was in the parcel.

'Cucumbers, sir. The first baby cucumbers from my garden,' replied the Arab. 'I am taking them as a present to the Emir.'

'A present? Do you expect nothing in return for such generosity?' asked the Emir, guessing the reply.

The Arab winked again and tapped his nose. 'Expect? What might a man expect from the most generous, hospitable, and courteous Believer who ever squandered money on the poor? He will ask me what kind of gift he could make in return for such trouble and effort and thoughtfulness on my part, and I shall think for a moment and say, ''What would you care to give me? A thousand dinars?'' And if he does I shall be the happiest man in the Sahara.'

'And what if he says No?' asked Muin, amazed at the Arab's impertinence.

'I shall say ''800 dinars'',' replied the Arab, 'and if he gives me them I shall be the happiest man in the region.'

'And what if he says no to 800 dinars?'

'''600 dinars.'' That would make me the happiest man in Utria, my home-town.'

'And what if he says no to 600?'

'''400 dinars.'' That would make my wife happy, at least.'

'And what if he says no to 400?' asked the Emir.

'''200 dinars'',' replied the Arab, 'which would pay for a new donkey.'

'And if he says no to that?'

'''100'' and then ''70'' and then ''40''.'

'But what if he says no to 40 dinars?' asked the Emir.

'Then I shall throw my cucumbers on the rubbish heap,' said the Arab, 'and say that the stories of Muin ibn Zaid were all lies and curse my donkey for taking me there to waste my time on misers.'

'Well, I hope your plan prospers,' said Muin, safely grinning a grin behind the folds of his burnous.

When the Arab was out of sight, the Emir turned back to his court so as to entertain his guest without delay. He changed into his robes of cloth-of-gold, bordered with red velvet, and received his humble visitor in an audience chamber roofed with stippled silver.

The Arab crept in, his packet of cucumbers folded to his chest, looking about him at the woollen tapestries and the sayings from the Holy Book inlaid in gold on the black lacquer furnishings and marble pillars. The Emir's voice ringing from the far end of the room startled him: 'The blessing of Allah be upon you, sir. What have I done to deserve the honour of a visit from . . .'

The Arab supplied his name: 'Ali ibn Ali. Lord and master of all that floor which lies under the ceiling of the sky, I have travelled a day and a night from my little house in the province of Utria to bring you the first fruits of my garden. When I saw these baby cucumbers hanging among their yellow flower-trumpets and green leaves, I said to myself: the Emir Muin ibn Zaid must have these if I have to travel a day and a night to give them to him.'

'How kind,' said Muin. 'To do such a selfless thing— without thought of reward—you must indeed be the most generous, hospitable, and courteous Believer ever to grace Allah's Sahara.'

'No indeed,' simpered Ali, 'I fall far short of the generosity, hospitality, and courtesy of the Emir ibn Zaid, for your fame has spread like a priceless carpet to the four corners of Arabia's floor.'

Muin took the cucumbers and looked at them thoughtfully, then laid them back in the Arab's hands. 'I cannot accept these delicate fruits unless you will allow me to reward your kindness in some way. But I ask my heart, and my heart confers with my stomach, and they cannot decide on the correct price for baby cucumbers so early in the season. What should an emir of great wealth give to a man as worthy as Ali ibn Ali?'

'1,000 dinars?' said the Arab, unable to mince matters for another moment.

'No, I shan't give you that,' said Muin.

'No, of course not, master. What am I thinking of? 800 dinars?'

'I could, but I shan't give you 800.'

'Why should you indeed!' said Ali. '600?'

'I shan't give you 600 dinars.'

'No, sir, of course not,' said Ali, his neck beginning to sweat. 'Would 400 dinars seem fair?'

'No, Ali ibn Ali, not for baby cucumbers.'

'200 then?'

'Not 200, Ali ibn Ali.'

'100?'

'Yes, but I shan't give you 100 dinars.'

'You could perhaps spare 70 dinars, though,' said the Arab.

'I could but I won't.'

'40 dinars for your humble servant.'

'No, Ali ibn Ali, for that would insult you.'

'Yes, sir,' said Ali, getting up off his aching knees. 'It would insult me as I would insult you if I had words enough in my ignorant head. But I curse the donkey that brought me here and will never believe again the stories of Muin ibn Zaid's generosity,' and he shuffled off towards the door.

'But it would seem a waste of delectable baby cucumbers to throw them on the rubbish heap, would it not?' said the Emir rising from his throne. 'If you won't eat them yourself, perhaps you could give them to the Arab you met riding in the desert.'

Each of the Emir's words sounded in the Arab's ears like the clanging of a prison door or the sharpening of an axe. He peeped back over his shoulder at Muin ibn Zaid who had covered his head with a burnous so that only his eyes were showing. The Arab fell on his face where he was, and trembled like a joint of meat that smells the cooking pot.

'Please don't lie on the cucumbers, friend Ali ibn Ali. We haven't decided on a fair price for them yet.'

'A present has no price,' mumbled Ali. 'Yours. All yours.'

But the Emir insisted. 'Would you not agree, friend, the thoughts which moved you to come here do deserve some kind of reward?' (Ali the Arab covered his head with his arms.) 'Let me see what I shall give you,' said Muin. '1,000 dinars, you said. I replied that I would not give you 1,000.' And he counted out 1,000 dinars onto a plate. 'And even though you asked me for a further 800 dinars, that was still insufficient to repay you for your thoughtfulness.' And he counted 800 dinars onto the same plate. 'Not even the addition of another 600 dinars was enough to repay your generosity; nor was another 400 dinars enough to repay your courtesy. And if I add to it the 200, the 100, the 70, and the 40 dinars by which you so modestly increased your estimate, I would still insult a truly generous man with the gift.'

And he counted out each of the sums—400, 200, 100, 70, and 40 dinars—onto the plate. 'A man's thoughtfulness and selfless act of love cannot be repaid with this paltry sum of 3,210 dinars.' (Ali ibn Ali was beating his forehead on the floor as he waited to hear what reward awaited a greedy confidence trickster.) 'But perhaps a scoundrel like Ali ibn Ali of Utria is not so easily insulted as an honest Believer.' And, laughing, Muin ibn Zaid carried the plate to where Ali lay rigid on the floor, and stood it down beside his head. 'But please don't lie on those cucumbers another moment, sir, for if there is one dish I relish it is baby cucumbers. Won't you share them with me?'

'And if there is one dish I relish, sir,' said the Arab, raising his face, 'it is that one,' and he nodded towards the plate of dinars the Emir had given him. 'May Allah bless you for your generosity, hospitality, and courtesy, but chiefly for your sense of humour, O Emir Muin ibn Zaid.'

When Shahrazad finished the story called The Price of Cucumbers, her husband was free to cut off her head, for the sun was straining its neck to see over the horizon. But given the admirable example of Muin ibn Zaid's generous dealings with the Arab, Shahryar could not immediately and peevishly condemn her to death.

Besides, his anger had soaked away while she spoke, as the angry wave bubbles on the sand's surface for a moment then soaks into the soft and shifting gold and leaves only a dark, cold trace of its shape. The dark, cold trace of Shahryar's bitterness still lay over Shahrazad, but she lived to tell another tale on the six hundred and thirteenth night after her wedding.

CHAPTER NINETEEN
The Wonderful Bag

On the six hundred and sixty-sixth night Shahrazad told a story (told to her) of a man whose name was too unimportant to remember, but who told his story to others in these words:

I was looking after my stall in the Baghdad bazaar when an Arab with eyes as sharp as spears and fingers as sticky as a tree frog's, boldly lifted a bag off the counter and walked away with it.

'Put that back, you son of a bluebottle's maggot,' I said, 'or I shall have you taken before the Wali and he'll cut off your hands.'

'Hold your tongue, you reminder of a moulting duck,' he replied calmly over his shoulder. 'The bag's mine.'

'It's no more yours than the Caliph's left ear!' I cried, pursuing him down the street. 'Put it back at once, you flea on a cockroach's knee-cap.'

In brief, I called on the neighbouring stall-holders for

help. They seized the Arab and carried him to the Wali's court, where the bag was placed on the judge's bench.

'There is a simple way of solving this matter,' said the Wali. 'The true owner will certainly know what the bag contains.'

'Why then, the matter is solved,' said the Arab, 'for I can tell you down to the last item what is in the bag. There is a knife, a fork, a spoon, three figs, a bottle of milk, four cheeses, a book, a camel driver's whip and a flag.'

'But that's quite absurd,' I said, curling my lip at the Arab. 'I know full well the bag contains a box of chalks, four dates, a twist of sherbet, two daggers, four hundred and twelve dinars, a mirror set with zircon, a pair of clogs, and some seaweed.'

'You did not give me time to finish,' said the Arab, flaring his nostrils at me. 'I did not mention the saddle, the three lamps, the small pond, the laundry basket, and the carved chair.'

'Your interruption proves that you have no more manners than honesty,' I said, jabbing a finger towards the Arab. 'As I was saying, there are five ducks, a candlestick, eight turbans, seventy-four ostrich eggs, my mother-in-law's left leg, a compact tent, and one whirling dervish.'

'Do you expect the judge to believe such monumental lies?' said the Arab, shaking his fist at me across the court. 'His eyes will shortly prove that the only contents I have yet to mention are the six red camels, the Chief of Police, the gate-house from Cairo's eastern wall, a platoon of horse, and sixteen small volcanoes—oh, and of course the troop of scantily dressed dancing girls.'

We glowered at one another across the court until I said: 'I trust only in Allah and the evidence of those twenty-four just sheikhs in the bag and the waiters who serve them their meals in there, along with the seven moonlit gardens, sixty-eight-and-a-half palaces, the pregnant ox, the snow-covered mountain range, and the modest quarter-section of the Sahara desert. I think that leaves only the Red Ocean and twelve of its beaches unlisted.'

At this point the Wali closed his gaping mouth and opened the wonderful bag, shaking out on to the bench some old pieces of orange peel, and three pips. There was a great silence in the courtroom.

'I really must apologize from the lowest rib of my chest,' said the Arab, bowing to me across the court. 'I seem to have made the most unfortunate mistake: this is not my bag at all. Can you forgive me the inconvenience you have been caused?'

'Do I not know as well as anyone here,' I said, returning the bow, 'how easily the mistake is made? I too mistook this bag for my own. I hope you will forgive me for treating you so barbarously in my ignorance.'

'Think nothing of it, friend,' said the Arab, and we left the courtroom arm in arm, leaving the Wali to scratch his head and dispose of the orange peel, the three pips, and the Wonderful Bag.

CHAPTER TWENTY

The Tale of the Anklet

'What tiny feet you have, Shahrazad,' said King Shahryar one night.

Shahrazad was astonished, for there is no greater compliment in all the language of Arabia than on the size of a lady's feet. Just as no one admires the moon on a cloudy night, she had thought King Shahryar's eyes were too cloudy with sorrow to admire her beauty. The King saw that she was pleased and said: 'If you had had big feet, wife, I would have cut off your head before the rose petals your bridesmaids threw had fallen to the ground.'

So Shahrazad did not trust her safety to the smallness of her feet or the greatness of her beauty, but to the quickness of her tongue and the glory of her stories.

'What dark stable would you find for your camel of a wife,' she said, 'if you were ever to see Delilah of the small ankles, in the Tale of the Anklet. How glad I am that she lives far away in the land of stories where no man may travel on foot but only by ear.'

148

'Take me to the land of stories,' said Shahryar, 'and show me Delilah in the Tale of the Anklet.'

'To hear you is to obey,' said Shahrazad.

If a reader were to search through the Stories of Three, he might find there Delilah who was the youngest of three sisters. Perhaps I should say step-sisters, for their father had two daughters before his first wife died. Then he married, in his old age, the beautiful mother of Delilah, and his third daughter grew up with her mother's beauty of face and soul. But when the old man and his young wife died, the three sisters lived together as happily as two scorpions and a mouse.

Delilah's two sisters were jealous of her face, which was as lovely as the tamarind flower, of her hair, whose waves gleamed like the night sea under a moon, of her hands, as long and delicate as fronded leaves, and of her little feet, as small and delicate as a baby fawn's. She tried to ease their jealousy by dressing in very plain and modest clothes, but it became their sport and pastime to make her as unhappy as she was beautiful.

They set her to work in a dark corner of the house, and Delilah sat and span the fluff of wool and the floss of cotton, and looked at the wall until she knew every brick, stone, dent, crack, and cockroach as well as her morning prayers. From what she earned, the sisters allowed her to keep the few pennies she needed to buy food.

But one day, instead of buying her usual sesame bun, she came home with a little vase instead, and put some wild flowers in it, and put it in front of her while she worked. The sisters laughed and jeered at her for buying such an ugly little vase, but Delilah placidly went on

149

spinning, while they went out to the bazaar to spend all the rest of the money she had earned.

'And what is so magic about you, little vase?' she said as the door closed behind them. 'The old man who sold you to me said that you were magic. Was I foolish to believe him just because of the length and whiteness of his beard?'

'No,' said the vase. 'Ask for any luxury and I will bring it to you.'

So Delilah lifted the flowers out of the vase and asked for a little something to eat (since she had gone without food to buy the vase). Immediately, a fountain of dates, apricots, sweetmeats, grapes, almond cakes, and all manner of good things poured out of the neck of the vase and arranged themselves in front of her.

Delilah's happiness was lovely to see. But only the little vase saw it.

Whenever her sisters went out, Delilah would ask the little vase to brighten her weary day, and the vase would fabricate gorgeous clothes, delicious tit-bits, enthralling books or the music of enchanting instruments. It was particularly adept at making jewellery—bracelets and necklaces more beautiful than Delilah knew how to request. Her happiness was as lovely as the jewels. But only the little vase saw it.

For fear of making her sisters more jealous, Delilah would change back into her cheap, drab clothes before they returned to the house, and hide or give away the little vase's produce.

One day, however, the joy she took in her ordinary work and her extraordinary vase seemed too large for the little house, and she decided to chance a small adventure. Asking the vase for a costume more fabulous than any before, she dressed herself in more finery than the sun does at sunset and pattered on her little feet all the way to the royal palace. No one barred the way to a lady as splendid and bejewelled as she was, and she found her way to the very heart of the King's harem. Women as lissom as waving grass and as fair as stooks of wheat decorated every chair and cushion, but they all clapped their hands and drew sharp breaths at the sight of Delilah. Her clothes set off her natural beauty as a clear, navy sky sets off the crescent moon.

'Are you to be the Prince's wife?' they asked. 'Emissaries have been scouring the realm for a beauty befitting the Prince's nobility and wealth, his breeding and good taste. Surely you are the answer to their prayers!'

Delilah only laughed to herself that they could be so mistaken. At their heartfelt description of the young Prince, she asked if she might be allowed to glimpse the Royal Heir. So they took her to a lattice window that overlooked a courtyard and below her she saw a group of young men playing football. Delilah thought to herself, The Royal Prince might be as high-born as an eagle of the mountain-tops, but I would dance from here to China across the sharp bed of the sea for a kiss from the young man in wine-coloured velvet.

'Which is the Prince?' she asked.

'Why, he's the tallest of the young men—the one dressed in wine-coloured velvet.'

Just then, beyond the courtyard and beyond the palace wall, Delilah glimpsed the two towering hair-styles of her step-sisters as they rolled home from the bazaar, crushing every caterpillar and beetle under their impressively monumental feet.

Empty of all thoughts but the thought of getting home

before them, Delilah fled down the palace stairs and across the courtyard to the nearest gate in the palace wall. The Prince was dimly aware of a jag of colour of the kind the eye sees if shut very tightly. He turned to see what lady of the palace would leave it in full flight with evening already approaching, but Delilah had already gone.

She leapt the shallow trough dug in the courtyard for the horses to drink from: she leapt it like a gazelle. But the anklet of diamonds she wore round her ankle slipped over her tiny foot and dropped into the water. Her feet were as quick as they were small, and she reached the house before her sisters and changed out of her clothes before they clattered in at the door. It did not show, but her throat was still damp with the running and her heart was still sore for the young man in wine-coloured velvet.

The following day there was a commotion at the palace when the sun reached its height, for the palace horses would not drink from the trough. A flashing in the water made them shy away, flaring their nostrils. When the Royal Ostler removed the diamond anklet from the trough, the Prince was standing close by with his horse.

'Look at the size of it!' said the Prince, holding it up on the tips of three fingers.

'Look at the cut of the diamonds,' said the ostler, as the rainbow-coloured light spilled on the ground in all directions.

'Look at the quality of the silverwork,' said the King when his son showed it to him.

'Yes, but look at the *size* of it,' repeated the Prince. 'If any mortal woman has a foot so delicate that it will pass through that anklet, I could die for love of her!'

'What would that achieve?' said the King who had forgotten about such things as love. 'Tell your mother if you want to marry the owner of the anklet. I have forgotten about such things.'

'Mother, I want to marry the girl who wore this anklet,' said the Prince to the Queen.

'Allah finds baffling ways of pairing a man and a woman,' said the Queen. 'I suppose the smallness of a woman's foot is as good a reason as any. I shall order a search of the city. Can we assume that the anklet will fit no one but the lady to whom it belongs?'

'Could there be two women with such delicate ankles?' asked the Prince by way of reply.

House by house, the Queen's emissaries carried out their search for the owner of the anklet. What washing of feet took place among the women of marriageable age! What shrinking of feet in bowls of cold water! But no one could fit the anklet over their feet until the emissaries came to the house of Delilah and her sisters.

'She never goes out,' said one step-sister, pushing Delilah into a corner and pulling up her own skirts.

'She has no jewellery at all,' said the other, sitting down on Delilah's lap to try on the diamond anklet. But the emissary looked sidelong at the four gigantic feet held out towards him and only lifted the folds of material covering Delilah's feet.

'The Prince's bride,' he said simply, before even slipping the anklet over her foot.

As Delilah prepared for the wedding, her happiness was almost a pain inside her. In secret she requested a wedding dress—in crimson and gold—from the magic vase and put it on, but she could feel the jealousy of her two sisters beating against her like black bird-wings. She knew their jealousy was hurting them more sharply than her happiness and was very sorry that they could not be as happy as her. So she told them the secret of the magic vase and wished them much joy of it, for she said she had magic enough in the Prince's love.

The sisters huddled together over the vase, asking it for this and that, all raucous with laughter when their wishes came true. But when Delilah went to show the neighbours her wedding dress, the one said to the other, 'Watch me, sister, and see if I can't put a stop to this selfish girl's wickedness and all the vile happiness that is clogging up the house like leaves clogging a drain . . .'

When Delilah came back from showing off her wedding dress, her sisters offered to dress her hair for the wedding. They braided it with gold and scattered it with pearls—all given them by the magic of the little vase.

'Now, a pin here and a second here and another to fasten your plait, my beautiful little sister, and your head will be so exquisite that the Prince will forget he fell in love with your feet.'

But as the last pin sank into her glossy hair, the hair became wool-white and feathered into the herls and quills of a young dove. The jealous sisters had asked the magic vase for three enchanted pins which would transform any living creature into a bird.

The step-sisters sent word that the bride-to-be had so hated the thought of the Prince that she had fled the country rather than be married to him; and they turned the dove off the window-sill and pelted it with dry rice when it fluttered back towards the house.

The Prince's disappointment felt almost like a sickness inside him. He refused to eat or leave his room, and he would hear no mention of alternative brides, though the King and Queen promised to send emissaries on their hands and knees to measure all the feet in the kingdom. His only comfort came from the visits of a crested dove at his window. The little wool-white bird crooned so gently and sorrowfully that the Prince felt befriended and set out food for the bird.

She would not touch it. Soon she seemed so weak that the Prince picked her up in the palm of his hand and stroked her head and neck. The crest seemed spiny to the touch, and when the Prince lifted her head feathers it seemed that three pins were sticking deep into her delicate skull. Pulling them out, his hand thought it would break from his arm for he found himself supporting the weight of a full-grown woman in crimson and gold wedding raiment. She might have weighed more, but for the incredible slimness of her ankles and the smallness of her feet.

Delilah told the Prince her story, and the wedding took place before dark, to the great astonishment of the King and Queen and the emissaries who were already searching the land on their hands and knees. When the noise of the festivities—the clamour of cymbals, the blowing of reed pipes, and the clatter of drums—wreathed down into the city, and the people began dancing, and benches were laid in the streets to celebrate the marriage of nobility to loveliness, then the two sisters of Delilah feared for their lives. They asked the magic vase to rescue them from the Royal Guards and the Palace Police.

'Hide us somewhere where no one can see us,' they begged, little realizing that the guards were already at the window with the Prince's orders to fetch them to him in chains.

The magic vase opened its neck and swallowed up the two sisters with a satisfied gulp. And the Palace Guards carried the little vase—at arm's length—to the Prince and his royal bride.

'Shall I order the vase to give up your sisters so that they can be beaten soundly and turned into jackdaws?' asked the Prince.

'No,' said Delilah. 'Place the vase on the highest shelf in the palace and if someone should discover its secret in years to come, they can decide what to do with two big-footed girls and enough envy to fill a barn.'

'A splendid story!' cried Shahryar. 'You said the Tale of the Anklet came from the Book of Threes. What is that?'

'The stories in it are all of three sisters or three brothers or three friends, my attentive and observant lord,' said Shahrazad.

'Can you find in your memory a story of three brothers as pleasing as the Tale of the Anklet?' he asked.

'Oh certainly, dearest husband, for the story of the Prince and the Large and Lonely Tortoise is far more wonderful than the Tale of the Anklet. But the air is yellow with morning, and there is not time to tell it now.'

'Unless you would rather bow down to my headsman than to me, tell it tonight when my day's work is over.'

'To hear you is to obey,' said Shahrazad, bowing low to the King.

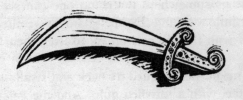

CHAPTER TWENTY-ONE

The Prince and the Large and Lonely Tortoise

'Allah's ways of pairing a man and a woman are many,' said the King of Inner Araby to his three sons, 'and pure chance is as good as any. Fetch your bows and arrows and meet me on the balcony in less time than it takes the heart to fall in love.'

So the Princes of Inner Araby met their father on the palace balcony, and there he instructed each to fire one arrow high over the city below.

'Wherever your arrow falls—on whatever house—a bride will be taken for you from under that roof.'

The oldest Prince's arrow fell on the house of a wealthy merchant whose eldest daughter was as beautiful as the ash tree by moonlight. Everyone was well pleased.

The second Prince shot an arrow which fell on the house of a respected and respectable sheikh whose only daughter was as beautiful as the larch tree in sunlight. Everyone was well pleased.

But when the youngest Prince—the King's favourite son—fired his arrow over the city, it fell among the thatches and tiles on to a wholly unremarkable house occupied by no one but a large and lonely tortoise.

'Shoot again,' said the King as hurriedly as a cat climbs out of water, 'Allah has made a slight mistake.'

But the second arrow fell on the self-same house.

'Shoot again,' said the King as hurriedly as a cat climbs out of fire, 'Allah has made a terrible mistake.'

But the third arrow fell on the very same house, to the excitement of the large and lonely tortoise inside.

'Either tell me the King's wishes or stop shooting arrows into my roof,' she said as the foot-pages arrived with ladders to retrieve the third arrow.

'Clearly Allah intends you never to marry,' said the King to his son, overcome with sadness.

'Far from it, father,' said the youngest Prince. 'Allah clearly intends me to marry this large and lonely tortoise, and I will not defy heaven's decision.'

So the tortoise was fetched to the Royal Palace on a large red cushion by four liveried foot-pages. She was a very ancient, horny, and repulsive tortoise who mumbled her food to pieces between lips as hard and toothless as the rims of stone jars.

'Allah cannot expect a man to marry that!' said the King bursting into tears. 'Think of the bed linen!'

At this the tortoise retreated into her shell, and out of courtesy the young Prince went forward and exchanged a few words with her, looking in at the neck of the shell.

'I am more certain than ever,' he said, returning to the King. 'I must marry this large and lonely tortoise. And if I am a just and gentle husband, I am sure I shall be rewarded with a loyal and gentle wife.'

The wedding of the three Princes took place on the same day: the oldest to the merchant's daughter who wore a crimson and gold robe; the second to the sheikh's daughter who wore white and silver; the youngest to the large and lonely tortoise who wore a purple bow round her neck.

The apple of the King's heart rotted to its core, and he cursed his idea of the fateful arrows. When his young son patiently accepted his bride and lived in apparent peace and cheerfulness with her, the King took it upon himself to grieve on the boy's behalf. His inward sighs clouded the windows of his eyes, and soon he was gravely ill and almost blind.

His three loving sons were anxious, and doubtful of the quackery and magic practised by the royal physicians.

'Father,' they said, 'from today onwards our wives alone will feed and nurse you, for their love is to be trusted better than your lazy and ignorant doctors. By turns, the ladies will prepare you meals to tempt your appetite and renew your strength.'

At once the royal Princesses set about preparing tasty broths to delight the sickly King.

'Here is an opportunity,' said the royal ladies, 'to shame the detestable animal that married the stupid young Prince. Perhaps when she lays some foul-tasting concoction in front of the King he will send her back where she came from, or spit and roast her over an open fire.'

Then the large and lonely tortoise sent a maid to the palace of her sister-in-law, the merchant's daughter, saying: 'May I have all the grease from your kitchen ceilings and the dust from under your carpet, to flavour the King's soup?'

The merchant's daughter curled her lip with disgust. 'That's just what I would expect from that *creature*,' she said. 'Tell it I have need of every drop of grease and speck of dust for my own cooking and it must make do with its own household dirt.' And she laughed contemptuously.

Then the Tortoise sent a maid to her other sister-in-law, the sheikh's daughter, saying:

'May I have all the dead mice from your traps, and the used straw from your stables, to flavour the King's broth?'

'Typical!' said her sister-in-law. 'I can hardly be bothered with sending a reply. Tell that beast that royal mice are too good for her sort, even when they are dead.'

When the maid brought back the messages, the tortoise, far from being angry, was spun about by laughter and she rolled on the rim of her shell like a coin spinning to rest.

For breakfast the next morning the merchant's daughter brought a steaming bowl of broth covered with a linen cloth and offered it to the King on a silver tray.

'Here, father, I prepared this with my own hands from the very best herbs, spices, honey, and fruit.'

But when the King lifted the linen cloth, the greasy grey swill in the bowl, all coated in fluff, was enough to make him turn green.

'I don't understand . . .' began the Princess, but the King had already fainted.

By mid-day he had recovered enough to be offered food by the second Princess. She brought him a bowl of broth covered with a linen cloth, and presented it to him on a golden tray. 'Here, father. I prepared this with my own hands from the very rarest herbs and spices with the leanest of meat.'

'Are you all trying to poison me?' the King exclaimed, for before he even lifted the linen, the smell was utterly appalling. And when he did so, three dead mice and a handful of dirty straw were floating in a milky swill.

'I don't understand . . .' began the Princess, spilling the bowl all over the bed. The King fell back on his pillow in a dead faint and was not well enough to receive anyone until the evening.

When the large, lonely, but royal tortoise crawled into the King's bedroom with a bowl of broth balanced on top of her shell, the King turned his face into his pillow and groaned. 'What mess have you mixed me with your horny left foot?' he asked disgustedly. But when he caught a scent of the Tortoise's broth, it so delighted his taste buds that the juices flowed in his old mouth like sweet water into a dry river bed. One mouthful, and the warmth came back to his skin; two mouthfuls, and his brittle old bones flexed amidst their plaited muscles; three mouthfuls, and his brain drew back the curtains on his eyes to see what deliciousness was restoring him to health by the spoonful.

Day by day, the King's health and eyesight were restored by the Tortoise's food and by knowing that the young Prince had at least married a wife who could cook. Still, he shuddered to see the huge mound of the tortoise-shell heaving along the palace corridors or mumbling a lettuce on the palace lawn. Although the two lady-Princesses could not understand what had happened to their cooking, they felt that the Tortoise was in some way to blame, and their loathing for her grew.

To celebrate his recovery, the King invited his family to a grand dinner. He gave orders that the guests should wear their most glorious clothes and arrive—as ships sail into port—to much waving of hands and cheering of crowds.

'I shall arrive on a foam-white horse with a golden mane and tail,' said the merchant's daughter, 'seated on a saddle of red leather with silver stirrups and red ribbon reins. And I shall humiliate that grotesque sister of ours.'

'I shall arrive on an ebony-black stallion with white star and ankles,' said the sheikh's daughter, 'seated on a saddle of yellow leather with brass stirrups and copper-corded reins. I'll shame that four-footed sister of ours for being so ugly.'

The sister-in-law in question sent word to them, asking first one for the loan of a goose, then the other for the loan of a goat on which she could arrive at the party. Their answers were so rude that the Tortoise drew her head into her shell to hide her blushes, but then she laughed and rolled about on the rim of her shell like a plate spinning to rest on a floor.

In the palace dining-hall, trumpets sounded to welcome the three Princesses, and all eyes turned towards the great oak doors which swung open grandly. From the farthest end of the corridor a shriek was followed by a rhythmic slapping on the stone floor. A moment later a huge goose as large as a baby rukh flapped into the hall at a gallop, the merchant's daughter clinging to its neck and screaming so much that the poor bird grew all the more excited and flapped its wings, smothering the Princess in loose feathers.

The goose was closely followed by a small tip-toeing goat, jutting its beard and tossing its horns in disdain at the great weight of its rider. The sheikh's daughter ran, to keep her feet from dragging along the floor, and the goat's hind hoofs tore through the hem of her white robe. The two animals deposited the Princesses in a heap at the King's feet, and ran out again, slap slap, tap tap tap.

'Are you trying to shame my sons, your husbands?' demanded the King, but his daughters-in-law had not the breath to explain that they had left home on a golden palamino and an ebony black stallion. As the eldest began to pant out an apology, the whole room fell silent at the sound of the third Princess coming. Some covered their faces with napkins; some tried to sit with their backs to the door so as not to see.

A little foot-page came in under the weight of a large red cushion. On it lay the tortoise-shell, but the sun shone through the leg-holes and out through the neck-hole: it was unoccupied. The King's mouth gaped at the very prospect of a *naked* tortoise lumbering in through the doors, but his amazement doubled when a horse, white as elderflowers and dappled with elderberry-black, carried bareback into the room a lady whose beauty flamed like the sun's burning corona. Her unplaited hair cascaded over the horse's flanks like dark water breaking over a rock; her eyes were as black as an eclipse and fringed like the tapestries of Iram.

The youngest Prince, showing no surprise at all, went forward, lifted his wife down from the horse, and seated her at table opposite the King.

'Are you trying to kill an old man?' said the King, clutching his favourite son's hand. 'My creaking heart aches at the sight of such unexpected beauty. I would have given half my kingdom to see you married to a bride like this. Explain or I shall burst with impatience!'

'Calm yourself, father,' said the Prince. 'If you remember, I spoke words with the Tortoise when she was first brought to the palace. I leaned down to the neck of her shell and saw inside this moonrise of a lady. But until today I have not had her permission to show the world my undeserved treasure. Only in the privacy of our own palace and the candlelight of our own bedroom has the Lady Tortiosa shown herself to me in this shape.'

The Lady Tortiosa said: 'I find that I can judge the true worth of a person so much better on first acquaintance when they think they are meeting a large and lonely tortoise. Can you wonder that I loved your noble third son at our very first meeting? But I must apologize: I was as slow as a tortoise in preparing myself for this happy celebration. I have left my hair unplaited and undecorated.' And she picked up the bowl of green pea soup that stood in front of her and tipped it over her head. As it fell, the drops of soup changed into sea-green emeralds which spangled in her hair and lodged in every fold of her gown. With one breath, the assembled guests gasped their admiration.

But the other two Princesses, livid that all eyes were not on them, and bruised in both bottom and pride after their undignified arrival, sniffed haughtily and snarled angrily.

'Hocus pocus,' said one.

'Stuff and nonsense,' said the other.

'Nothing to it,' said one.

'Easy as winking,' said the other.

And both ladies picked up their pea-green soup and tipped it over their hair. The soup squelched through to their scalps, ran down their foreheads, and dripped off their noses. Lentils and squashed peas slid down each hair and dropped in at the necks of their dresses.

The King laughed and the Princes laughed and the Lady Tortiosa laughed, then she presented her two jealous sisters with the empty tortoise-shell—to remind them in the future of what loveliness can often be found under a humble exterior, and how ugly jealousy can make a woman.

CHAPTER TWENTY-TWO

The Ass and his Ass

One story goes—and I do not doubt it is true, for there is such stupidity in the world—that there was once a peasant with more cobwebs than brains between his ears. He was the owner of a rather fine ass with large, loppy, leaf-like ears.

Two rascals saw him pass by one day, trudging ahead of his ass, lost in his usual daydream.

'Let me show you how we can steal this idiot's donkey without him even objecting!' said one of them.

'I should like to see that!' replied his friend.

The thief crept up behind the peasant until he was walking alongside the donkey. Then he slipped the bridle off the beast and looped it over his own head and neck. His accomplice took charge of the stolen ass while the rascally thief trotted along behind the peasant.

'Not far now,' said the peasant over his shoulder. 'Gee up, old ass.'

'Very well,' said the thief, but the peasant did not

notice. 'Cough, cough,' said the thief. 'I'm thirsty. I hope it isn't far to the next town.'

Slowly understanding dawned on the peasant and he turned round to stare at his talking donkey. He stopped so suddenly that the thief collided with him.

'Why are you looking at me like that?' asked the 'donkey'.

'You . . . you're a . . . you've changed into a man!'

'Ah,' said the 'ass', 'you've noticed. You obviously don't miss much, my friend. Let me tell you my sad story.' And he loosened the cheek-straps of his bridle so as to speak more easily.

'My wife's brother is a magician, and it has always seemed to me that she thought more of him than she ever did of me. Her cooking was the cause of much annoyance and indigestion in me, for it was always bad. As often as she burned my dinner, I would lose my temper and beat her.'

'If you beat your wife my sister once more,' her brother said, 'I shall turn you into an ass for other men to beat.'

'As you can see, kind sir, I was tempted to beat my wife again and my brother-in-law was tempted to turn me into an ass. Now it would seem that the spell has worn off, and I am restored to my proper shape. Allah be praised!'

'Allah be praised in all things,' agreed the peasant, believing every word. 'Please don't feel you have to wear my bridle. I would not have any Believer wear a bridle of mine. I'm sure you are very sorry for beating your wife: how happy she will be to see you in man's shape again.'

So the men shook hands and parted company. The peasant apologized for any ill-treatment meted out. The 'transformed' donkey vowed never to beat his good wife again.

In the market square of the next town the two thieves sold the donkey for an excellent price. They were doubly pleased to have made a profit out of an ass and an ass out of its master. The beast was roped in a row of several mules and donkeys but was quite easily distinguished by its large, loppy, leaf-like ears.

The peasant came by, as dreamy as an afternoon siesta, but was startled out of his daydream by the sight of his own donkey. 'I recognize those large, loppy, leaf-like ears!' he said, starting to lose his temper. Going up to the ass he lifted one of the large, loppy, leaf-like ears and, to the astonishment of the donkey-seller, shouted into it: 'You've obviously been beating your wife again, you wicked rogue. Well I shan't be foolish enough to buy *you* again!'

CHAPTER TWENTY-THREE

The Tale of Ala al-Din and his Wonderful Lamp

O ne morning, King Shahryar's sleep was disturbed by the hooting and shrieking of young boys playing football in the palace yard. Their noise grated on his ears as a knife scratching down a pane of glass, and he woke in an unreasonable rage.

'I shall cut out their noisy bawling tongues and, for fear they still set up a caterwauling, I'll make them play football with their own raucous heads!' he shouted, leaping out of bed.

Shahrazad saw that today she had more lives to save than her own, and she followed her husband to the window and laid her hands on his shoulders. 'Oh be gentle, Shahryar, King of Sasan and father of all the people of Sasan, for who knows but that Allah has planned a future for one of those boys as happy and fortunate as Ala al-Din. You may have heard what a useless waster of a child *he* was before the adventure of the Wonderful Lamp.'

The King felt the warmth of the sun on his chest and the warmth of his wife's hands on his back, and he was sorry for his words: 'My temper is like the jinni held prisoner in that small copper bottle, for it is a huge thing packed up inside a small vessel,' he said, turning away from the window. 'Coax my anger back into my chest, fair Shahrazad, by telling me the Tale of Ala al-Din and his Wonderful Lamp.'

'Willingly, my lord.' And so Shahrazad began the story on the morning of the six hundred and forty-fifth day and continued it that evening.

If Ala al-Din had been a cat, he ought to have been drowned at birth, for he was *bad* from his nose to his knee-caps. Indeed, this son of a tailor was very like a cat in the way he roamed the city all day long, achieving nothing but mischief, and working as hard as the shadow of a post which lies along the ground all day. His father was dead, and his old mother's words of advice penetrated to Ala's heart as often as rain penetrates a stone.

One day, while he was teasing a kitten by holding it over a well by its tail, he was noted by a black dwarf who followed him with great interest for the rest of the day. The dwarf asked questions about the boy from his friends. Shortly after Ala al-Din arrived home that evening, demanding his supper and resting his feet on the table, there was a knock at the door and the black dwarf stood on the step.

'Is my brother Mustafa at home?' he asked. 'For I am here to fill his eyes with the sight of his long-lost brother.'

The old lady explained that she was the widow of a man who had no brothers.

170

'Your words grind my hopes between them like millstones grinding flour,' said the dwarf, 'for I know this is the house of my brother Mustafa, and you are telling me that he is dead.' Then he fell full-length on the floor and burst into tears: the old lady did not have the heart to say that her dead husband had in no way resembled this black midget. His pretended grief was so convincing, however, that she soon believed that this man was indeed a brother-in-law of whom she had never heard tell.

'For thirty years I have travelled about in Egypt, Morocco, Ind, and Sind,' said the dwarf. 'Not until my joints stiffened with age did I think of finding my brother again and sharing with him the fortune I have amassed over the years. I rode for a year to find this humble house—only to discover that my dear brother is dead. Oh Allah be praised that he left a fine, strong son to carry the family name and help his mother by working hard.'

Ala al-Din choked on his food. His mother shook her head and smiled wanly. 'The parents who look to their child for help and happiness are like the fisherman who looks at a river: he needs a rod before any good will come of it. This lazy son of mine does as much work as the shadow of a post which lies along the ground all day.'

The black dwarf shamed Ala al-Din with a look of his eyes, but then spoke to the boy as though he was the most gentle and promising child to rock in the cradle of a mother's heart. 'You are too old still to be playing with children and wasting the days. I must have you apprenticed to learn a trade.' (Ala al-Din turned pale at the thought of work.) 'Well then,' said the black dwarf, undeterred, 'if that is not to your taste I shall buy you a shop and goods to sell in it. But first you must be fitted out to look the part of a wealthy merchant, for within the year you will undoubtedly be the richest of them all.'

So the next morning the black dwarf took Ala al-Din by the hand and led him to a tailor's shop where he bought the boy silk and linen robes. Ala al-Din triumphed in his imagination: all the luxuries and sweetnesses of the good life crowded into his thoughts, and he thanked his black uncle from the lowest rib of his chest.

'I want to complete the boy's education,' said the dwarf to Ala al-Din's mother that night, 'by walking him among the leisured and polished people who will be his customers when he opens his shop. Tomorrow we shall walk through all the gardens which surround the city— places of greenery and flowers where the working people never find time to set foot.'

The mother turned her palms towards heaven and thanked Allah for sending this generous and cultured man to be a father to her poor, fatherless boy, Ala al-Din.

Beyond the trim rose gardens were the water gardens; beyond the water gardens were the wild gardens of bush and shrub; and beyond the wild gardens, a tame wood of little trees, though few people walked out as far as the wood. Beyond the wood was the desert, and a barren valley bare of all but thorn-bushes.

'My stomach protests that there is no more food to fuel my legs,' said Ala al-Din, sitting down. 'Surely we have seen all the gardens, dear uncle, and observed all the people walking in them?'

'And what have you learned?' said the black dwarf, moving all the while out into the desert as though it was tugging him by the sleeve.

'I have seen how the rich dress and I have heard how they speak to one another, using the largest words to clothe the smallest thoughts. Can we not go home now and eat?'

But his supposed uncle had moved so far out into the desert that he could no longer hear Ala al-Din, and the boy ran after him rather than be lost. The black dwarf was close to his goal now. For this he had measured one year in camel's footsteps, travelling from Ind and Sind to find *Ala al-Din, son of Mustafa*, and the barren valley.

'Fetch dry wood. Build me a fire here,' he commanded, and his eyes bored into the boy as a skewer bores into meat.

'Yes, uncle.'

Ala al-Din built the brushwood fire: the black dwarf lit it and threw incense into its heart.

And suddenly the hills round about shook to their ankles, and the whole valley flinched at the touch of the dwarf's fire. The ground was wrenched open, and the burning wood of the fire tumbled down a cavernous flight of steps and guttered to a smoke on top of a great slab of stone—a hinged slab with a great brass ring set into it for a handle.

At the sight of all this, Ala al-Din hitched up his expensive new robes, held them in his teeth, and ran away.

Who would have thought that the grizzled little villain could move so fast? He fell on Ala and knocked him to the floor with one blow.

'Cowardly son of a rabbit,' the dwarf said. 'Is this how you repay me? I have not come this far to let you rob me of my prize!' When he knew that Ala al-Din was sufficiently terrified to do what he was told, the dwarf became more friendly. 'I'm sorry, child,' he said, 'but you have grown up too much in the folds of your mother's skirts. Be a man and do what I tell you without trembling in face and leg.'

'Certainly, uncle. Forgive your worthless girl of a nephew.'

The black dwarf instructed Ala al-Din to go down the stairs and open the stone trapdoor. 'Behind it you will find a red copper door which will open at the sight of you. Behind that you will find three halls—one is full of treasure jars which you must on no account brush against. In the next hall is a garden of fruit trees. Do not dawdle there, but go straight through to the third hall which is lit by a worthless little lamp. Take this lamp, tip out its oil, and bring it back to me here. If you must fetch out a souvenir, pick some of the fruit off the trees in the second chamber on your way back.' Lastly, the black dwarf took out a ring and pushed it on to Ala al-Din's finger: 'That will keep you safe from all but the danger of touching the great jars. Be quick now.'

'But uncle,' said Ala al-Din. 'How can a smallish boy lift that huge stone slab on his own? Won't you come down and help me?'

'Your name is written on the copper door and on the door beyond it. Allah alone knows why this magic place has been sealed with your name, boy, but no one can enter this place who does not carry the name of *Ala al-Din, son of Mustafa*. The magic of your name will help you open the stone trapdoor.'

It was true. Ala al-Din pulled no harder on the brass ring than he would pull on a horse's bridle to lead it from its stable, and the door opened to reveal more steps and a glowing red copper door studded with copper nail-heads.

Oh open your ears now, all you who hear this story, and understand that the black dwarf had learnt of the

174

barren valley and its magic underground caverns from evil magic he practised while he was still in Ind and Sind. He had read in books that the name written on the doors below ground was *Ala al-Din, son of Mustafa*, and had searched the city daily until he found the tailor's son. Then he had pretended to be the boy's uncle, thinking (in the dark, cobwebbed corners of his heart) to use the boy's magic and then kill him there in the lonely valley. Imagine now how his hopes were growing—as fire spreads in wheat—to a heat that scorched his black heart to a blacker black.

The keyhole in the copper door looked Ala al-Din up and down and recognized his magic. The door opened as he approached it. Inside was just as the dwarf had said. Huge jars bulged out from the shadows—full of liquid gold, gold dust, or gold coins. Ala al-Din tucked the skirts of his robes into his belt so as not to brush against the jars as he passed. In the second hall he barely stopped to look at the trees whose white, red, blue, transparent, green, gold, and purple fruit was ripening without help of the sun above ground. In the third chamber he found with ease a small niche in the far wall where a cheap little lamp was burning. He tipped out the oil and splashed himself in doing so—but the oil left no mark on his new silk robe. So he did not hesitate to tuck the lamp inside his shirt and return to the central orchard with both hands free to pick fruit.

To his great disappointment, Ala al-Din found that he could not sink his teeth into the glorious coloured fruit. How could a tailor's son recognize rubies, cornelian, emeralds, jade, aquamarine, sapphires, lapis lazuli, turquoise, amethysts, jasper, topaz, agate, opal, aventurine, peridot, jet, or chrysoprase? He thought that their prettiness might please his mother and friend, but he would have much preferred to harvest apples or pears. He filled every pocket with these precious jewels until he bulged like the treasure-jars in the first chamber. Squeezing past these dangerous pots of gold, both hands full of glassy fruit, he set one foot on the stairs. But the narrow copper door-posts gripped his bulging sides and would not let him through.

'Give me the lamp, you dear, good, obedient boy,' said his 'uncle', leaning down through the open trapdoor. Ala al-Din grunted and strained, but the door was too narrow.

'It's inside my clothes, uncle,' he called, 'and my hands are full. Help me up the stairs and I can give it you.'

'Give me the lamp, you greedy swelled-up bullfrog, or I shall crush your head like an egg!'

'Allah defend me!' said an amazed Ala al-Din. 'Are these the words of a kind uncle? Come and help me out through this door and you can have your tin lamp and welcome.'

The black dwarf thought that Ala al-Din must have discovered the secret of the lamp and wanted to keep it for himself. He dared not enter the cavern, and when he shook his fist and drew a dagger as if he would throw it at Ala al-Din, the boy backed into the hall of gold and closed the copper door as quickly as he could, refusing absolutely to come out.

'What wishes wasted! What hopes unhinged! What dreams dashed! What gold gone!' the dwarf raged, tearing his hair. 'You shan't enjoy the lamp if I can't!' and he poured more incense on to the hinge of the stone trap-door, which immediately slammed shut. 'Lie there and starve in your new silk clothes. May all magic be cursed for carving the name of such a worthless, greedy clod on the treasure-doors. Who will miss the son of a poor, dead tailor? Tell me? No one!'

So the black dwarf travelled back to Africa where he was born, and planted his dark, poisonous, and twisted anger in the dark, poisonous, and twisted jungle, where it grew.

Below ground in the lonely valley, Ala al-Din had time to sit and reflect on the small heap of goodness he had swept together during his childhood and the small store of happiness he had left at home with his good, kind mother.

CHAPTER TWENTY-FOUR
Ala al-Din and Badr al-Budur

'Did Ala al-Din live to change his ways?' asked King Shahryar the next night, 'or did he starve to death, trapped in the treasure-cave?'

'He fully expected to, my shining lord,' replied Shahrazad, 'but listen and I will tell you how chance or the hand of Allah freed him from a terrible death.'

Overwhelmed with unhappiness at the thought of his mother watching and waiting for his return till all hope shrivelled in her eye and heart, Ala al-Din fell on his face on the stone steps and wrung his hands together. In doing so, of course, he rubbed the ring which the dwarf had put on his finger to protect him from evil magic. Suddenly, a heat like the opening of an oven door fanned his back, and the cavern was filled with black smoke. No, nor *was* it smoke, but the vaporous black body of an

178

ifrit with flaming red eyes, who crouched over Ala so closely that he thought he would drown in fear.

'I am the slave of the ring,' it said, 'and slave of any who wears it. What do you want, master?'

The passing hours had accustomed Ala al-Din to the idea of dying in that underground cave, and no fear was greater than that. So he summoned his voice into his mouth and said: 'O ifrit, I want to get out of this cavern if you please!'

In the breathing of a breath, the ground overhead opened, and Ala al-Din found himself standing in the barren valley. The city on the horizon was such a welcome sight that Ala al-Din ran all the way there without looking back for the ifrit or the spot where he had built the brushwood fire.

He fell over the threshold of his house, and his mother fed him every morsel of food in the larder before his hunger was satisfied and before he would begin his story. Then, calling the black dwarf liar of liars, dog of dogs, and devil of all devils, he described his adventure and emptied proof of it out of every pocket and cuff.

'To think that I almost died because of these *baubles*,' he said, turning the glassy fruits over with one hand. 'Mother, I have been of less help to you than the dust you sweep out of the back door. But tomorrow I shall find work, for with every strand of thread that you spin to earn pennies, you spin out my shameful, worthless childhood.'

Unfortunately, there was no breakfast to be had in the morning, because Ala al-Din had already eaten all the food in the house.

'Wait a while,' said his mother, 'and I will sell some of my spun thread to buy a loaf of bread.'

Ala al-Din stopped her: 'Sell some of these worthless trinkets,' he said, pointing to the jewels, 'or sell that old lamp for half a dinar.'

She agreed: 'If I polish it, though, I may get a better price.' So she rubbed her sleeve across the tarnished metal.

An ifrit of gigantic size poured itself out of the lamp's spout and stood down, bellowing: 'I am the slave of the Lamp and of any who holds it. What do you want, lady?'

Ala al-Din's mother was not used to entertaining such strange, unexpected company, and fell in a dead faint on the floor. But Ala al-Din snatched up the lamp out of her hand and held it up towards the ifrit. 'Bring me some of your most excellent food, please.'

One flash of invisible fire and the ifrit disappeared and reappeared—all in the same second. On his head was a massive silver tray laid with twelve dishes of food fit for angels. In one hand he carried a little table inlaid with ivory, and in the other, two silver cups full to the brim with aromatic wine.

The delicious smells alone revived the old lady, and Ala al-Din and his mother sat down to the finest meal ever served since al-Hasan Ali ibn Ahmad of Khurasan served al-Mutasid Billah. But towards morning the old lady rested from eating and wondered why the ifrits had appeared to her and her son.

'They come whenever we rub the ring or the magic lamp,' said Ala al-Din.

'I think that kind of magic may be evil in the eyes of Allah,' replied his mother. 'Don't use the magic again, my son.'

For several days Ala al-Din had no need to use the services of the ifrits. He took one of the gold serving-dishes to a pawnbroker who, seeing the boy had no understanding of precious metals, offered him just one dinar. (He wished afterwards that he had offered less, for Ala al-Din was delighted with the paltry sum and bought a day's food with it.) So it was with the other eleven gold plates. Then Ala al-Din took the huge silver tray—which must have been worth two thousand dinars—to the pawnbroker who offered him just two. But the trusting, ignorant Ala al-Din was so pleased that he threw in the silver cups along with the tray.

When the serving-dishes were gone, however, and his mother was out of the house, Ala al-Din summoned a trembling heart to his throat and rubbed the magic lamp.

'I am the slave of the lamp and of any who holds it,' said the ifrit who poured from the spout of the lamp. 'What do you want, master?'

The rich man, if asked what he wants, asks for palaces and pavilions and principalities because they are the pictures in his dreams. But the poor man dreams only of food and shelter and asks only for dinner and dinars.

'Bring me the same food as before,' said Ala al-Din. A silver tray with twelve gold dishes and two silver cups all filled with deliciousness were set before the boy at once, on a table inlaid with ivory. And when his mother returned, and the feast was eaten, he prepared to sell the golden plates as before.

Ignorance is ugly in the eyes of Allah, so as Ala al-Din made his way through the bazaar to the pawnbroker's shop, he chanced to drop the gold plate he was carrying in front of the stall of a reputable, honest jeweller.

'Boy!' said the jeweller, 'I have seen you going to and fro to the pawnbroker, but surely you won't sell anything as beautiful as this to anyone but a jeweller?'

'Ah, but my head is not as empty as a blown egg, sir,' replied Ala al-Din, determined not to be tricked by any quick-talking stall-holder. 'I'm quite sure you won't give me such a good price. I got one whole dinar from the pawnbroker . . .'

So it was that Ala al-Din discovered the true value of the gold and silverware and became really rather rich. Moving more among the merchants and the wealthy tradesmen of the city, he also had cause to see precious jewels change hands for great weights of gold coin, and realized what priceless treasure he had brought home from the underground trees-of-glassy-fruit. He soon had reason to be very glad of harvesting such a treasure. In the mid-morning of Ala al-Din's young and promising life, he was walking through the city centre when two heralds holding long staffs came down the street shouting a proclamation.

'O citizens, draw aside for the love of beauty, and take your eyes home to your houses. Draw down your blinds and lock up your shutters, for the King's daughter, light of our Sultan's heart, Badr al-Budur, is passing this way to the baths. The Sultan begs you not to scorch your eyes with the sight of the Princess's glorious beauty. He furthermore commands that any who dare to look on her will be hung, burned, or put to the sword—or all three! Make way! Take away your eyes . . .'

Now Ala al-Din had heard such proclamations every time the Princess Badr al-Budur went to the baths. But a streak of wilfulness was left in the heart of Ala al-Din despite his changed ways, and he took it into his head to see the Princess (for he suspected that her reputation for beauty was much exaggerated). Instead of taking his eyes home, he ran to the Turkish baths and hid behind the big wooden doors—where those entering from the bright street were momentarily blinded by the dark interior.

A crunch of gravel, a snort of horses, the setting down of a palanquin—and then a fragment of sunlight broke from the brightness outdoors and pattered in through the doorway on tiny white feet and dressed in cloth of gold. Badr al-Budur at once cast off her veil.

All those who have travelled to see the day-lily which blooms for one hour in ten years in the remotest jungles of the world; all those who have climbed to the white forehead of the earth to peep over the world's rim and glimpse the sun dressing herself before she enters the sky; all those who have passed through cream-white surf to see the wheat-white harvest of sea pearls rolling where the air is aquamarine—surely they have glimpsed the face of Badr al-Budur and have run distracted through the world, looking for a second such sight.

Ala al-Din stumbled home, sighing out loud and repeating the name of the Princess over and over again. 'I wish I had never seen her,' he said to his mother, 'for if I cannot marry her I shall undoubtedly die!'

His mother tried to comfort him. 'Are you not rich enough to woo any Princess?' she said. 'Let me go to the Sultan on your behalf and ask him to consider your request to marry Badr al-Budur.'

Ala al-Din was wildly grateful to his mother but was afraid that the King would not believe that a man of no title or Royal blood truly owned a fortune in jewels. So he placed some of the precious tree-fruit in one of the golden bowls, and his mother carried it, covered in a linen cloth, to the Sultan's audience chamber.

Never having set foot outside the working quarter of

the city, she had no idea how many people came and went at the Royal Palace of the Sultan. The audience chamber was as full of people as a glove is full of hand. Everyone with a suit to the King was jostling and pushing in an effort to be near the front. A hundred elbows wagged between her and the King whose crown she sighted only twice in four hours' standing. Ala al-Din's mother returned home, exhausted and downhearted, but told her son that she would go again the next day.

By arriving very early in the morning she found herself fenced from the King by only thirty rows of elbows. Then the crowd closed in behind her, and she could neither leave nor move forwards but was pressed and jabbed from morning till late afternoon. She sat down on the floor in tears and let a hundred pairs of feet shuffle out round her at the command of the Royal Guard.

'Who is that old woman?' said the King to his wazir. 'Find out what she has brought me, for clearly there is some gift under the cloth, and even if it is only a few loaves of bread, it may be a large gift from a woman whose eyes seem to have known great poverty.'

'O Sultan, lord of minutes and centuries,' said the lady, falling on her face at the King's feet. 'Hear my son's message and accept his gift, for even after a long day's standing my old bones do not ache as much as my son's poor heart: I fear for his life if he does not unburden his heart through me.'

'Sit down, old lady, and tell me why your son did not bring his own suit, but sent his mother.'

'Does a man go to his would-be father-in-law to ask for the hand of his daughter? No, he sends his mother. My son Ala al-Din begs leave to marry your daughter Badr al-Budur. He sends you this gift, which is a mere fraction of the marriage gift he would make, should you accept him as a bridegroom.'

Out of courtesy, the Sultan hid his smiles. 'What fine family does your son come from, madam? Who was his father?'

'His father was Mustafa the Tailor. I promise you, there was no finer tailor or kinder man in the whole city.'

Out of courtesy again, the Sultan hid his laughter and deigned to look at the present under the cloth. His amusement changed to amazement when he saw the precious tree-fruit, and he looked closely at Ala al-Din's mother for the mark of royalty in her cheeks—in case she was a Queen in disguise.

'Indeed, this offer is larger than any we have received from the princes and caliphs ruling the coastal kingdoms of the world's Central Sea,' said the King in private to his wazir (whom he trusted as a hand trusts its fingers). 'It is larger even than the offers which have come from Ind and Sind.'

But the wazir, riding so high in the saddle of the King's respect, had hoped to marry his own son to Badr al-Budur. So he said: 'The man may be a bandit, and the royal blood of your family may mean no more to him than the pedigree of his horse! Marry the Princess to someone whose background you know as well as your own.'

'If this Ala al-Din is a bandit, wise friend, he will not waste time and sighs on waiting. I shall say that my daughter is too young by a birthday to marry anyone. In three months she will be seventeen and then I may accept his offer.'

For three months Ala al-Din sent presents day after day to his beloved Badr al-Budur—presents fetched for him

185

by the slave of the lamp and boxed magically in gold, silver, and platinum. And with letters so laden with love that the Princess felt the scorch of his love through the paper before she saw the words. Without the light of her glimmering eyes, she saw the loveliness of Ala al-Din and loved him.

After two months and twenty-five days Ala al-Din's mother was shopping in the casbah for scents to perfume her son's wedding clothes.

'Perfume for a wedding,' she explained to the stall-holder.

'Oh, are you and your son guests at the Princess's wedding?' the man replied. 'I hear it's to be a magnificent occasion. The wazir's son was lucky to have his father to recommend him to the King. For truly his evil looks would not win him so much as a goat for a bride!'

Amazed past speaking, Ala al-Din's mother dropped the perfume and ran home. 'Son, son! Wall up your heart to protect it from my bad news: the Sultan is marrying your beloved Badr al-Budur to his wazir's son tomorrow. He has forgotten his promise altogether . . .'

At this point, a cock crowing in the palace yard proclaimed the marriage of the old night with the young day, and dawn sang in the window. Shahrazad fell silent.

CHAPTER TWENTY-FIVE

Ala al-Din: the Marriage of Badr al-Budur

The Sultan was hardly to blame for breaking faith with Ala al-Din. For two months he had listened to the wily persuasion of his wazir (and it must be remembered that he trusted his wazir as a hand trusts its fingers), and after ten weeks he had given in and betrothed the beautiful Badr al-Budur to the wazir's gruesome son.

The bride was as sad as the little clouds that cluster together on hilltops and cry. But Ala al-Din was thrown into a despair deeper than the black mud on the Nile's riverbed. He could not eat, and he hid his head from the world under the sheets of his bed and under the blankets of Sleep. Soon his mother feared for his life and, while the town outside was dancing in the streets to celebrate the Princess's marriage to the wazir's son, Ala al-Din lay curled up on his bed like a hedgehog that has died in hibernation.

In one last effort to rouse him, his mother brought the magic lamp and placed it in his hands. 'Get up and try what your magic will do. It has already changed the course of a life or two, perhaps it can change more.'

Meanwhile, the wazir's son strutted up and down in front of his bedroom mirror thinking how lucky Badr al-Budur was to marry such a fine figure of a man. Behind him his bride went quietly to bed, wishing her wishes in the private places of her mind.

Suddenly there was a silent bang, as loud as the clap of a man with one hand, and the room filled with smoke. When it cleared, a pale but handsome young man dressed in a djellabah of white wool stood holding an old brass lamp. Behind him, an ifrit as tall as the ceiling had the wazir's son dangling under one arm.

'Carry this man seventeen miles from the city, if you please,' said Ala al-Din to the slave of the lamp. 'Then fetch me away from here just as dawn breaks.'

When the ifrit had gone, Ala al-Din sat down at the foot of the bed and signalled to Badr al-Budur that she should go to sleep in peace. She stared at the young man, with astonished eyebrows raised in the shape of two flying birds. But such peace and harmlessness flowed from his eyes that they washed her down the river of drowsiness to the Sea of Sleep.

When the wazir's son found himself seventeen miles from the city, on the far side of the Nile, he had no choice but to begin walking home. It took him all night, and his face was one-third black with temper, one-third black with Nile mud, and one-third black with his usual ugliness when he trailed into the palace courtyard. He tried to reach his rooms unnoticed, but from a window the Sultan saw him coming home, all dishevelled and down in the mouth.

'Where have you been on your wedding night?' demanded the Sultan.

The wazir's son knew that his story was too far-fetched to be believed, so he simply said: 'Oh, I went for a walk, father-in-law, to walk off all the food I ate at the wedding feast.'

'Peculiar young man,' said the Sultan to himself.

The wazir's son asked his wife what had happened while he had been gone, but she only said: 'I went to sleep, of course, husband. Was it not the night?'

The very same thing happened the next night. Just as the wazir's son was climbing into bed beside Badr al-Budur, Ala al-Din and the ifrit appeared in a clatter of silence, and the miserable bridegroom was carried seventeen miles out of the city and obliged to spend all night walking home. Ala al-Din, on the other hand, seated himself at the foot of the bed, smiled at Badr al-Budur (so that her heart rose up and flew around her chest) then told her to sleep. In the morning his magic carried him away again.

'Where have you been while your wife slept alone the night after her wedding?' demanded the King hotly, as the wazir's son crawled home past the breakfast table.

'Don't ask,' said the bridegroom rudely. 'My feet hurt too much for my mouth to give answer. I'm going to have a bath.'

On the third night the ifrit threw the wazir's son over his shoulder and was about to disappear when Ala al-Din spoke to his rival. 'Do you wish this to happen every night of your life, good sir?'

'Allah forbid!' replied the wazir's son as best he could from an upside-down position. 'I thought that married life would be a lot more fun than this!'

'Well, the Sultan already thinks that your brain has run aground on the rocks of madness,' said Ala. 'If you tell him some story about ifrits and clashes of silence, he will certainly lock you up. I suggest you tell him that you find the Princess too ugly to look at and cannot bear to stay in the same room with her at night. I think that should save you from a lifetime of nightly walks.' When the ifrit and the wazir's son had gone, Ala al-Din bowed to the Princess and sat down as usual for his night's vigil over her. But this time she hazarded a word with him:

'Young man,' she said, 'I don't know who you are, but you must know that it is a terrible thing for a man to see the face of a young woman to whom he is not married.'

'Truly, it *is* a terrible thing,' he replied, 'for the sight of your face has tortured me for three months and will continue to do so until we are married, you and I. I make you one promise, Badr al-Budur, and swear to keep it. If you are angry with me for keeping your bridegroom from spending one night in your arms or even from kissing you, I will not do to the wazir's son what I said I would do. I shall leave you both in peace.'

Badr al-Budur did not reply, but lay down and went to sleep while Ala al-Din watched her—as the moon watches over the world—until morning.

'Send for Badr al-Budur!' cried the Sultan next morning in a great rage. 'And fetch a bath to wash this brain-loose boy in. Where have you been all night, son of my wazir, to be so filthy by morning?'

'I went for a walk, dear father-in-law,' whispered the bridegroom, who was covered from head to foot in Nile mud.

'Badr al-Budur, daughter of my heart,' said the Sultan.

'What have you to say on the subject of your husband's strange night-time *walks*?'

'I have so much puzzlement in my heart, dear father, that there is little room for words,' said Badr al-Budur. 'I only know that I was married three days ago, but as yet no man has kissed me. And I should have liked to be kissed.'

'Explain yourself, nincompoop, son of a nincompoop,' the Sultan shouted at the wazir's son, outraged that his daughter had been so ignored by her new husband.

'Well, sir. Well . . . it's quite easy to explain . . .' mumbled the wazir's son. 'An ifrit came every night and carried me seventeen miles outside the city, while a young man dressed all in white did I-don't-know-what in my bedroom.'

'He's mad!' gasped the Sultan. 'Tell me he's mad, daughter!'

'I only know that no man has kissed me since I married three days ago,' said Badr al-Budur.

'Lock up this madman!' cried the Sultan.

'But it's quite simple to explain,' said the wazir's son hurriedly. 'I simply can't bear the sight of your ugly daughter. Her face gives me indigestion . . . and I think that if I have to spend one more night in that bedroom I shall *die*!'

'Lock up this insulting wart-hog,' raged the Sultan. 'No one insults my family, and no one but a madman could find Badr al-Budur ugly. Consider yourself divorced, Badr al-Budur. I wish I had married you to that stranger Ala al-Din whom my wazir persuaded me was such a rascal.' (There was one to whom Badr al-Budur wished she could be married. Even her earlier love for Ala al-Din was forgotten in her new love. But she did not know the

191

name of the youth who had come to her bedroom for three nights, and she could never never say that he had been there.) 'Indeed, I think that I *shall* marry you to Ala al-Din if he will still have you after the snub I gave him.'

So Badr al-Budur and Ala al-Din were married, and one morning the Sultan woke to see a new palace opposite his own which the magic of the lamp had built under cover of darkness. The young couple breathed in happiness with every breath, and breathed out time until three years had settled on the floors, carpets, and walls of the magic palace— a palace of nine hundred and ninety-nine windows.

The love around them seemed more magical than a magician's magic hoops, so Ala al-Din put away the lamp on a high shelf and never troubled to tell Badr al-Budur what ifrit-friend had brought her her bridegroom and her palace.

If only he had. She would have crossed the Nile daily using alligators for stepping-stones rather than betray her husband to the black dwarf of Africa. But in her ignorance, she almost brought Ala al-Din to ruin.

The black dwarf's ambitions had all festered in Africa, and after three years he came back to gloat over the body of Ala al-Din. For he believed him to be long since dead, buried in the underground treasure-cave. The black dwarf soon heard tell of the Prince Ala al-Din, son of Mustafa the tailor, and realized that the boy had escaped and discovered the secret of the magic lamp. His jealousy ate into him as the lamprey eats into fellow fish.

On a day when Ala al-Din was away hunting, the dwarf disguised himself as a seller of lamps. He carried a tray of shining brass and copper lamps to the Prince's palace wall, shouting: 'New lamps for old! New lamps for old!'

This was such a generous offer that servants from all over the palace looked out their old lamps and brought them to the lamp-seller to exchange for new ones— without a penny's expense. Soon all the new lamps would be gone, and still the Princess had not heard his voice.

'There's some foul-faced salesman at the palace gate giving away new lamps for old,' said Badr al-Budur's handmaid. 'How does he make his living, offering such a bargain!'

Badr al-Budur began to run her eyes along the shelves of her own apartments until she spotted the cheap brass lamp from the treasure-cave. 'This old thing should have been thrown on the rubbish heap long ago. Take it to him, Zabudah, and see if his offer is as good as it sounds.'

'At last!' cried the black dwarf, dropping his tray as Zabudah handed him the magic lamp. 'Now we shall see whether Ala al-Din, son of Mustafa, was born to enjoy all this luxury instead of me!' And he rubbed the lamp with his sleeve until the air around him was quaking at the sound of the ifrit's voice.

'I am the slave of the lamp and of any who holds it. What do you want, master?'

At this point Shahrazad begged leave to continue the story the following night.

'But that is such a long time to wait!' Shahryar protested.

His wife replied: 'The future is impatient to become the present, the present to become the past. One thing is certain, my dearest lord: tonight will come without fail.'

CHAPTER TWENTY-SIX

The Terrible Fates decided for Ala al-Din and Badr al-Budur

The Sultan of the city rose next morning and looked out of his window to delight in the sight of the palace of nine hundred and ninety-nine windows. As he did so the sap dried in his bones and the hand of Fear gripped his throat.

'Allah has named the day of my death if what I see is true. Where is Ala al-Din's palace? Where is the roof that covers the head of my priceless daughter, Badr al-Budur? Where is my daughter?'

Nothing remained of the palace of nine hundred and ninety-nine windows but narrow holes where the foundations had stood. The black dwarf—though none knew it then—had commanded the slave of the lamp to carry the palace and Badr al-Budur and himself across the Seas of Separation to his native Africa.

194

The Sultan called for his wazir, who had been in great disfavour since the disastrous three-day marriage of his son to Badr al-Budur. Consequently the wazir fell on his face at the door and crawled to the feet of the Sultan in fearful respect.

'Where is the palace of Ala al-Din and my daughter?' asked the Sultan, trembling with anguish.

'About five furlongs from your own, my devastating lord and master,' said the wazir.

'Have you seen it today?'

'I never look on it, awesome lord and master, for to speak the truth it sickens me to my stomach.'

'Look at it now and give me your opinion.'

So the wazir crawled to the window and peeped over the sill without rising from his knees. After a minute or so he said: 'It is my opinion, sir, that Ala al-Din's palace has disappeared.'

'Fool! Idiot! Son of a camel-flea! I can see that it has disappeared. Where has it gone?'

A happy thought broke like an egg in the wazir's heart, for he hated his son's rival more than flies or scorpions.

'It is my opinion that Ala al-Din has spirited away his palace and your daughter to Hell. For he is undoubtedly a devil simply disguised as a Believer.'

Now it must be remembered that the Sultan had at one time trusted his wazir as a hand trusts its fingers, and in these sorry circumstances, he believed the wazir's words. The Sultan said: 'If the devil Ala al-Din should ever set foot inside the walls of this city, seize him and bring him in chains to a place where I may see his head struck from his shoulders.'

The wazir did not for one moment believe that Ala al-Din was a devil, but he now had the Sultan's voice in his mouth. When Ala al-Din rode back from his hunting trip, the wazir and a band of soldiers met him on the desert road. They arrested him and had him bound in chains and dragged through the city's streets to the King. The poor prisoner had no knowledge of what had happened, and called out for someone to help him or tell him why he was in chains.

There was one flaw in the plan of the envious wazir. He had forgotten how much the ordinary people of the city loved this tailor's son who had risen, by his own deserving, from bitter hardships to ownership of a palace of nine hundred and ninety-nine windows. As Ala al-Din was brought before the Sultan, crowds were already gathering around the palace walls.

'Where is your palace, Ala al-Din, son of a murdering thief or a thieving murderer?' said the Sultan.

'Five furlongs from your own, O incomprehensible father-in-law!' replied Ala al-Din.

'Liar! Fiend! Enough! Cut off his head!' commanded the Sultan.

But as the Sultan's Headsman flourished his sword above his head and it flashed in the sun, the citizens gave one outraged shout and began to storm the palace.

'Hold off your hand,' said the Sultan, frightened of a revolution if he did not give the people back their Prince. 'Tell me what you have done with my daughter. Then take your face out of my country and leave behind nothing but the grief you have given me and my kingdom!'

When Ala al-Din saw the hole where his palace of nine hundred and ninety-nine windows had been, his heart shrivelled inside him as a grape shrivels to a raisin.

He said: 'You are welcome to my life, O my poor, distracted father-in-law, for I have no use of it now that

Badr al-Budur has been stolen away. For four months I shall search the world for my palace and my wife. Then I shall return to place your foot on my head and beg for a speedy death if I have failed in my search.'

Where was he to look? Where could a palace of nine hundred and ninety-nine windows be hidden? In the sands of the desert? or the mountains of the north? or the twisted jungles of the South? He could search for four-times forty months and never find trace of Badr al-Budur.

Arriving at a river bank, Ala al-Din took it into his heart to drown himself in the waves. But the holy words of Allah forbad him to jump in. So he bent down to wash the tears from his face. He finished by washing his hands in preparation for morning prayers and, in doing so of course, he accidentally rubbed the magic ring given him three years before by the villainous black dwarf.

Suddenly a heat like the opening of an oven door fanned his back, and the huge black ifrit with red eyes stood bellowing into his ear: 'I am the slave of the ring and of any who wears it. What do you want, master?'

'O ifrit, what a handsome monster you are! Allah has sent you to rescue me from my sorrows. Bring me back my palace and Badr al-Budur, the spine of my body, the beat of my heart, the iris of my eye.'

The ifrit lifted one foot as if to depart, but then put it down again. 'I cannot do that master. Your palace was carried away by the slave of the lamp on the instructions of the black dwarf. My magic is not as strong as the magic of the slave of the lamp, and I cannot oppose it.'

'Then carry me wherever my wife is, even if she is over the world's edge or in the locked cellars of the sea!'

Meanwhile, the nine hundred and ninety-nine windows

of Ala al-Din's palace looked out on the fleshy leaves and strangulating tendrils of the African jungle a thousand and one miles from the eye of any man. Inside its walls, Badr al-Budur sat straight-backed behind locked doors, surrounding herself with a moat of tears.

Outside the door the black dwarf laughed and said: 'It is no use, Badr al-Budur. With my magic I can transform these doors into sheets of paper and tear them in pieces. Open the door of your own free will and say that you'll marry me. Your husband Ala al-Din is dead: the Sultan has cut off his head for the crime of mislaying his wife. Now my heart is set on having you, and since you will spend the rest of your life here—one thousand and one miles from the eye of any other man—you really ought to be grateful for an offer of marriage. Soon you will be old and your beauty will fade, and even I may not want you.'

'Oh go away, you black plague-rat, or send me poison to drink, for I would rather die than marry you, the cause of my dear husband's death and the ugliest sucking-pig in this whole continent!'

'Think about it, sugar mouse,' said the dwarf in a grinning voice. 'Death is far uglier than I am!' His sandals slapped off along the corridor, and Badr al-Budur prayed to Allah for a Third Choice. 'I may choose to marry the dwarf, or choose to die. Allah send me a third choice.'

In the time it takes the eye to see, Ala al-Din was transported by the slave of the ring from the river bank to the African jungle and his palace of nine hundred and ninety-nine windows. He found himself standing in front of his wife, his feet wet with her moat of tears.

'Are you so amazed to see your husband?' said Ala

al-Din, seeing her face. 'Didn't you know I would come and rescue you?'

'O marrow of my bones, beat of my pulse, blood of my veins, the wicked black dwarf told me you were dead—beheaded by my father for the crime of mislaying me. And now he has sworn to have me for his wife and slave, to wash all the nine hundred and ninety-nine windows and sweep all the seven hundred and seventy-seven stairs, and polish all the silverware every day. Is your magic powerful enough to save me from him, dearest Ala al-Din?'

'I have only the magic of the slave of the ring,' he said thoughtfully, 'and that conjuror's box which Allah calls brains and hides in every man's head. Let me think how we can take the lamp from him . . .'

When he had formed a plan, Ala al-Din summoned the slave of the ring and asked him for a strong sleeping potion, which he put into Badr al-Budur's hand. Then he hid himself behind a curtain, and his wife combed out her hair all around her so that she looked like the loveliest of willow trees.

'Open the door, Badr al-Budur,' cried the black dwarf in a grinning voice. 'For I have come to marry you, and nothing will stop me.'

'The door is open, my dear,' replied Badr al-Budur, though the words stuck in her teeth like caramels. 'I have quite overcome my silly sorrow for the dead Ala al-Din. Even though his beauty has gone from the world, there still remains the beauty of the black dw— the Acclaimed Magician of Africa. I count myself fortunate. Come in now, my love, and let me comb your shining hair and give you sherbet to drink and kisses to eat.'

Like a cockerel with nine hens, the black dwarf strutted

into the bedroom, stroking his moustaches with one finger. Badr al-Budur prepared him a drink and sprinkled the sleeping potion into it while her back was turned to him. Then she forced herself to comb his greasy hair (which was as coarse as porcupine quills) until the hairs themselves went limp and the black dwarf was lying face down in his sherbet, fast asleep.

Ala al-Din leapt from behind his curtain, pulled the magic lamp from the folds of the dwarf's shirt and rubbed it.

'I am the slave of the lamp and of any who holds it,' said the ifrit who appeared. 'And may I say how pleasant it is to be working for you again, master. What do you want?'

'Carry my palace back to my native city, and plant its foundations in the holes which are waiting.'

With a gentle vibrating of pillars and shaking of eaves, the palace was freed from the jungle vines which had entwined themselves around its walls, and it flashed through the night to where morning dyed the sky's skirts with blue and yellow.

When the Sultan looked out of his window the next morning, he went back to bed because he thought he must still be asleep and dreaming. He lay looking up at his bed's canopy, waiting to wake up. Then there was a knocking on the door.

'Go away, I'm having a pleasant dream: I dreamt that Ala al-Din's palace had reappeared overnight.'

'They say that dreams often come true, dearest father,' said Badr al-Budur, opening the door . . .

Celebrations were arranged which would occupy twelve orchestras and three hundred cooks and a tribe of dancing girls; but still they could not express the Sultan's joy at being given back his daughter and at hearing the truth about Ala al-Din.

One thing remains unsaid: what became of the black dwarf? Ala al-Din searched his heart for a fitting punishment and, finally, summoned the magician from the deep prison cells and took the wonderful lamp on to his lap.

'You have studied evil magic all your life in order to lay your hands on this magic lamp,' said Ala al-Din. 'Is that not right, little gargoyle?'

The black dwarf did not answer, but as his eyes rested on the lamp, his mouth watered and his tongue hung out. Ala al-Din rubbed the lamp.

'I am the slave of the lamp and of any who holds it,' said the billowing ifrit in a rather weary voice (for he had done much appearing and disappearing in the last few days). 'What do you want, master?'

'Does your life content you, O ifrit,' asked Ala al-Din.

'Content me, master? I often wish that I could say something different when I appear, if that's what you mean.'

'No, I mean do you enjoy being a slave? Do you enjoy being coiled up inside that lamp through all eternity?'

The ifrit scratched his head: 'One gets used to anything in time, master. I don't mind being *your* slave. It was rather different working for this scoundrel,' and he charred the dwarf a little with the heat of his smoking tail.

'Thank you, sir,' said Ala al-Din. 'But are you willing to destroy this lamp and thereby free yourself completely?'

In the saying of the words, the slave of the lamp seized the brass lamp from Ala al-Din's hands and swallowed it whole: it was seen sliding edgeways down his bulging throat. Then the ifrit flew three times round the ceiling, sang the song of the hump-back whale, then disappeared in a deafening silence.

'Now leave this land and study how to be content without ambition or greed or evil magic,' said Ala al-Din, and the black dwarf, his every dream undone, crept out of the city and walked back to Africa.

'Come, Badr al-Budur, my white magic, conjuror of all my dreams,' said Ala al-Din, turning to his beloved wife. 'Let me rub your cheeks between my hands and see what magic comes of it!'

'O lord of Sasan!' cried a voice outside the bedroom door. 'O King Shahryar, who excels all men as the lion excels the mole, as the albatross excels the duck: shall I tell the sun to stay down or will you allow the day to begin?'

'All right, Chancellor,' replied the King. 'I'm awake.'

Shahrazad added: 'And how are you this morning, Chancellor?'

The Chancellor was so surprised by being asked such a question that he gave an honest answer: 'As happy as a man can be who has a wife, my lady,' he said through the door.

Then Shahrazad wished she had not asked the question.

'You see, wife? Another man whose life has been ruined by a woman!' said Shahryar triumphantly. 'I dare say his wife is in love with his brother, or the water-carrier, or a sailor.'

'She nags, my lady,' said the Chancellor's mooing voice through the door. 'Nag, nag, nag, all day long . . .'

'Oh, you should simply tell her the story of The Man

202

with Three Wives,' said Shahrazad. 'She would soon realize how fortunate she is to be married to such a fine man as the Chancellor of Sasan!'

'Oh tell me that story, your ladyship, carpet of my king's feet. Do tell it me!' said the Chancellor.

'Be off with you!' shouted the King. 'I shall hear the story from my wife's lips tonight, and if it has any merit I shall tell you it myself. The impudence!' he exclaimed. 'Expecting his ear to swallow the words of my wife's mouth before I have tasted them!'

CHAPTER TWENTY-SEVEN

The Man with Three Wives

I f we are to talk of nagging wives, then how can we begin without mentioning the wife of Sidi Ahmad? She nagged like a blackberry bush which sinks sharp thorns into a man's skin: every time he tries to move, the thorns tear and the pain grips him tighter.

At the same moment that sunlight crept in under Ahmad's lashes, his wife's nagging blasted in at his ear. And it did not stop until he was out of earshot on his way to work. At night he went to sleep amidst as much peace as a man sleeping out in a hailstorm or curling up in a wasp's nest.

'Must you spend so long at work? Why don't you work harder? Then perhaps we could pay these bills. Have you seen these bills? No, of course not, you're too busy ignoring me. Don't pretend you don't ignore me! Have you said how pretty my hair is this evening or complimented my cooking? No! Too idle to open your mouth, that's you. I don't know why anybody buys wood from a woodcutter who treats his wife so abominably. I wouldn't mind if I hadn't married *beneath* myself. My mother always said I deserved better. My mother knew something, and it's no good looking like that: I know you hate my mother however much you deny it. I think a man who hates his mother-in-law doesn't deserve a good wife. Allah knows, you don't deserve me . . .'

And so it went on, day in, day out. The only peace Ahmad enjoyed was in the green bowl of the forest where even the birds flew away at the sound of his axe and the only noise was of his breathing, his sweating, and his axe working.

So when his wife complained that he spent too much time working and too little time with her, he saw his last pocketful of happiness drop out of sight like money falling through the slats of a pier.

'Yes, I shall come with you from now on and see that you keep hard at work and not lie around sunning yourself like the dog you are.'

He tried to dissuade her, but it was useless. She mounted his donkey and goaded them both into the forest. She pelted him with words as small boys pelt coconuts to bring them down from a palm-tree. 'What kind of a miserable forest do you call this? When are you going to start work? Can't you keep this donkey on the path? It brushed me against that tree. Didn't you hear me?'

'Yes, dear,' he said, but in his head he said, 'O Allah, forgive me for shattering the silence of your quiet places, but why have you sent down this punishment? What have I ever done that deserved it?'

An idea came to him—Allah alone knows where it dropped from—and he stopped the donkey. 'My dear, since you have insisted on coming with me, I cannot keep secret the treasure I found yesterday. I was going to fetch it up today, sell it a little at a time, and bring home the money as if I had earned it by simple hard work.'

His wife, of course, beat him around the ears and demanded to see the treasure.

'It's at the bottom of a deep, dry well over there. If you lower me down in the bucket, I shall fetch it up to you, dearest.'

But his wife pushed him aside. 'Out of my way, you worthless object. *You* lower *me* into the well, and I shall inspect the treasure to see that none of it finds its way to the inn instead of into my housekeeping!'

Sighing many sighs, Ahmad helped his wife sit astride the bucket and lowered her down to the bottom of the well—then brushed his hands together and began work. 'Allah hear me: I may die for this tonight when I pull her up again, but at least I shall have one last day of peace and pleasant solitude.'

When the trees' arms dropped the sun and it rolled over the evening horizon, Ahmad returned to the well and wound up the bucket. It was a damp, smelly well: his wife would be covered in rotting leaf-mould and spiders with possibly a toad or two in her pockets. 'How I shall suffer for this!' he groaned as he turned the handle. 'But Allah be my witness: it was worth it!'

'Rescued! Name your reward!' said a voice. 'I'll give you a king's daughter to marry or a king's purse to empty.'

At the sight of the head emerging from the well, Ahmad dropped the handle, but the Jinni of the Well clamped his huge teeth over the rim of the well and pulled himself out.

'I'm a quiet soul,' he said, hugging Ahmad warmly. 'I've lived for hundreds of years down that well, minding my own business. But—would you believe it?—this morning someone lowered a dreadful woman down on my head in the bucket and she has nagged me from that moment to this. My eardrums are ragged! My nerves are in tatters.' And taking Ahmad under one arm and his donkey under the other, the Jinni flew as far away from the well as his brown magic would carry him.

'Where are we?' said Sidi Ahmad. 'I must be getting into town. I have firewood to sell.'

'China, I should say,' replied the Jinni. 'But there is still the matter of your reward for rescuing me from that woman's nagging.'

It was reward enough to be taken three continents away from his wife, so Ahmad only said in joking: 'I could not ask for gold from a stranger, and as for a King's daughter to be my wife—I fail to see how *finding* a wife could make a man happier than *losing* one!'

'What! No beautiful face to look at as you wake up? No delicate hand to prepare your favourite meals? No lash-lidded eyes to see all your good points and none of your faults?' To persuade Ahmad of the delights of marriage, the Jinni carried him to the chandelier in the great hall of the palace of the Emperor of China. From there Ahmad could see all the faces of the women in the royal household and how well they treated their husbands.

Sidi Ahmad at once fell in love with the Emperor's only daughter—a single girl whose skin was the colour of almond paste, whose eyes were the shape of almonds, and whose waist was as narrow as the almond tree. She was as different from his wife as the yellow jasmine is from the nettle.

Since the commonest Believer is allowed four wives in

the wide-tented land of Arabia, Ahmad's heart turned towards the Chinese Princess as a compass needle turns towards True North. 'I must marry her, friend Jinni. Help me or I shall die of ecstasy!'

'It is harder to butter a slice of bread than for you to have this Princess. Listen and obey . . .'

A handful of minutes fell like leaves from the tree of Time.

The Chinese Princess was one moment playing bowls with her friends and the next was lying on the ground under her cloud of hair. Her body was as stiff as the mast of a ship, with her arms stretched out like spars on either side; her eyes were open, but scarcely a breath escaped her. The palace physicians were called but they could do nothing.

The heartbroken King of China ordered his whole palace to be painted black in mourning, and sent messengers along the length of China's Great Wall to search for doctors who could cure his daughter.

Then Sidi Ahmad presented himself at the palace door, carrying a doctor's bag. 'I see that the palace is being painted black, and I hear that sickness is the reason. May I offer the knowledge of my country, which is wise in such matters as the sickness of Princesses?'

On being taken to the Princess's bed, Ahmad allowed himself the pleasure of feeling her pulse and laying a hand on her forehead, then he rubbed his jaw sagely and said: 'There is no question about it: this young lady has been possessed by a jinni. Such creatures roam about the world without tent or luggage, looking for a pleasant place to shelter out of the rain and wind. Look, I'll demonstrate.' And he spoke to the wild-eyed, rigid Princess who, up to that time, had been as silent as the dead. 'Now, you old buzzard; you've chosen quite the wrong nest to winter in. Come out of there immediately.'

'Ah but it's so warm and cosy in here!' replied the Princess in a voice as deep as any mine. Hearing this, the King of China threw himself along the floor and begged Ahmad to tell him if there was any remedy.

The Princess growled: 'Do I have to go?'

'Indeed you do,' said Ahmad. 'Come on now. Be off with you! You can see the distress you are causing these kind and honourable people.'

The Princess's body made three somersaults, then cracked like a whip and fell limp on the bed. The Jinni of the Well wreathed out of her nostrils in the form of smoke, and plunged through the wall, leaving an outsized hole shaped like a giant ifrit.

Before the King had risen from the floor, the Chinese Princess blinked her eyes and sat up as if from a heavy sleep.

To be brief, the King's gratitude gave Ahmad his heart's desire. He was married to the Chinese Princess, and she proved to be as sweet in temperament as she was sweet to look at.

Now whether Ahmad would have stayed in China and overlooked a certain package he had lowered into a certain well cannot be judged with certainty. It is related that he was still living comfortably in the Chinese palace when messengers arrived from India. They threw themselves at the King's feet.

'O King of the Yellow Seas and the jasmine-coloured peoples of the world's greatest continent—we are the messengers from the King of Ind, father of one dear daughter. Our King's palace has been painted black out of grief, for the King's only daughter has fallen sick with a strange sickness. News reached us that your daughter was stricken with a similar sickness during the shining of the last moon, and that she was cured by a mighty physician from the Western Wildernesses.'

Ahmad guessed that his happiness was doomed before his father-in-law even spoke.

'Say no more,' said the Chinese King, holding up one hand. 'I shall send the physician, who is now my son-in-law, to heal the Princess of Ind. May your journey be speedy, for I know all too well how tightly the King's heart is clenched in sorrow.'

It was useless to say that the miraculous cure of the Chinese Princess had all been a conspiracy to win Ahmad a pretty wife. The truth would rob him of his wife—and his head too! So with his heart dragging behind him like a bent ploughshare, Sidi Ahmad went to India with the messengers and was presented to the King of Ind.

'Cure my daughter, O physician of the Western Wildernesses, O teacher among the wise, and you may have any reward up to half my kingdom,' said the King.

'I shall try my best,' said Ahmad who, as a woodcutter, had less science in his head than an empty hazelnut and less courage in his heart than a coward.

At first sight, however, he loved the Princess of Ind— a girl whose skin was the colour of cane sugar, whose hair tangled like burnt spun sugar, and whose lips promised a sweetness more than sugar.

'Oh, I am so sorry, Princess,' he said when he was left alone with her. She could not hear him, of course. But he still felt he should say, 'I would cure you if I had the art, but I have no knowledge of medicine: I am only a misguided rascal.'

'So they have sent for you, have they?' said the

Princess in a voice as gruff as any lion. 'How embarrassing for you, my friend. How very regrettable.' The voice of the Jinni of the Well was instantly recognizable.

'Come out of there, you rogue,' said Ahmad, 'or I shall be separated from my head within the hour.'

'Sorry, little woodcutter,' said the Jinni. 'It's very comfortable in here. This Indian Princess is even more cosy than the Chinese girl.'

'Oh *please*, friend Jinni! Don't rob me of my life when it has just become pleasant for the first time!'

'Very regrettable, friend woodcutter,' said the Jinni, 'but I'm not leaving this little body and that, my friend, is that.'

Sidi Ahmad went to the window, thinking to jump into the moat and run away. The King would be knocking at the door at any minute, expecting to find his daughter cured. How was Ahmad to persuade him not to behead the unfortunate 'physician' who had failed to cure her? Voices drifted up to him on the sultry breeze: the cook and his wife were squabbling: the wife was nag, nag, nagging . . .

'Well, well, well. Look who is coming!' said Sidi Ahmad, peering down the road as if someone was approaching the castle. 'Speaking of wells, do you remember how I rescued you from the tongue of a fearful woman who was lowered into your comfortable, peaceful, damp well? This seems the right time to admit to you: that woman was my wife, and rumours reached me in China that she had escaped from the well and was roaming the world in search of a certain jinni. It seems that she fell desperately in love with this jinni, having spent one day with him in a deep, dank well. I see that the rumours are

211

true, for she has found her way here. Shall I go and tell her that her search is over? Husband or not, I shall not object if she wishes to sit here beside you and talk to you day after day, telling you her problems, encouraging you to come out of hiding and marry her . . . begging you for money to buy herself a new yashmak. Yes, knowing you both so well, I think you are made for each other!'

'Oh have mercy, little woodcutter! What can I bribe you with? What do you want to keep her away from me? I've never met such a tormentor as that woman! The Caliph of Baghdad's whip is less dreadful than her nagging tongue!'

'No, I've quite made up my mind,' said Ahmad. 'It's been a pleasure knowing you, friend Jinni. I'll just go and greet my wife; she has reached the bridge already.'

'I'm off!' cried the Jinni. 'Let no man stand in my way.'

The body of the Indian Princess made three somersaults then cracked like a whip, and the Jinni of the Well wreathed out through her nose and leapt through the window.

'Good-day, Princess,' said Sidi Ahmad to the waking girl. 'Let me introduce myself: I am the Prince of China, and your future husband if you will have me.'

So it was that a woodcutter with a nagging wife became the Prince of India and China, and the husband of three wives—one was as fair as the almond tree, another was as sweet as sugar-cane, and the third was as biddable, obedient, and silent as a kite on its string. For when Sidi Ahmad sent messengers to the forest near his first little home, and the woodcutter's wife was drawn up in her bucket, the damp surroundings had given her a chill and she had quite lost her voice. Before it could recover,

Ahmad used some of his great wealth to have wells dug in every acre of Ind and China and ordered his wife's name to be painted on every wooden bucket.

People said that Ahmad loved his first wife so deeply that he had wells dug all over Ind and China and painted her name on every wooden bucket to show how her sweetness refreshed his life like a drink of cool water. The woodcutter's wife encouraged this rumour, and perhaps in time she came to believe it herself. But she never nagged her husband again: the Chinese Princess and the Princess of Ind saw to that.

'Will you tell my worthless story to the Chancellor?' asked Shahrazad when she had finished the story of The Man with Three Wives.

'It's far too good for him,' said Shahryar with a laugh. 'If I couldn't rely on the Chancellor's wife to keep him in his place, he might start behaving like a Prince of China or India!' And they laughed and laughed, the two of them, until the Chancellor came to tell the King that his Court was assembled and waiting.

CHAPTER TWENTY-EIGHT

The Scrounger's Tale

Morning broke like a phial of mercury.

'More greed, more scroungers,' said Shahryar one morning. 'All day long I listen to men pleading for a judgement, cadging for money, begging for mercy, asking for their lives. They all want something from me, Shahrazad, and you are no better.'

Shahrazad rose from sleep as a pearl-diver rises to the surface. 'What have I done, my wakeful, persecuted lord, for if it is anything I can put right, tell me immediately.'

'Oh, I know you have never pleaded for your life in so many words . . .' grumbled Shahryar, 'but your stories plead to be heard and your beauty pleads to be preserved.'

'You know that my life is entirely at your disposal, my most beset lord, judge of all living judges. Sentence me to live or die according to your pleasure. But if Allah, to His amazement, finds me still alive tonight, I could tell you the story of a magnificent scrounger and you would hear his side of the argument. But perhaps it would offend you to hear of such wickedness from the mouth of a sponger?'

King Shahryar decided in his mind to hear The Scrounger's Tale and thought to himself, Perhaps if I hear the cadger's point of view, I shall be better able to like the people who creep and cringe round my throne every day.

So on the seven hundred and seventy-seventh night, Shahrazad began:

Tufail the Sponge lived entirely by scrounging. He cadged all his meals at the houses of friends—or should I say 'acquaintances', for quite soon he had no friends left. He borrowed money for absolutely, positively, unquestionably the shortest of times and best of reasons, but somehow the loans were never repaid. But I must tell you this story in the words of Tufail himself, for how can I, an honest Believer and a mere woman, understand such people?

They call me Tufail the Sponge because I soak up their food and money. But truly there is such meanness in the world these days that anyone wringing out *this* sponge at the end of the day will often find it dry!

Take, for example, my noble and esteemed friend Kalifah al-Walid . . . He gave a dinner the other night for a few friends, and served a table of fish dishes worthy of the greatest cook among the mermaids. There was far too much for so few to eat without discomfort and indigestion, so I thought it my duty to go along and help eat up the meal.

I suppose al-Walid recognized my voice as I spoke to his doorkeeper, for when I entered the dining room there was much shuffling of plates going on. There was only one empty chair by the table, and all the smallest, most miserable-looking fish had been arranged on the plates within reach of that chair. Someone has seen me coming, I thought to myself, but sat down in the empty chair with a cheerful smile.

I touched nothing—none of the food—except for a stick or two of celery and a crust of bread. I noticed that the fattest, greasiest, most delicious fish had been tucked away on the far side of the table—and no Believer with manners may reach across a table, as you know.

'You seem to have lost your appetite,' said al-Walid, thinking he had insulted me so successfully that I would not visit *him* again in a hurry.

'I have to admit to a certain loathing of fish, O mighty Kalifah. Ever since my father drowned in the sea, I have never been able to stomach a sea fish. These savage beasts on the table probably ate him, after all!'

'Surely this is the perfect opportunity to avenge yourself,' joked al-Walid, knowing full well that my father had been hanged for stealing seventy-four camels.

'Perhaps you are right!' I exclaimed and picked up the smallest, most bony, fleshless, twig of a sprat from the plate nearest me. Holding it up to my ear, I rattled it a little. 'Do you know what this little fellow says?' I cried; leaping to my feet.

All but al-Walid were now quite spellbound, and their jaws dropped: 'How should we know unless you tell us?'

'It says, "I'm far too young to have eaten your father, but if you want revenge, look to those big fat mullets lolling on that plate over there. That plate beside the noble Kalifah's hand. For they are the very fellows that gobbled up your father!"'

216

Then al-Walid—may Allah bless him for a mean, cunning old buzzard and as big a rogue as I am—he laughed so hard that he fell off his chair. And when he had picked himself up, he set the biggest red mullet in front of me—it was so big that it hung off either side of the plate—and said: 'Eat it, enjoy it, and I hope it gives you indigestion for a week! Your tongue's as slippery as any fish on this table!' So we shook hands and ate until three in the morning.

'Such greedy gluttons deserve each other's company,' said Shahryar. 'I enjoyed your story, but I hate people who keep their brains inside their stomachs like the octopus. As the poet says:

> *I do not live to eat—as does the glutton*
> *Who stuffs himself with bread and meat and pies—*
> *For when the glutton finds his way to heaven,*
> *The gates are all too small to take his size!'*

'That is perfectly true,' said Shahrazad thoughtfully. 'Greedy people never reach a happy ending. Take the example of the Fox in the story of The Crow and the Fox. He ate so much that he emptied a whole valley of everything that ran, crawled, flew, or jumped.'

'Is this another of your stories told in the animal language, Shahrazad?' said King Shahryar, already determined to postpone her execution another day and hear the story.

'If the new day spared me to see moonlight again,' she replied, 'I would speak it in Arabic for your delight and convenience.'

CHAPTER TWENTY-NINE

The Crow and the Fox

A story is told—though only the animals can tell if it is true—of a greedy fox who retired to live in a secluded valley with his wife and children. But he ate so ravenously anything that ran, crawled, flew, or jumped that soon there was nothing left alive in the valley but the Fox and his family.

It was then necessary to eat his wife-fox and all the little children-foxes. After they had all been digested, the Fox grew desperate and decided he would have to leave the valley.

Unfortunately, old age (which eventually chews on all Allah's creatures) chewed on the Fox's bones and made them ache when he ran. His sensitive nose, having smelled more smells than the dustbins of Baghdad, was clogged with dust, sand, and pollen, and the pads of his paws were as hard as stone. When his stomach had been empty for a whole day, the Fox said to himself: 'This is a tragedy for an animal of my rank. Steps must be taken!'

His steps took him to the foot of a tall acacia tree where, from the topmost branches, a crow was scanning the countryside.

If I can persuade this scrawny, evil-faced, sin-coloured bird to work for me, thought the Fox, I can save myself a great deal of running. She can fly ahead of me and spy out dead rabbits and knock-kneed chickens. Then, if her directions are good, I shall let her peck the bones after I have eaten my fill. So he polished his tongue on the inside of his cheeks and said, in words as slippery as ice, 'O most fair-faced, free-flying bird of the blackest wing— more purple-black than the purple-black raven—the golden curve of your beak is more beautiful than the new moon against the blackest night sky.'

'Aawwkk, aawwkk, aawwkk!' said the Crow, laughing until she was hanging upside down by her feet. 'That's the funniest thing I've heard since the scarecrow saw my brother and died of fright! What was the purpose of that poetical outburst, you foul-faced, flat-footed fool of a fox?'

'Before you insult me, sweetest eagle of the morning sky,' said the Fox, and the smile on his mask never wavered, 'you ought to hear the wonderful plan I have for our future lives together . . .'

'What's this? A proposal of marriage? Put your cunning back between your teeth and your bald brush back between your legs, and remember the words of the poet:

> *Let every creature keep to his own—*
> *Those who are eaten and those who eat;*
> *For if Allah intends*
> *All beasts to be friends*
> *Why did he give the Lion its teeth*
> *And why has the Tiger never flown?*

219

But the Fox did not give up: 'Your wisdom and education convince me all the more of the wonderful good we could gain from knowing one another. Let me compose a verse now in praise of your ravishing left wing . . .'

'O Fox, O flea-farm, O liar of lies, a crow has never trusted a fox before today and I don't intend to be the first. I know what you want, but you are like the Vulture in the story, and I won't help you.'

'I don't know the story of the Vulture,' said the Fox.

So the Crow told it:

'There was once a Vulture so ravenous and cruel that he emptied the sky around him. The little birds took to walking on the ground rather than fly into the claws of the Vulture. But even there they were not safe, for he stooped out of the sun and mangled many a delicate bird, biting off its head with one closing of his beak.

'But all things grow old except for Time itself. The Vulture's baldness spread to the very tip of his tail, and his dragging wings unravelled on the ground, and his beak rotted on his nose. Then he blustered and stormed at the little birds who flew overhead and the chickens who pecked grain right up to the edge of his shadow. ''Bring me food, you nests for a thousand fleas.'' But having known him for a lifetime, no bird went near him. This was not through fear, you understand, for there was nothing left to fear. The Vulture was simply beneath contempt. Because they had watched out for him when he was young, they scorned to notice him when he was old, and he crumbled into a heap of feathers and bone, which blew away in the next sandstorm.'

The Crow's words fell out of the tree on to the Fox like so many pebbles, but none of them bruised his hard heart. He went on relentlessly:

'Crow among crows, I can understand this wise and wordly argument, every word chosen with the care of a brilliant storyteller. But when you hear my plan, you are certain to change your mind, just as the weathercock is certain to turn when the wind changes direction. Listen. My days of rabbit-eating are over, and I shall not stand for another frog leaping around in my digestion. What separates the hill from the mountain, the Duck from the Eagle, the tribe of Fox from the tribe of Wolf? Ambition! Together you and I will ambush Man-kin when he passes by with his caravans of five hundred camels, with his wife riding in a silk palanquin. I shall tear out his throat and then stand aside while you feast on his eyes and tongue.'

The Fox roared wheezily and stretched to his full height against the acacia tree. But it only served to display his hungry ribs sticking through his skin like the frame of a worn-out tent.

'Wreck of a fox,' said the Crow. 'Go to a river bank and look in. If you are fortunate, the mangy fox you see in the water may tell you the story of the Sparrow, and you would do well to learn from it.'

'You tell it, O masterful storyteller,' said the Fox, his ears beginning to crumple.

'Very well, old furry-bones. There was once a Sparrow who lived in a field where a farmer kept his sheep. Once in a while, the Sparrow would see a great golden eagle hurtle down, and seize one of the sheep with its massive talons, and carry it off to the mountains—fleece, meat, and hooves. The Sparrow said to himself, "I am as good as any eagle. I shall do the same." So he spiralled up on eager, ambitious wings to a height where the thin air whistled in his throat. Then he plunged down on to the back of a big, woolly ram—the biggest of the flock. In the beating of a wing, he found himself inextricably tangled in the long, shaggy fleece, and lay there flickering and peeping until the farmer came to shear his sheep. When the farmer found the little bird caught up in the wool, he threaded a string through one wing and gave the Sparrow to his little son to whirl around his head as a toy.

'Any fox who thinks he can imitate his brother the Wolf is not fit company for a wise young bird like me,' said the Crow in conclusion. 'You thought that you could persuade me to fly ahead of you and spy out an easy supper. But I am young and my eyes are still as sharp as my beak. By the law of Nature, that makes me as high as the Eagle and you as lowly and stupid as the Sparrow.'

'May your feathers drop as you fly! May your beak rust! May the Eagle overhear your despicable story, you foul-faced, flip-flapping, flying flea-circus!' said the Fox, and he ground his teeth until they all broke between his jaws.

After a lifetime of cruelty and overeating, the Fox ended his days in the city alleyways, scavenging from the dustbins along with the stray city cats and the black gnawing rats.

CHAPTER THIRTY
The Two Wazirs

In the mornings, Shahrazad would often see her father standing in the courtyard with a silver tray. It was the tray on which he would one day carry Shahrazad's head to the King when she had at last failed to delight him with a story.

The old Wazir was as bent with worry as a blade of grass is bent by a wasp. If he raised his hopes they would be crushed one morning; and so he stood there in the courtyard, hopeless and miserable, and Shahrazad felt his sorrow as if she were carrying it in the folds of her own dress.

Even King Shahryar took note, and he was generally as thoughtless of other people's feelings as the Arab is thoughtless of the floating ice at the world's poles. 'Is your father sick, Shahrazad?' he asked one night. 'For lately his face has become as white as leprosy, and his hands shake whenever he brings me papers of state.'

'He has worries,' said Shahrazad simply, 'but no doubt Allah will smile on him again in the future.'

The King's thoughts seemed to circle the old Wazir for several minutes. 'Shahrazad, it is normal for a King's Wazir to pass his wisdom on to his son, so that the son can in turn become Wazir to the King. What will your father do, having only two daughters?'

'I don't know, my lord, master of all Wazirs,' she replied. 'But I hope he finds a better solution than the King in the story of The Two Wazirs, who was faced with the same problem.'

'Tell me the story, Shahrazad, and perhaps you will be of help to me—for it is I who must appoint a successor to your father when the time comes. Be my Wazir, wife: advise me.'

There was once a King whose Wazir had no sons, so when the Wazir died the King invited candidates from all over his kingdom to apply for the post of Royal Wazir.

If the light of their intellect shone too dimly, or their past life was dark with some crime or other, if their clothes were too colourful, or their imagination too dull, they were sent home with no more reward than the cost of their journey. And soon only two candidates remained— men of the same age; men of the same height; men of the same education; men of the same reputation; men of the same standing in the eyes of Allah. The King could not choose between them: they were as alike in merit as two petals from the same flower. So he asked the same question of both men:

'Supposing there were a king who found himself obliged to interview candidates to fill the post of Royal Wazir. He found two of the candidates so equal in merit that he could not choose between them. Advise me, since you would have the position of my adviser—which should I choose?'

The first applicant replied: 'Why not choose both, your majesty? For as the poet says—''Two heads are better than one.'' '

The second candidate said to the King: 'I would advise you to appoint both men, my lord, for as the poet says—''Why keep one dog when your kennel is big enough for two?'' '

The King was delighted with their answers and immediately employed both men to be his Wazirs.

When they were introduced, the Wazirs took an immediate liking to one another.

'I can see that we shall be marvellous friends,' said one. 'Our lives will hold hands like dancers in a ring.'

'No doubt about it,' said the other. 'We shall be like two gloves on the King's hands: you on his right and I on his left.'

'I dare say,' said the first, 'that our lives will now follow the self-same pattern. We shall both marry ladies of the court and live in neighbouring apartments of the palace.'

This kindred life-style so appealed to the second Wazir that he said: 'I promise you, friend, that I shall not even marry unless our weddings can be on the very same day.'

'In that case,' cried the first Wazir, who was fast becoming his firm friend, 'our sons will be conceived at the same moment and born on the same day.'

With ecstatic delight the second Wazir took up the story of their future lives: 'Our sons will both marry ladies of the court and we shall arrange their weddings for the self-same day. And then, having seen our children well settled in life, we can light our pipes from the same candle, grow old in the same hour, and die within the breathing of one breath. I shall see to it that when my son becomes Wazir in my place, he finds a comfortable and well-paid job for your son . . .'

'Pardon?' said the first Wazir. 'Did you say when my son becomes Wazir, he will find your son a comfortable and well-paid job?'

'Not quite, dear friend,' smiled the second Wazir indulgently, 'for I cannot imagine that the King or his heir would favour your son above mine in the choosing of a Wazir.'

'I can see no reason,' said the first Wazir, throwing back his shoulders, 'why the King or his heir or anyone with judgement should favour *your* son above *mine*!'

'Why, because he would be the superior man, O ignorant, short-sighted friend. You're not suggesting, surely, that your miserable offspring could possibly stand higher than the shoulder of my handsome, honourable boy?'

'What!' screamed the first Wazir. 'Your runt would not pass the elbow of my arrow-sharp, spear-tall son and heir, you frog-faced son of a tadpole!'

'If we are to talk of faces,' said the second Wazir, 'I can only imagine that any boy born with the evil fate of being your son would inherit your evil looks, poor lad! I have seen potatoes with better eyes, and prunes with a better skin.'

'I'm not staying here to listen to the growling of a three-toed sloth like you,' ranted the first Wazir, 'and no son of mine will come within a thousand miles of the smell of *your* children! I shall see to that.' And he stormed out of the palace in a passionate rage, which did not cool until his camel had galloped into the upper Rif and forgotten the taste of Arabian water.

When only one Wazir woke the King with the chant of prayers and with respectful greetings, the King asked: 'Where is my other Wazir?'

The remaining one took great delight in recounting the whole quarrel, word for word. But his voice faded to a silence as he saw the King's face darken with fury.

'Go to your camel and pack your bags!' cried the King, trembling like a tree in heavy rain, 'for you advised me to employ the both of you. Now I see that your advice must be as bad as your temper, and your counsel as sour as your pride.'

When King Shahryar had heard the story of The Two Wazirs, he said to Shahrazad: 'I sometimes think, when I hear your stories, that your father should name *you* his heir to the robe of authority, so that *you* become the Royal Wazir when he dies.'

'Alas, my lord,' she replied jokingly, 'despite my youth, it seems that I shall be dead long before my father the Wazir, or I might just prove to the men of Sasan that an ignorant woman is often wiser than a clever man!'

Then, unaccountably, a large ache appeared in the heart of Shahryar, and he could not smile at Shahrazad's joke.

CHAPTER THIRTY-ONE

The Two Lives of Sultan Mahmud

King Shahryar remained so melancholy during the next days that his courtiers realized how many clouds Shahrazad had previously lifted from over the Royal Palace of Sasan. He sat in his throne with his head in one hand and seemed neither to hear nor see the babble of voices, the herd of faces, that streamed past him in the audience chamber.

No suits were satisfied, no judgments were given, the whole routine of the court fell into disorder. Finally the King's Wazir became so concerned for the King's health that he went to his daughter, Shahrazad, and said:

'Dearest daughter, wife of my King, can you tell us any reason for the King's latest gloom? For indeed it seems that all the music has left his soul, and sudden autumn has stripped the tree of his heart of all its leaves.'

'Oh, I am lower in his esteem than any prisoner who sits in prison waiting for the day of his execution. I simply wait outside prison,' said Shahrazad. 'But if I can, I shall devise a story tonight which will change his mood for the better.'

'A funny story, to make him laugh?' asked her father.

'I think not,' replied Shahrazad, 'for if a man is melancholy, laughter is as far from his heart as land from a drowning man.'

'A sad story, then, to use up all his tears?' suggested the Wazir.

'Certainly not,' Shahrazad answered. 'For what danger will I be in if the King becomes one shade darker, one frown more melancholy. I shall tell him the story of a melancholy king who learned to appreciate his boundless good fortune.'

Shahrazad began:

When King Ratafia of Rif was born, Allah heaped on him every good fortune a man could wish for. His wit and good sense were housed in the most handsome of heads; his health and energy were housed in a tall and agile body. His wife's gifts as a cook, a hostess, a musician, and a writer of love poems were only surpassed by her beauty. And her beauty, in turn, was only surpassed by that of his three little babies—two sons and a daughter.

During his reign, the walls of his Chancery were demolished and rebuilt to make room for the vast quantity of gold and silver coin that represented his wealth. The stables were rebuilt because all the royal mares foaled and the royal herd tripled in size. All the members of his staff were, without exception, honest, loyal, and dedicated, for they knew that King Ratafia was loved by every subject in his widespread Kingdom of the Rif.

In short King Ratafia had everything, and there can hardly be a man who has heard of his good fortune and not envied him his happiness. Did I say happiness? No. One thing was lacking. King Ratafia did not have the ability to enjoy all that he owned. For long days at a time the King would be plunged into the blackest of depressions. He would sit in his throne, his head in one hand, sighing sighs until the windows of the palace were all clouded. He would kick his wazir in the shins, and shout at his wife if she kept him waiting for as much as the third part of a second. If he played with his children and made them laugh, he would complain that they were too noisy. If he refused to play with them and made them cry, he would again complain of their noise.

During one of the King's blackest moods, a strange visitor came to the Palace. He inspired such respect that at the sight of him all the courtiers and officials fell back: no one barred his path to the King. If anyone had guessed his age, it would have been measured in hundreds of years. He had a beard which had never seen a razor or scissors and he wore it wrapped round his body in place of clothes.

Swathed like this in his beard, he approached the King's throne but did not make the customary bow of obeisance. Instead he took the King by the wrist and pulled him towards the window. Now the throne room was situated in a high tower and had four windows overlooking the whole city. From the first there was a fine view of the palace moat; from the second, a view of the city; from the third, a view of the Nile; and from the fourth, a prospect of gardens and parkland. But when the strange old man threw open the first window, the King ducked down below the sill, for he saw an army of men in the very act of storming his palace. Catapaults were showering boulders against the walls; men in chain-mail were throwing across the moat grappling hooks, which clutched and clawed at the masonry; battering rams were splintering the doors of the keep; and a sleet of arrows was driving against the face of the building.

'Alert the army! We are under attack!' cried the King. But no one seemed to believe him, for of all the courtiers and officers standing near by, not one made a move.

The gnarled old man slammed the window shut and dragged the King by the wrist to the second. But as he opened it, the reeking stench of smoke scorched the King's nostrils and the glow of fire lit up his whole city. Buildings were crumbling into dust like the ashes of a smouldering log fire. His own bronze statue was melting into a shapeless mass from which a river of molten bronze flowed into the gutters. Shreds of burning cloth blew this way and that in the air, raining down soot on the heads of a thousand citizens as they fled their burning houses, screaming for help.

'Carry the horse-troughs to the city! Tear the blankets off every bed! My people's homes are burning down—will no one help them?' But no one among the King's courtiers or officers went to their assistance.

Slamming the second window shut, the raddled old man opened the third, just in time to reveal the River Nile bursting its high banks and washing away two cotton farms and a rice paddy. Fishing boats were swept prow-first through the walls of the riverside houses; alligators writhed in the streets, devouring those who stumbled about trying to escape the flood.

'Throw life-lines from the windows! Take the palace doors off their hinges and make rafts of them for the drowning to cling to. The Nile has burst its banks and my people are being washed away. Oh, will no one act to help my poor citizens!' But no one moved except the grizzly-bearded old man who slammed shut the third window and opened the fourth.

The last fruit in the palace orangery was shrivelling to the size of raisins and dropping from the trees. The trees themselves were knotting and shrivelling as the garden prospect was invaded by the blast of the sun, and the scouring sand of the Sahara swept in to swamp the flower-beds and bury the lawns. As sand-dunes formed in drifts along the palace walls, nests of scorpions broke from every tussock of remaining grass, and knots of black vipers suddenly festooned the bleaching bushes. Locusts carpeted the ground for as far as the eye could see, crackling their bodies and devouring one another when there was no greenery left to devour. And yellow hyenas shrieked with laughter below the window to see the destruction of Sultan Mahmud's parklands and all the surrounding farms.

'Locusts and the desert are swallowing us up!' cried the Sultan. 'Take your hands off me, old man, and help me make these heartless people act to save some lives.'

The old man, though he seemed frail, had the strength of ten in his grip. He had no difficulty in dragging the King to the drinking fountain in the centre of the room, where he placed a second hand in the nape of the King's neck and plunged his head beneath the water.

Down, down and down he went, until seven colours were flashing in his eyelids and the spent air was fluttering in his lungs. The fearsome grip slackened on his neck and arm, and he was released to struggle back to the surface. Up and up he swam, arms and legs driving through the water, and he lost consciousness just as his mouth tasted air again for the first time.

Washed ashore by the surf, he lay with a strange beach under his back for fully an hour, until the sound of voices stirred him to consciousness.

'Here's a strange fish!' said the peasants who found him. 'What foolish and impractical clothes for a working man.' Many unfriendly hands stripped Mahmud of his satin djellabah and golden crown, and dressed him in a shirt of coarsest yellow sailcloth and breeches of roughest hessian.

'I wish the sea had washed up a new donkey,' said one voice as the Sultan stumbled to his feet.

'Don't be ungrateful,' said another voice. 'Allah has sent you a foreigner. And foreigners can be made to work almost as hard as donkeys.'

'Where am I?' asked Sultan Mahmud. 'Will no one here treat me with the respect I deserve?'

'Yes indeed, foreign dog, son of a cur, I shall use you with the respect you deserve, for my donkey died yesterday and I shall set you to work in his place at my mill.'

Before Mahmud could make anyone understand that he was a Sultan and the ruler of a great kingdom, he found himself trudging round inside the tread-wheel of a flour-mill.

His bare feet grew hard against the splintery wood, and it almost seemed that they had been turned into hooves. His unkempt hair became so matted with sweat and dirt that it hung down on either side of his head almost like ears. The owner of the mill congratulated himself: 'My friends were right: having a foreigner is almost the same as having a donkey.'

233

The miserable Mahmud received only a bucketful of beans to satisfy his hunger and a trough of sun-warm water to quench his thirst. 'Will no one release me from this terrible wheel?' he moaned daily. 'Will no one have pity on a Sultan who has been almost changed into a donkey?'

One day a shepherd boy was passing the mill and heard Mahmud cry out like this.

'Good-day, foreigner,' he said. 'Is this kind of work not to your taste?'

'O good shepherd, unfasten me from the wheel, or go to my master and plead with him to let me go,' said Mahmud, hanging his panting head through the spokes of the treadwheel.

'I suppose you realize,' said the shepherd, 'that legally only foreigners can be set to work like this? And I suppose you realize that you would no longer be a foreigner if you took a local girl for a wife?'

'Oh, fetch me a slave-girl, fetch me a milk-maid, fetch me your sister, gentle shepherd. Fetch me some woman whom I can marry and so escape this terrible work,' begged Mahmud.

'I see that your bad fortunes have brought you a great distance from your native land, for you do not understand the laws in these parts. In order to take a bride, you have only to stand at the doors of the public baths. As each lady comes out, ask her if she is married or single. It is written that Allah will send you the wife of your deserving. The first single woman you question need only say ''No, sir, I am not married'', and the two of you will be man and wife immediately.'

That evening, when the mill-owner led Mahmud out of the wheel to feed him his bucket of beans, the

Sultan bolted off across a field and ran all the way to the city, sleeping on the steps of the public baths until late the next morning. The first thing he noticed on opening his eyes was that the women of the country went unveiled.

The first female to leave the public baths was a radiant young girl with foaming golden hair falling to below her waist. She smiled encouragingly at Mahmud as he gabbled his words: 'Are you married, child of honey, for if you are not . . .'

'I married only last week,' she said and patted his sleeve. 'May Allah send you a fair wife.'

'You are married, aren't you?' he asked the next woman who emerged from the Turkish baths. She was of about his mother's age with the shape of a bag of bricks and a face as fair as the bowl of a baobab tree.

'I wish I were not,' she said, pinching his cheek and winking hugely. 'I could eat you up, you handsome boy!'

'Are you married?' Mahmud shouted into the shadows of the bath-house as the next slap of feet approached the doors. The footsteps quickened into a run, and a voice called back—like the call of a baboon through the shadowy rain-forests:

'No, sunshine, light of my future life! Let me look at you, my lover, my scrumptious little baby boy, my big masterful bridegroom! No, sir, I'm not married.'

The head like an ox had been joined to the body of a hippopotamus, or so it seemed to Mahmud as his bride galloped towards him into the light. With arms spread wide, with hair still damp and sticking out in spikes, with face still red from the steambaths, her feet thudded closer like Unavoidable Fate. As she went to take him in her arms, he ducked underneath her mace-like fists and fled headlong into the hammam. Women in baths screamed and clutched up towels; masseurs shouted and grabbed at him as he scampered past; steam swallowed him up; and the slapping of sandals on stone floors pursued him, shouting, 'Come back, sweetie sugar-cake. I don't mind if you look like a donkey. We're married now. Come back, sugar-lump!'

He ducked down a side corridor which had no end door. So he slipped behind a curtain part-way along, skidded on the wet floor with flailing arms and a prayer to Allah, and plunged over the edge of a sunken bath full of large, pink ladies.

Down and down he plunged until seven colours were flashing in his eyelids and the spent air was fluttering in his lungs. The fat pink ladies seemed to be holding him under the water with the strength of massive hands, and as recent misfortunes gathered in his memory, Mahmud wondered if it was even worthwhile to struggle . . .

Lifting the Sultan's head after dipping it into the drinking fountain for only a few moments, the bearded old sage called for a chair and seated Sultan Mahmud while he recovered his breath.

Mahmud looked around him at the anxious faces of his wife, children, and courtiers. But they all burst out laughing when he spluttered: 'Where is my hideous wife? Where are all the fat, pink ladies? Where are my ears and hooves?'

'Listen, Sultan Mahmud,' said the old man wrapped round in nothing but his beard. 'I have shown you the life you might have led, the twists of fate that might have overturned your happiness, the evil luck which many suffer every day.'

236

'Has the city been saved? Have the flood-waters dropped? Has the fire been put out? Have the locusts gone?' asked Mahmud, rushing from one window to another to look out over his tranquil kingdom.

'Those things happened only in your imagination, Mahmud, which I am able to paint as the artist paints canvas,' said the old man, lighting a paper spill at the open log fire. 'But all of them could have happened to you had Allah decreed it. If all and every one of these disasters had fallen on your head, you silly king, then you might have had cause to be sad. But none of them are written in your Destiny. Therefore be happy or you will shame Allah with your ingratitude for His priceless gifts: a lovely wife, beautiful children, a thriving kingdom, a powerful throne and a time of peace—and a body more lovely to box up your soul in than the old frame I have to house my magic wisdom.'

So saying, the gnarled, raddled old man lit the trailing tip of his beard and a spiral column of green fire burned where his beard had coiled around his body. The green vapour made everybody turn aside to cough, and when they turned back, the old man was gone, and nothing but a scrap of yellow sailcloth lay at Mahmud's feet.

'I would weep for the loss of a good friend,' he said to his wife as their eyes met, 'but I have banished all tears out of my eyes and banished all my blackness out of the kingdom. I now declare that any one of my loyal subjects—however lowly their position—is granted the right to banish me, Sultan Mahmud, if ever I sulk or brood or mop or mow or fail to thank Allah hourly for all the good things life has given me. Come now, there has been much time wasted in moping and moods. I wish it written, in letters a hundred inches high, all along the Palace wall:

THE SULTAN MAHMUD IS THE MOST FORTUNATE MAN ON ALLAH'S GOLDEN EARTH.

And I will fight to the death any stranger who disputes it!'

As Shahrazad finished the story of The Two Lives of Sultan Mahmud, she trembled for fear her husband mistook the story for criticism. But his eyes rested on her as a brown bird rests momentarily on a fence and then flies away. 'I'm sorry, Shahrazad,' he said, 'my ears have delighted in your story like strains of music heard through a wall, but my thoughts have not travelled with your story tonight. I have not been listening. Promise me you will tell me another story tomorrow, and I shall apply my ears to listening.'

'To hear you is to love you and obey,' replied Shahrazad, but she shook her head as she walked slowly back to her rooms, and inside her her heart shook of its own accord.

CHAPTER THIRTY-TWO

The Tale of the Leg of Mutton

On the nine hundred and ninety-seventh night after her marriage Shahrazad said to Shahryar: 'Have you not said to me, "A woman looks into a man's purse to judge how much she can love him"?'

It is said that there was just such a woman in Cairo—though who can tell if it is true?—who loved money so much that she could not find a husband rich enough to satisfy her. The girl, whose name was Raiya, was wooed by two men: one a robber called Haram, the other a pickpocket called Akil. Now Haram (like the hyena) worked at night, breaking into houses and stealing from the boats that rocked along the Nile. Akil (like the jackal) worked by day among the crowds of the bazaar and the jostling pockets of the cattle market. Consequently, Haram slept and ate by day, and Akil slept and ate by night.

On the day Raiya agreed to marry Haram, she took him to an empty house near Victory Gate and said: 'The rent on this lovely house is only two hundred dinars a month. We shall live here in love and prosperity all the days of our married life.'

The next day she took Akil, the pickpocket, by the hand and led him to the same house near Victory Gate.

'Dearest Akil,' she said, 'the rent on this lovely house is only two hundred dinars a month. I will marry you if we can live here.'

So Raiya married both Akil and Haram (though neither bridegroom knew that he was sharing the bride). And since Haram worked, like a hyena, at night-time, and Akil worked, like a jackal, by day, they were never at home at the same time. Raiya received housekeeping money from both husbands, and every month both gave her two hundred dinars to pay the rent. Raiya's wardrobe, as a result, was the finest in Cairo, and her throat and wrists were decorated with finest Indian silver, and her hair was braided with coloured silk.

Her two husbands gloried in their delightful wife and prided themselves on finding a woman who could eke out her allowance to such good effect. At the inn in the city Haram bragged about the valuable prize he had locked away at home. At the Turkish baths Akil bragged that his wife was the prettiest treasure any man ever locked in his treasure chest.

The following summer a great and infamous bandit in the mountains of the Rif organized a congress of thieves and villains, and invited all the burglars, footpads, robbers, bandits, pickpockets, confidence tricksters, and horse-thieves for a week of festivities.

'I must leave the city on business for a while,' said Haram to his wife.

'O roof of my heart, keel of my body's ship! What shall I do without my beloved husband?' said Raiya. But she packed him a meal for his journey, kissed him warmly, and waved him goodbye from the door.

When Akil came home that evening he gave her the purses he had stolen that day and said, 'It breaks my heart, but I must leave Cairo on business for a while.'

'O floor of my heart, mast of my body's ship! What shall I do without my beloved husband?' said Raiya, but she packed him a meal for his journey, kissed him warmly, and waved him goodbye from the door.

At the end of a day's travelling, Haram the robber built a camp fire and settled down for a sleep. He was woken by the shadow of a passing camel thrown across him by the firelight.

'Stranger!' he called to the rider. 'The blessings of Allah on your head. Will you share food with me and tell me news from the desert?'

Akil got off his camel and sat down beside Haram. 'I have only come from Cairo today,' he replied, and as is the custom of the desert they emptied out their parcels of food to share them equally.

'No wife in Cairo can pack a meal as appetizing as mine can!' said Haram. 'See here, she has given me dates, grapes, half a leg of cold mutton, half a loaf of sesame bread she baked herself, and a slice of cake, some almonds, and a melon!'

'Allah akbar!' exclaimed Akim. 'Do you know what my wife has given me? Dates, grapes, half a leg of cold mutton, half a loaf of sesame bread she baked herself, and a slice of cake, some almonds, and a melon.'

241

They looked at the portions laid out on the flaps of their saddlebags and marvelled at the coincidence. Then Haram reached across and took Akil's half leg of mutton and held it against his own joint of cold meat. Lo and behold—they fitted together exactly.

'Our wives must shop at the same butcher. Is it not remarkable that neighbours should travel this far in order to meet for the first time? Where do you live?'

'Near Cairo's Victory Gate,' replied the pickpocket.

As they spoke they both reached for some sesame bread. Akil caught Haram's wrist. 'Tell me something, friend, does your wife buy her bread at a baker's?'

'No indeed. Her thrift is a shining example to other men's wives. I woke to the smell of *this* loaf baking. Our wives must be the best of friends—even to sharing the food of their kitchens.'

Akil took the half loaf out of Haram's hand and fitted it end to end with his own half. 'But I had the smell of this loaf in my nostrils as I fell asleep yesterday. Tell me, if it will dispel my fears, exactly where your home is at Victory Gate.'

'Mine is the third house from the laundry, with a small oak door and a rent of two hundred dinars a month. Now tell me, if it will dispel my fears, exactly what your wife is called.'

'She is called Raiya, as is yours, sir, and I believe we slept in the same bed yesterday.'

Both men thought at first to seize the other man by the throat and kill the rival who had robbed him of half his wife. But as they tumbled into the ashes of the fire, Akil pushed Haram away and said:

'Wait, friend, why are we quarrelling? We have more

in common than two brothers with the same mother: we have both been tricked by that hussy, Raiya.'

They saddled their camels and galloped back to Cairo, swearing vengeance on the woman who had emptied their four pockets for a whole year.

'The shame of it!' cried Haram as he pushed the door open of the little house near Victory Gate.

'The extravagance! The waste!' cried Akil, climbing the stairs.

'The wicked, deceitful treachery of women!' cried both the wronged husbands as they seized Raiya, each by a wrist.

'For love of Allah!' she cried. 'What will you do to me!'

'We shall tear you in half like a chicken's wishbone and see which of us wins the larger portion. Then we shall see if there are two men in Cairo so foolish as to buy two halves of one worthless woman, as we did. When we have finished with you, the two halves of your body will not fit together as neatly as did the leg of mutton or the sesame loaf you used for our meals.'

But the time that an angry man spends in shouting at his wife only gives her time to think of an answer. Raiya looked at first one husband then the other, and her brown eyes ran salt tears. 'Houses of my heart,' she said, 'you are welcome to my life at any hour of the day or night. But will you be so heartless as to let me die in ignorance? What have I done to offend you?'

At these brazen words Akil and Haram were so shocked that they let go of her wrists and fell off their feet.

'I loved you both equally,' she said, 'and could not choose between you. So I found a means to squeeze happiness enough for three out of the fruit of one small wife. Have you not bragged at the inn, Haram, that your wife is the best dressed woman in Cairo because of her thrift? Have you not bragged, Akil, that your wife could do more with her housekeeping than any woman in Cairo? Do you think the takings of one petty thief could keep him in linen shirts and his wife in Indian silk and silver? Get along with you. Go to my brother's party in the Rif and say that his sister sends her love to the greatest bandit of all, and is happy and well with two good husbands to look after her in her old age.'

Now no one in Cairo discovered the secret of Akil the pickpocket and Haram the robber, for if they had, both men would have been shamed into exile. Those who tell the Tale of the Leg of Mutton say that the two husbands were so afraid, when they discovered their brother-in-law was the Great Bandit of the Rif, that they lived on in the little house near Victory Gate just as if nothing had happened. Others say that they saw the wisdom of Raiya's words and went on bragging of their thrifty and beautiful wife. But that is absurd, for who could think that one silly woman could outwit two clever Believers who earned their living by roguery?

King Shahryar stared at his wife in disbelief that she had dared to tell him such a story.

'Are you sick of life, Shahrazad, that you remind me of woman's deceitfulness? Do you think I haven't seen what trick you are playing to keep your head on your shoulders night after night? I deny myself the pleasure of cutting off your head for the sake of the greater pleasure of hearing your stories. But now you have reminded me that a woman's love for a man is no greater or smaller than the size of his purse. Why did you tell it, Shahrazad?'

His wife stood up and threw her hands back, like a swan rising up in the water on a beat of its wings. For the first time, she addressed her husband without looking at the floor: 'I know other stories, Shahryar.'

'But will you be able to tell them after I have cut off your head this morning?' said Shahryar, opening the window.

'What, my lord, will you hear only the story of a bad woman and not stories about the other kinds? For are there not as many kinds of woman as there are trees or flowers or birds?'

'What sort could interest me?' he asked, banging on the palace wall below his window with his metal dagger. The Royal Swordsman in his room below, rolled out of bed and ran to fetch the sword that had stood unused for almost a thousand nights.

'Are there not women who love like the deer loves its mother—even after it has stopped drinking her milk?'

'No!' shouted Shahryar.

'It is time indeed, then, to cut off my head, lord, before I prove you wrong.'

No one had ever spoken with so little respect to the ruler of all Sasan. King Shahryar was so astonished by her insolence that he stopped banging on the stone wall.

'Hurry, Shahryar,' she said, 'for I prove you wrong by simply drawing breath. I am a woman who loves her husband better than money or clothes or ornaments, and one who will love him tomorrow as I love him today. Be quick and cut off my head or I shall prove you wrong in every syllable, by loving you all your life.'

'Yes, O King?' said the Royal Swordsman, looking up at the King's chamber window for instructions. Shahryar uttered a roar of vexation and threw the dagger at his Swordsman before slamming the window.

His mouth began to frame the word 'Liar', but Shahrazad interrupted him again. 'In the Story of the Ebony Horse, isn't Shams al-Nahar as different from the deceitful woman Raiya as the holly is different from the willow or the wren from the vulture? Now *there* is a woman I understand, for I love you as much as Princess Shams al-Nahar loved the Prince Kamar al-Akmar, rider of the Ebony Horse.'

'And how much is that, pray?' Shahryar shouted at his wife. But he was so troubled by her ferocious declaration of love that he silenced her answer and would not let Shahrazad begin her story until the night of the nine hundred and ninety-eighth day.

CHAPTER THIRTY-THREE

The Tale of the Ebony Horse

Before the winds of Time blow, and every trace of Man is covered with Sahara sand, let me name the name of King Sabur, ruler of all Persia, who had one son and one daughter.

Every year King Sabur's birthday was celebrated more lavishly than the year before. The fame of the festivities spread like the circular sound of a gong echoing to the very rim of Persia: the dervishes who danced, the slave-girls who served, the chefs who cooked, and the presents that were presented. But in the year of King Sabur's fifty-fifth birthday, the celebrations reached new splendours, and every road in the kingdom was littered with the presents that fell from the overfull saddlebags of camel trains streaming into Tehran.

One gift surpassed all other gifts. It was brought by an old sage as twisted and stunted as a pollarded tree, who lived in the mountain caves of Persia. The gift was carried into the court under a white canopy with curtains on all sides, and unveiled in front of the King's throne. There stood a life-size ebony horse. Its saddle was of red morocco with stirrups of chased gold, and its flanks were dappled with inlaid ivory in the shape of flower-heads. Its mane and tail were of the finest strands of raw silk ever coaxed from the slow silkworm; and its eyes were many-faceted diamonds encasing brown and black striped tiger-eye.

'There is more wonderful artistry here than in any statue in my entire realm, sir,' said the King. 'You have honoured me greatly.'

'You see only its shape, and not its purpose, O best of kings,' said the sage in a voice like safflower oil. 'This horse has the power of flight: it can leap the rainbow and bring you safely to earth on the far shores of the sea.'

'If this were true,' said Sabur, 'it would be the present to shame all other presents, and I would reward your generosity by granting as many wishes as your heart could think to express.'

So the sage demonstrated his magic ebony horse. Although it required six slaves to lift his twisted body into the saddle, once there the old man was little less than an angel. He flicked a key in the saddle's pommel, and the horse lifted its front hooves and plunged into the air, which buoyed it up as water buoys up a swimmer. Over the balcony rail and round the garden it flew, until the sage brought it back to rest in front of the King's throne. The King was astonished:

'It is written that Alexander of Macedon had a flying horse called Bucephalus. With this horse I would be a second Alexander! Sabur the Great! Ask anything of me, gentle sage, for if your wishes were as many as the grains of sand in a dune, I would grant them all!'

But the old man had only one wish. How then could the King refuse him? He asked for the hand of the King's only daughter, and at once received permission from Sabur to marry her.

The Princess's cry could be heard throughout the palace when she was given the news and told to prepare herself for her immediate wedding. She ran distractedly to the eastern wing of the building and fell down at her brother's feet in a monsoon of tears.

'Whatever is the matter, little sister?' asked Kamar al-Akmar. 'Nothing can be so terrible that your brother cannot remedy it.'

'Then plead with my father, O brother among brothers, and beg him not to marry me to the foul, twisted old man who gave him the magic horse! I would rather die than marry a man whose face alone terrifies me!'

'What old man? What magic horse? Hush, little sister,' said the Prince. 'Our father will grant me anything, for I am his only son and heir. Put away your wedding clothes and do not think another thought concerning this repulsive suitor.'

'Father!' said the Prince as he entered the throne room. 'What is this I hear about you marrying my little sister to a black-faced baboon in return for some childish rocking-horse?' He stopped short as he saw the horse in question, and walked round it admiringly. The King introduced the old sage who (can you wonder at it?) immediately hated Prince Kamar. He realized at once that Kamar al-Akmar would dissuade King Sabur from giving away his daughter in return for a birthday gift. But this hatred showed no more on his face than the sourness of a lemon shows on its skin. As the King explained how the magic horse flew, the sage smiled and bowed and nestled close to the Prince.

'I must ride this wonderful beast!' exclaimed Kamar al-Akmar, and leapt into the saddle.

Still the sage smiled and made little respectful bows towards him. 'If you would raise it from the ground, simply flick the key on the right hand side of the saddle, O delightful one, beat of your father's heart.'

With a click and a whirring, a mechanical jolt, and a rushing slipstream the magic horse bounded over the balcony rail and soared into the sky while Prince Kamar was still feeling for the stirrups. Half in and half out of the saddle, he was heaved up into the sky faster than an arrow aimed at the sun. The air thinned; he struck the separate sunbeams like a stick clattered along a fence; a little cloud fell past him on the right side like a lamb dropped from the claws of an eagle.

'Down, boy! Whoa!' he shouted. But the horse's ears were of solid ebony and deaf to all commands.

He was riding towards the sun as the moth rides on its wings towards the destruction of a candle flame.

'Fetch back my boy!' cried King Sabur, dragging on the Sage's clothes. 'Bring down your horse or you will rob the whole kingdom of Persia of its Prince and heir!'

'As you would have robbed me of my rightful prize—the hand of your daughter. I know that it was already in your heart to withdraw your offer. Kamar al-Akmar had decided that the marriage was not to be. Well, now your son has gone to marry the world's sun, and may the warmth of that marriage char his skin as black as mine!'

King Sabur threw the Sage into his deepest, most crawling dungeon, but revenge did nothing to ease his sorrow, for he was certain that Kamar al-Akmar was flying to his death . . .

Kamar al-Akmar spoke severely to his quaking heart. 'Man was given mastery over all animals. Use those powers given you by Allah to control this mechanical beast, for as the poet might have said: *What flies up must fly down.*'

He searched the saddle for another key and, finally, as the silk mane of the horse began to shrivel in the sun's heat, found a switch no larger than a pin, on the left-hand side. One flick, and the horse's climb slowed—stopped—reversed—and Kamar al-Akmar was plunging towards the open sea beyond the rivers of Tigris and Euphrates and the Shatt al-Arab. Having mastered both keys, Kamar was able to save himself from galloping into the sea, and crossed both water and land. His delight in the pleasures of flight had carried him to a land rich with many cities. And the fairest of these was Sana.

Seeing the palace of Sana amidst the tree-lined avenues of its surrounding city, Kamar al-Akmar thought to himself: 'This seems like a place where a young Prince of blood-royal might be offered meat and milk. But I shall land on the roof first and make certain that I am in a land friendly towards Persia, for I shall not eat off the table of my father's enemies.'

The roof was not flat, as the roofs of Araby are flat. The ebony horse had to pick its way between a hundred minarets and sloping dormer windows, but was hidden from all eyes when the Prince dismounted and climbed into the palace attic through a small fanlight.

Below the palace dovecot and several storerooms, Kamar came to the uppermost staterooms of the royal apartments and accidentally walked into the bedroom of the kingdom's only Princess. (Believers in Love would say that Allah guided his footsteps.) There she lay, sound asleep on a satin bed hung with voile curtains and roofed with a carved rosewood canopy. Her golden hair covered all but her little white feet and her small white hands, and her face was turned towards him.

'This is how the sun must feel when the white and purple passion flower turns its face towards the light,' thought Kamar al-Akmar, and his heart waded into the quicksand of love and was swallowed up wholly, completely, instantaneously.

'My heart is a swinging bell and you are its clapper,' he said to the Princess Shams al-Nahar as she woke to his kisses.

'Your kisses are rain and I am a little parched flower,' she said and wrapped him in the golden cloak of her hair as her soul cloaked him in love.

'You are my destiny, the reason for Allah's gift of sight,' he said.

'You are my fate, and the reason for Allah's gift of hands,' she replied.

'You are my sea, let me lay my shore alongside you,' he said.

'You are my husband, let me lay my life beside yours,' she said.

'You are a bee stealing the honey of the kingdom, and I shall wrench out your sting and crush you underfoot,' said the King of Sana, entering the bedroom among a dozen armed and armoured soldiers. The Princess hurriedly caught up a veil. 'How did you come here past the hundred guards on the stairs and the twenty ferocious dogs in the palace grounds?'

252

After some moments, Prince Kamar al-Akmar managed to tear his eyes from the face of Shams al-Nahar and said, 'Why do you offer such violence to your future son-in-law? For I am a Prince of the blood-royal and I have decided to marry your daughter even if, for the bride-price, I must pay you a whole half-hemisphere of the world.'

'Enough words from a miserable house-breaker. Get up, or your blood will dirty my daughter's bedspread when my soldiers kill you,' said the King between his teeth. 'This girl is promised to my cousin's third nephew's uncle—a venerable man of seventy-four respectable and noteworthy years. And what are *you*?'

The Princess Shams al-Nahar put her arms round Kamar al-Akmar and begged him not to rise and fight.

'I am the Prince Kamar al-Akmar and I am not a coward,' he said, prising himself free from her, 'but I think your father is lacking in courtesy if he will not bide by the most basic rules of chivalry.'

'How have I broken the rules of chivalry, runt of a thousand pig-litters?' demanded the King (who was, in truth, a highly chivalrous man).

'Either you should offer to fight me in single combat, my lord, father of my lover,' Kamar replied, 'or you should send your whole army against me on a field of battle. But you insult me by sending a mere dozen against me like dogs set loose on a burglar.'

The King of Sana looked the youth up and down as a woodcutter sizes up a tree for felling. He quickly decided that he could not fight such a leopard of a boy himself: 'Very well, young civet cat. I shall range my army on the northern plain and place at your disposal a pitched tent, a horse, and some armour as soon as the mid-day heat has slackened.'

'Armour is unnecessary,' said Kamar, 'and I have my own horse with me: I left it on your roof.'

Then the King feared greatly for his daughter's honour: the young man who had seen her with her face uncovered and wearing only her hair was clearly as mad as a bareheaded man in a desert. 'There are seventy stairs between each floor, and this is the topmost floor. Did your horse climb all those stairs or simply leap the two-hundred feet to my roof? Come away, daughter, for this young man's wits have gone, and his wits will be followed shortly by his life.'

When Prince Kamar al-Akmar was left alone, he climbed back to the roof and watched the army of Sana assemble on the field below. At a distance, the King had placed a pavilion and a horse, and a set of shining armour was laid out on the grass. Kamar mounted the ebony horse, flicked the key on the saddle, and together they leapt over the roof's parapet, somehow settling on the battlefield without being noticed by the milling soldiers.

'There he is!' one of them shouted. 'Poor baby's only got a toy horse!' And wheeling their iron-shod horses towards Kamar, they galloped down on him like the unholy Turks when they stormed the Holy City.

As the first whirling sword shortened the hairs of the silken mane, Kamar flicked the key and the ebony horse lifted into the air, above the soldiers' heads and came to rest behind them. With a cry of astonishment, the whole army tried to turn, and some of the horses collided and fell over. Kamar met the return charge in just the same way, lifting out of reach of their lunging swords. Back and to, to and fro, the army rushed up and down the field with Kamar hovering a little above their heads on his magic, mechanical horse, teasing and enraging them. He never even drew his sword.

The Princess Shams al-Nahar watched spellbound from a window, thinking she must be in love with the ghost of Alexander of Macedon, rider of Bucephalus. At last he rose so high into the air that the arch of the window prevented her seeing his movements.

'What an amazing thing!' exclaimed the King, bustling into the room behind her among several soldiers who were red with heat and embarrassment. 'A truly amazing thing! Did he tell you that his horse could fly, my dear? What an astounding young man! Send for the Royal Historian and have the story set down in writing.'

'But where is Kamar al-Akmar?' his daughter interrupted. 'Please tell me, father, for he taught not only his horse to fly, but my heart also.'

'Was that his name? Kamar al-Akmar?' asked the King. 'Oh well, he has gone, of course—flew away into the sun after he had shamed my fighting men sufficiently. Where's the Royal Historian?—Ah, there you are! Look now, you need not mention where we found him, but I want the story of this Kamar al-Akmar written down and . . .'

The King's voice grew fainter as he walked off along the corridor with his courtiers and officers, and Princess Shams al-Nahar found herself alone. But now she was alone as only ladies can be who have been unalone in the arms of Love. She vowed then and there that she would never marry any man but Kamar al-Akmar. And after a week of waiting, she had her maidservant burn the rosewood chest in which all her wedding clothes were stored. Little clouds came and went on the horizon, but the ebony horse and Kamar al-Akmar, it seemed, had ridden out of the whole realm of Sky.

Throughout the telling of the Tale of the Ebony Horse, Shahrazad stood to speak the words. When she had described the disappearance of Kamar al-Akmar from the life of Princess Shams al-Nahar, she said: 'Does this conclusion please you, sir?'

'No, Shahrazad, of course not!' said the King sitting up in bed.

'Then you may wish to hear the remainder of the story tomorrow night?'

'Certainly, if you will sit down to tell it,' said Shahryar.

'I would rather stand, lord King,' she said shortly, and then left the room and was not seen anywhere in the palace until the following evening.

CHAPTER THIRTY-FOUR

The Ebony Horse: The Sorcerer's Revenge

When Prince Kamar al-Akmar returned to his father's kingdom, the whole countryside was grieving and the palace balcony, where he set down the ebony horse, was strewn with ashes of mourning.

'Who has died?' he asked anxiously when he found his mother, father, and sister all weeping in one room. At the sight of him they leapt up and danced with delight.

'Where have you been, core of my heart's fruit, son of my old age?' asked King Sabur. 'For we saw you fly towards the sun and certain destruction, like a moth towards a candle flame. The Sorcerer who made that evil horse is locked in my deepest dungeon for he undoubtedly expected you to die.'

'Oh free him, father, for his evil intention brought me nothing but good.' Then Kamar told his story and begged

257

his father to send ambassadors to Sana to ask for the hand of Shams al-Nahar.

'No, no, son. For you were received there like a common burglar and entertained with violence. Besides, the daughter's tears will have long since dried, and your name will be to her nothing but a half-remembered sound heard through a wall. Woman's love is as short as the stride of a man standing still. No. We shall celebrate your return, select for you four of the fairest Persian brides, and lock away the ebony horse which so nearly robbed me and my kingdom of its most glorious Prince.'

Kamar could not believe in his heart that the King's words were true . . . But Sabur his father had great experience of the world, and the wisdom of an older man. So Kamar was obedient and allowed the celebrations to roll around him like an incoming sea. Seven whole days passed in festivities. Then the Prince spoke these words to himself:

'There is food on every table, and yet there is an emptiness inside me larger than hunger. There is laughter on all sides, and yet my throat is blocked with tears. There are presents given me with every passing hour, and yet I seem to have nothing.' He went to the storeroom where the mechanical ebony horse was standing, dragged it to a landing at the head of the stairs, and climbed into its saddle.

'I must fetch back my Shams al-Nahar!' he called out as he swooped low over the heads of his family and relatives and out across the terrace. 'I have starved my love but it will not die. I have denied my love but it will not set me free.' As he crossed the palace moat, Kamar could see the black, wrinkled face of the old Sorcerer, newly released from prison, watching him with open hatred.

'I have told my heart what you say,' said Shams al-Nahar to her father, 'but it will not listen. I have argued with my heartbeat, but I lose every argument. I will not marry my cousin's third nephew's uncle because he is not Kamar al-Akmar.'

'Why shed tears for a boy who has forgotten you already?' said her mother. 'The love of a man (and of foreigners in particular) is as short as your memory of tomorrow.'

But the Princess had cried herself to sleep between her parents, and they left her sleeping, and went downstairs with much cursing of Love and of Kamar al-Akmar.

'There is salt water enough in the Seven Seas, Shams al-Nahar. Why weep more?' said Prince Kamar, stepping from his hiding place behind a curtain to wake her with kisses.

'You are the songbird in my heart's cage,' she said on waking and seeing his eyes.

'You are my crescent moon flying through my night sky,' he said, 'and I have come back for you.'

She dressed, and braided her hair with the most valuable jewels and climbed with him to the roof, where they mounted the ebony horse. She sat behind him in the saddle, her arms round his waist, and sang this love-song as they flew:

> *I have been without my Kamar*
> *One long week, but not again;*
> *For without him I am summer*
> *Drought without the touch of rain.*

> *I am now without my mother—*
> *Father too—and far from home;*
> *But because I'm with my lover,*
> *Where in me shall tears find room?*

Shams al-Nahar did not unclasp her hands until they landed together in the water gardens of Tehran, a mile from the royal palace of King Sabur.

'Wait here: I shall go ahead and prepare the city to greet you as befits a Princess arriving to marry the Prince of Persia,' said Kamar. 'Look after the ebony horse.'

'Do not be long,' replied Shams al-Nahar, kissing his fingers, 'for no civic welcome can make up for the time we shall be apart.'

The Princess sat beside a fountain, singing love-songs and holding the bridle of the ebony horse as if it might gallop away of its own accord. This was the sight which met the eyes of the foul-faced Sorcerer as he left Tehran city. (When King Sabur had released the horse-maker from prison, he had made it perfectly clear that the Sorcerer would not be given the Persian Princess for a bride: 'Count yourself fortunate that Prince Kamar has begged me to free you!' Sabur had said. 'That is reward enough for an ugly jackal like you!')

Imagine the mixture of passions that seethed in his chest as he walked through the water-gardens. Imagine his joy at seeing the horse he had laboured long years to create!

'Child! You must be the Princess Shams al-Nahar from the city of Sana in al-Yaman. Let me kiss the ground between your feet.' (Shams al-Nahar let out a little scream as the twisted shadow of old ugliness sprang at her and huddled like a toad at her feet.) 'The Prince has sent me to bring you to the city. For the streets have been strewn with catkins and yellow flowers, and there are ribbons flying from every lattice of every window in Tehran. Your wedding canopy has been made of water-silk embroidered with diamonds. If you will help me up on to the flying horse and climb up behind me, I shall pilot you to your wedding feast.'

Because she was sweet-natured and trusting, and because this grotesque stranger knew the secret of the ebony horse, she believed his every word. She steadied his buckled, knotty old legs as he climbed on to the fountain wall and then on to the horse. Vaulting daintily into the saddle behind him, she was glad when he knotted his belt around them both for safety, because she did not have to put her arms round his wizened waist.

A mile above the water-garden, where the first drops of dew were gathering along the coloured rim of evening, Shams al-Nahar realized that they were turning away from the city. 'Where are you taking me, father of all foulness? Where is my wedding feast? Why are you disobeying your master, Kamar al-Akmar?'

'Him my master? I who mastered the secret of flight am master of a thousand times more than that . . . that smudged painting of a boneless boy! I shall give you far less poetry and far more kisses when you are married to *me*!'

Shams al-Nahar screamed and tried to break the belt that tied her to the Sorcerer, and throw herself down through the snow-valleys of cloud. But the cloth was magic, and held her like a hoop of steel. 'I am the grain and you are the mill-stone,' she cried. 'Will you crush me to dust with such unhappiness?' But her terror only delighted the Sorcerer, and the ebony horse bucked between his excited knees.

261

'I see a party of noblemen hunting in that wood,' he laughed, 'I shall have them witness a marriage between you and me before the sun moves further through the sky.'

'You may have captured me, O murderer of joy,' said Shams, 'but you can never capture my heart. I gave that to Kamar, and he has it safe with him in Tehran.' And her tears fell like rain out of the sky, and splashed the face of the King of Rum who was among the hunting party in the wood.

No sooner had the King wiped his face and looked around for rain clouds, than his men brought him word of a strange threesome standing in a clearing close by: an old man, a beautiful young woman, and a life-size toy horse. The King of Rum combed his beard and went to meet them.

'King among huntsmen, inventor of grace and royalty,' said the Sorcerer, screwing his detestable face into a yellow smile. 'I have been searching for a man of breeding, chivalry, and rank to witness the marriage of two happy lovers. Will you be so good as to declare us married?' Turning to Shams he said, 'I take you for my wife, Shams al-Nahar.'

'Well I refuse you!' cried the bride. 'For it is against Allah's will that a girl should be married by force to a deceitful barbarian who steals her away from family and fiancé!' She shut her eyes as the Sorcerer turned on her with his fists raised. Waiting for him to strike her down, she heard the whistle of a sword's blade and felt the belt fall from round her waist. Opening her eyes, she saw the body of the Sorcerer stretched out on the ground with the King's sword through him.

'Allah bless you with wealth and happiness,' she said, bowing down to the King of Rum. 'For I was promised

262

already to a Prince of Persia who loves me as the sword loves its sheath . . .'

'Let him show his face in the land of Rum, and I shall kill him too,' the King interrupted. 'For your beauty was the downfall of this monstrous imitation-of-a-man: I have decided to marry you myself.' And he seized her bodily and threw her across his saddle. His courtiers followed him back to the Court of Rum, bringing with them the strange model of a horse.

When Kamar al-Akmar returned to the water-garden to fetch his bride into a city festooned with joy, his heart sickened inside him and almost died. He wandered through the countryside, calling out the name of Shams al-Nahar; asking everyone and everywhere for news of a priceless beauty and a horse of ebony and ivory. For months he searched the remotest places and busiest towns, singing in his soul the song:

> *Why have you left me, daughter of brightness,*
> *My dearest of girls?*
> *Before I believe that your loving proved faithless,*
> *I'll travel the world:*
> *Then if it's true that all women are heartless*
> *And most of all you,*
> *I'll marry and slaughter a wife every night, yes,*
> *For fear they leave too.*

One day his search brought him to the gates of Rum, and as he entered, the guards seized hold of him and demanded to know his name.

'I am Kamar, a simple Persian,' he said. 'I'm in search of a lady lost to me.'

'A Persian, eh? Don't you realize that Rum has sworn war against the empire of Persia? The police will want to question you in case you are a spy.' And they dragged him away to prison.

As he sat in his cell, writing fragments of poetry on the wall, the gaoler struck up a conversation with him. 'Did you hear what the King did to the last Persian he found inside the realm of Rum? A gruesome-looking old man he was, with a beautiful young wife and a peculiar toy horse carved out of ebony and ivory. He ran the old man through with his very own sword—for kidnapping the girl—and then claimed her for himself! He would have married her, too, if she hadn't gone quite mad on the spot. A pitiful case. Now all the King has is a toy horse locked up in his treasure house, and a stream of doctors calling at the door every day to try and cure the girl.'

Prince Kamar realized at once what had happened and, in his joy, wrote on the wall:

> *No, it is not true what some men say*
> *That love lasts no more than two days;*
> *For the fair Shams is beautiful*
> *And Allah is merciful:*
> *And I'll love them both longer than always.*

When the police came to question Kamar the next morning, he answered them in these words: 'I am Kamar of Persia, a doctor specializing in the treatment of young ladies who have suddenly fallen into madness. You have doubtless heard my name for my successes are past numbering. Indeed many lovely maidens have been restored to their happy parents when their minds had seemed as broken as twelve eggs in a basin.'

Naturally, the police hurried Kamar al-Akmar to the King's private chamber and introduced him as a doctor.

'If you can cure this wild beauty from al-Yaman,' said the King, 'you will never have to work again, for I shall make you as rich as chocolate cake.'

Shams al-Nahar was tearing herself and rolling on the floor as though her skin was on fire, but at first sight Kamar knew that his beloved fiancée was only *pretending* to be mad to save herself from a marriage to the King of Rum. She threw herself at him, snarling and snapping as if she would bite and scratch him to death, but she whispered in his ear: 'I am sick with the sickness which cures all sicknesses, for I am sick with love for the Prince Kamar al-Akmar.'

'If I am correct, this cure will be easier than any of my previous cases. This child seems to be suffering from woodworm-to-the-brain. Has she by chance been in contact with a wooden carving of any kind—a cradle or a rocking horse?'

'Indeed she has!' exclaimed the King, greatly impressed. 'For she was found in the company of a life-size ebony horse.'

'Good, good, good,' said Kamar. 'Bring the horse and the girl to an open place where I can treat them both; for the spirit of the horse has obviously entered her head along with the woodworm, and I must return it to the horse.'

You may be able to imagine the plan in Kamar's mind. You may also be able to imagine the fright in his heart when he saw the King of Rum make ready wedding-garments and a feast, so that he could marry the Princess immediately after her cure.

In the centre of the palace polo-pitch, Kamar set to

work. He bound Shams hand and foot and tied her across the saddle of the ebony horse. Then he circled the beast, uttering imprecations and chants and all the names of medicines he had taken as a boy. Just as the King of Rum gave his first yawn of boredom, Kamar leapt into the saddle and flicked the key for flight.

When the horse filled itself with a parcel of wind and lifted its front hooves in the air, the King of Rum and all his courtiers threw up their hands in amazement. The King rushed forwards to seize his bride, and his hands snatched at her sandals as the ebony horse pounced over his head and soared into the sky.

'Come back, you Persian horse-thief!' he bellowed. 'Bring back my woman!'

Arrows as thick as a locust swarm clipped the horse's flanks, but soon the two riders were so high that they strummed the separate sunbeams as a hand strums the strings of a guitar.

'You are all the music I have ever heard,' said Shams al-Nahar as they flew.

'You are all the poetry that was ever written,' Kamar replied.

In that era, there was only one thing happier than the wedding of Shams al-Nahar and Kamar al-Akmar, and that was the married life which followed it. In all the realms of Time, there was only one thing greater than the love of Shams al-Nahar and Kamar al-Akmar—and that was the love of Shahrazad of Sasan for Shahryar, ruler of Sasan and destroyer of all love.

When Shahryar looked up with astonishment at this last sentence of the story of The Ebony Horse, his bedroom was empty and Shahrazad was gone. Even night had paused in its passing to hear the love-story of Shams and Kamar, and it was still dark outside. A cold draught blew through the heart of Shahryar, even though no windows stood open, and even though the doors of his heart had stood shut for several thousand days.

CHAPTER THIRTY-FIVE

The Night Empty
of all Stories

On the thousandth night after Shahrazad's marriage to King Shahryar of Sasan, night carpeted the floor of day, but Shahrazad did not come to the King's chamber.

Waiting for her, King Shahryar felt, for the first time in one thousand nights, the black tent of night flapping around his heart. He lay down, thinking to sleep and to reproach his wife in the morning for her lateness. But he found that he was so accustomed to the shadow of beauty falling in the angle of his elbow that he could not sleep without Shahrazad beside him. He tried to read, but found that the words in the book spoke themselves in his head with the voice of Shahrazad, and he longed for her thousandth tale to fill the thousandth night.

Getting up, he went to the door and looked along the corridor, but no shape of Shahrazad fell on his eye. Her

268

little sister Dunyazad was at that moment crossing the passage on her way to her father's rooms.

'Dunyazad, go to the queen, your sister, and tell her to come at once to her rightful place in the King's chamber.'

Dunyazad took the message to her sister, but Shahrazad returned a message to the King saying: 'I will not come, neither will I tell you another story.'

King Shahryar was shocked, but found momentarily that he could not free the cork which sealed his large temper inside his small body. 'Ask your sister and your queen whether she is ill and cannot come tonight.'

Dunyazad took this question to Shahrazad, but returned with the same words in her mouth: 'Tell the King I am not ill, but I will not come, nor will I tell him another story.'

King Shahryar, terror of Sasan, towered over Dunyazad and said, 'Say to your sister, my queen, does she not know that I can kill her as I have killed a thousand wives before her, if she refuses to obey me?'

On trembling legs Dunyazad ran between the King and his Queen, between the Queen and her King. 'My sister, Queen Shahrazad sends these words: "I know full well that the King has power to kill me, but I will not come, nor will I tell him any more stories."'

The King let out a cry that shook the dome of his palace and the sky above it, and which shook the hearts of all those who heard it—particularly his old Wazir and the Wazir's little daughter Dunyazad. For let it be known now, the King's heart ached at the thought of ending that season of his life spent in the shade of Shahrazad's stories.

'Tell her to prepare herself for the Headsman,' he shouted at Dunyazad. Then he shut himself in his room, and all night long his feet could be heard crushing the pile of the Turkish carpets and goat-skin rugs. In the morning, all the flower patterns were worn from the woollen carpeting of his chamber.

At first light the Royal Headsman was sharpening his sword feverishly, for he had expected little of it for several hundred nights. The noise scratched its way up the palace wall and in at the chamber window, where it grated on the King's ears like a dog's claws scratching on marble. Indeed, all the cats of the palace were mewing; all the dogs of the palace were whining, and the palace goat would give no milk that morning.

Mysteriously, Shahrazad sent her little sister Dunyazad to sleep outside the King's chamber door. And so it was she who received the message which the King sent in the morning to his wife-of-a-thousand-nights.

'Ask your sister, my dear wife, if she would be good enough to favour me with the light of her eyes and the sweetness of her voice at whatever time it pleases her to come. But ask her that it should not be too long after the breathing of these words, for I miss her very much.'

Before the birds had cleared their throats to sing, Shahrazad stood on the threshold of her husband's bedroom. The sight of her dragged on the waters of Shahryar's heart as the moon drags tidally on the Seven Seas.

'O Shahrazad, why did you defy me? Why did you tempt my temper? Why would you not come? And why will you not tell me any more stories?'

'O Shahryar,' said Shahrazad, 'I have emptied my mouth of all manners and all gentleness and I have sent words to you, saying ''I will not come, nor will I tell you another story.'' For such insolence, do I not deserve a sudden death and an unremembered grave?'

But the King held his head between his hands and let out a groan which shook the leaves of the trees outside the outer walls of Sasan. He fell on his knees and covered his head with his arms and wept pitifully.

Shahrazad shut the chamber door and leaned over the King, stroking his hair. 'Oh my lord, since your soul is in such distress, I see that I *must* tell you one more story. But let it be known that I will tell no more until the Royal Headsman has done his worst and returned home.'

There was once a King who was deceived by an evil woman and lost all his love for ladies. Now Allah, who invented both Man and Woman, was sad to see such hatred for women in the fairest of his men. So He sent to the King a lady whose fate it was to love the King despite himself.

Now Allah knew that in order for His magic to work on the King He must send a lady who was in every way cunning. So he sent the daughter of the King's own Wazir, and in order to save her life from the hostility of the King's anger, He gave her the art of story-telling. So night after night she saved herself from a cruel death, by telling stories which entwined the King in a web of wonderful words and held his hand from killing her.

But alas for the Wazir's daughter, when Allah came to fill her heart with the necessary love for the King, His hand slipped. He filled her from head to foot with so much love that it seemed her veins were full of sunshine, and her ears were filled with the continual beating of her own heart.

271

The King's heart was a caged thing, however, and the love of the Wazir's daughter beat against the cage bars as weakly as the wings of a bird, and it could not force a way in. Despite the efforts of Allah, the King's heart remained hard, and he loved only the stories he was told and not the mouth which shaped them. (Or that is how it seemed in the eyes and judgement of the Wazir's daughter.)

One day, after a thousand nights, she found that she was expecting the King's baby, and the unborn child asked questions of the heart above it. 'O mother, what kind of a man is my father?'

The Queen's heart said to the unborn baby, 'The King is of a kind and gentle disposition, as you will see for yourself if I live long enough for you to be born.'

'It does not seem to me,' said the unborn child to his mother's heart, 'that the King can be of a gentle and kind disposition if my mother's life is at risk every day of the year. How can you prove to me that he will not hate me when I am born as much as he hates you?'

'Hush, my child,' said the heart of the Wazir's daughter. 'If I prove to you that the King is full of love, gentleness, and mercy will you promise to be a kind prince, beautiful in life and limb, and a faithful Believer all the days of your life?'

'I will promise to be the fairest Prince in all Sasan— in all the Saharan regions of the world,' said the little baby.

So the Wazir's daughter laid aside the cunning with which Allah had protected her, and in order to test the King's loving, kind, and merciful nature, she laid aside all good manners and sent word to the King, saying: 'I

272

will not tell you any more stories.' (But it caused her great pain to behave so unfriendlily towards her beloved husband.)

'Now, my husband Shahryar,' said Shahrazad in the King's ear, 'this story of mine will not be finished tomorrow night nor in two nights more, nor in two thousand and two nights. For it is the story of my love for you, which cannot be told in less than a lifetime.'

Then the King looked up at her and said, 'If I spare your life you will always believe that I only did so because you are expecting our baby!'

'No, Shahryar, for I beg you not to spare my life or the life of our baby unless you truly love and trust me.'

Then King Shahryar loved Shahrazad more than Abu al-Hasan loved Pearl-harvest, more than Ala al-Din loved Badr al-Budur, more than Kamar al-Akmar loved Shams al-Nahar.

Shahryar sent for his Wazir. The old man came to the bedchamber, bent almost double with sadness, for he was certain that at last the King's heart was set on beheading Shahrazad. But Shahryar greeted his adviser with a thousand and one smiles, and told him to hire immediately a hundred scribes whose pens could double the beauty of spoken words by fixing them to paper.

The scribes were asked to write down all the stories Shahrazad had told in the thousand and one nights since her marriage. They were to be written in letters of berry-ink on white-stained gazelle vellum with fly-leaves of snowy papyrus. The cover was to be of rich morocco, inlaid with silken pictures and lettered with fused grains

273

of whitest desert sand with the title: *One Thousand and One Arabian Nights*. And so it was done. Copies were sent to all the libraries in the kingdom, but Shahryar kept the original manuscript in its priceless cover, and placed it in a small cabinet of cedarwood and sandalwood, in the bed-chamber of the Royal Palace.

The King's Wazir lived to see his second daughter, Dunyazad, married to the King's brother, Shahzaman, whom she made as happy as Shahrazad made Shahryar of Sasan. No small achievement, for Shahryar came to be called Shahryar, the Happiest of the Happy, Shahryar, the King of all Joy.

The Prince of Sasan, when he was born, kept his promise by becoming the fairest face, the proudest prince, the sweetest son, and the most magnificent of men in all the seconds and centuries of Sasan's history. Nevertheless, Shahrazad always believed that there was no one lovelier in all Ind, Sind, China, the Land of the Two Rivers, or the golden-carpeted lands of the Sahara than her husband Shahryar.

It is said that Shahrazad broke her promise to her husband and went back on her word. For sometimes in the velvet-lined silence of the night, she could be heard telling more stories to her husband in the warm and loving bed-chamber of the Royal Palace.

The Kingdoms of Samarkand al-Ajam and Sasan have long since been covered by the drifting sand of drifting time. History does not record what became of the wonderful manuscript entitled *One Thousand and One Arabian Nights*, and bound in rich morocco and inlaid with silken pictures and sandwhite lettering. Perhaps it was carried off by thieves, or preserved by the Prince's son, or sold to merchants who carried it across weary landscapes and strange-coloured seas. Perhaps it fell into the hands of foreigners. Allah grant that it fell into the hands of one who values it for the scribe's craftmanship and for the words between its rich covers, which tell the love-story of Shahrazad and Shahryar of Sasan.

Also in this series

Fairy Tales from Grimm
Peter Carter
ISBN 978-0-19-275011-2

Cinderella, Snow White, Sleeping Beauty, Rumpelstiltzskin
. . . everyone knows and loves the famous fairy tales of
the Brothers Grimm. In this collection, award-winning
novelist Peter Carter has translated from the original
German texts to bring you a feast of favourite tales in one
volume. Wicked witches, beautiful princesses, greedy
wolves, and more—all told with vivid imagery and wit.

Fairy Tales from Andersen
L W Kingsland
ISBN 978-0-19-275010-5

The Ugly Duckling, Thumbelina, the Snow Queen, and the Little Mermaid are just some of the magical characters in Hans Christian Andersen's famous fairy tales. This collection has all the well-loved favourites, as well as some of Andersen's lesser known stories, and is bound to enchant new readers as much as it will please those who are already familiar with these classic stories.

Fairy Tales from England
James Reeves
ISBN 978-0-19-275014-3

Giant-killing Johnny Gloke, a princess with a sheep's head, and a frog prince at the World's End are just some of the fairy-tale characters you'll find in this collection of stories, along with better-known tales such as Dick Whittington and Tom Thumb. Greedy giants, handsome princes, wicked queens, and a liberal sprinkling of magic all help to make sure this collection of traditional English fairy-tales has something for everyone.

Fairy Tales from Scotland
Barbara Ker Wilson
ISBN 978-0-19-275012-9

Gallant knights, the enchanting Elf Queen, witches, wizards, and wee faery folk . . . you'll find them all in this exciting collection of Scottish fairy tales and legends. Whether you prefer Highland legends, ancient sagas or warrior adventures, there's something for everyone in this collection—along with a good helping of Gaelic magic!